THE FALSTAFF VAMPIRE FILES

LYNNE MURRAY

PEARLSONG PRESS
NASHVILLE, TN

Pearlsong Press
P.O. Box 58065
Nashville, TN 37205
1-866-4-A-PEARL
www.pearlsong.com
www.pearlsongpress.com

Trade paperback ISBN: 9781597190381
Ebook ISBN: 9781597190398

Cover & book design by Zelda Pudding.
Bridge photo © Bryce Newell—Fotolia.com
Parchment graphic © Maksym Yemelyanov—Fotolia.com

Other Novels by Lynne Murray:

Bride of the Living Dead

The Josephine Fuller Novels
Larger Than Death • Large Target • At Large • A Ton of Trouble

The Ingrid Hunter Novels
Termination Interview • Death Flower

Library of Congress Cataloging-in-Publication Data

Murray, Lynne.
  The Falstaff vampire files / Lynne Murray.
     p. cm.
  ISBN 978-1-59719-038-1 (original trade pbk. : alk. paper) — ISBN 978-1-59719-039-8 (ebook)
  1. Women psychologists—Fiction. 2. Vampires—Fiction. I. Title.
  PS3563.U7716F35 2011
  813'.54—dc23
                                    2011020936

PART I

THE THING IN THE SHED

THE FILES

THE PACKAGE CONTAINED: a plastic spray bottle with a few ounces of cloudy liquid that smelled like onion juice; a grease-smeared menu from a Chinese restaurant; a rubber-banded file folder of typed pages with a few loose, handwritten pages on top; a red digital recorder/MP3 player; a simple black voice recorder; and a silver flash drive and digital recorder.

The contents are presented here in chronological order except for the first few pages of handwritten notes.

CHAPTER 1

KRISTIN MARLOWE'S HANDWRITTEN NOTES
AUGUST 5TH

MY NAME IS KRISTIN MARLOWE and I'm supposed to be sane for a living, but my ex-lover stole the one irreplaceable item I own, and God help me, I broke into his creepy old house by the ocean to get it back. As a psychologist I know a dozen techniques to calm down and think rationally. Sorry! Too angry to use any of them.

Technically I didn't break in. I had Hal's key, but before I could use it the front door flew open and the old woman caretaker came bustling out like a wool-clad force of nature. I caught the door and edged past her, mumbling something about getting my stuff.

She stopped right in front of me. "Don't go in the shed," she warned in a hostile tone.

"I have no reason to go there." Shivering from nerves rather than cold, I started to close the door, but she blocked me and stepped so close that I could smell her personal perfume of eucalyptus cough drops and antiseptic.

"I give you good advice. Take it." She turned and walked away, muttering something about the nephew changing the locks, the old lady being gone, and go ahead and take the light bulbs and hospital bed.

Okay, so I could be arrested and lose my therapist's license if the old lady called Hal or the cops. But I needed to get my property back and I was still enraged that Hal had taken it. I walked into the darkened foyer paved in red stone. It was late afternoon, but very little daylight filtered in and the lights mounted on the wall already glowed in their twisted copper fittings. The veins in the alabaster seemed to pulse like reptilian eggs.

Hal had told me on my first visit that his aunt lived in the ground floor flat on the right. "The corridor on the left leads to the back door. I keep my coffin in a shed out there. Did I mention that I'm a vampire in my spare time?"

Strange how I forgot those words until I stood on the red stone floor again. I started up the chilly staircase, also red stone.

A scrabbling sound nearby made me freeze in my tracks. I stopped to listen. The house seemed to shudder like a ship in the wind. The scratching sound was outside. The wind drove branches whipping against the walls. I went up to the landing. The first step off the stairs onto the floorboards creaked loudly.

Hal's flat sounded empty, with echoing hardwood floors.

When we'd come here before, he'd turned on a dim lamp and we'd walked past three closed doors down a hallway with a narrow Turkish carpet runner. Hal's apartment was as spare as I had remembered, furnished with solid vintage furniture he said he'd harvested from elsewhere in the old house.

An hour of searching yielded no trace of my property. I hated to leave without it. I went down the stairs. A corridor led past the ground floor flat to the rear of the building. I squinted as the setting sun lit up the entryway so that I seemed to be walking on dried blood.

No harm in looking at the shed.

At the end of the corridor a room with rows of west-facing windows led out to the back stairs and the yard where the shed sat. Rubber mats covered the floor against mud and a row of hooks poked out of the wall. Low shelves just inside the door held only a wind-scrambled umbrella and a single pair of rubber boots. The wind off the ocean had coated the windows with a scum of salt and grit.

The outside door creaked and stuck. I had to force it open and then pull heavily to close it behind me. Standing at the top of the weathered wood steps, I watched the Pacific Ocean gleaming for a moment and the red disk of sun bleeding into the banks of clouds to vanish.

At the bottom of the steps the masses of untended bushes and trees blocked the light and the yard seemed colder. The shed and the trelliswork wall next to it had the same grimy, blistered green paint as the house. The trellis shuddered in the wind that swayed a few clinging skeletal shreds of ivy.

The shed door held a padlock that had not been snapped closed. I lifted it out of the hasp, hung it on one side and tried the corroded doorknob. Frozen past repair, it didn't turn, but the door opened smoothly and felt as heavy as a safe door. I stepped inside and it slammed shut behind me.

Total darkness. Something brushed against my face. I jumped back and cried out.

The door creaked open when I hit it, letting in a sliver of twilight. A string hanging down from a light bulb on the ceiling touched my face again, swinging back and forth. Laughing a little shakily, I pulled the string and the shed was bathed in harsh yellow light.

It looked empty.

A patch with oil drips on the floor indicated where Hal parked his motorcycle. No sign of my property. Everything looked inches deep in dust. The place had an earthy, grassy smell, with a faint hint of pine shavings. In one corner an ancient hand-pushed lawnmower leaned on a pile of garden tools rusted beyond recognition.

The door slammed shut more solidly and the sound of the wind died away. The walls seemed thicker than an ordinary shed. My heart beat as fast as if I'd been running.

At least there aren't any coffins, I said to myself. *Not funny, Kristin—you should go with your gut and get out of here.* I took a quick look around. Where in this shed could Hal have hidden my property?

Half a dozen old fruit crates held piles of dust-shrouded junk. Next to them a huge crate sat, clean and free of dust. About eight feet long by four feet wide and equally as high. A piano case? I'd seen no sign of a piano in the house.

The big box was the only thing in the room that looked as if it were regularly opened. Could Hal have tossed my property in there? Maybe it was full of souvenirs stolen from other ex-girlfriends.

I eased across the cement floor, ready to run for the door at any moment. In the silence I could hear myself take a deep breath.

Walking past the fruit crates stirred up dust and I began to sneeze. More than once.

A sneeze exploded from inside the crate.

I jumped back violently—back into the cloud of dust, which made me sneeze again.

As if in answer, another sneeze and a series of coughs shook the crate. The hinges creaked as if something inside wanted out. The lid began to rise up and open.

CHAPTER 2

MINA MURRAY'S JOURNAL
RED DIGITAL VOICE RECORDER
AUGUST 4ᵀᴴ

TODAY IS THE DAY HAL ASKED ME to marry him. I celebrated by buying this cute little red recorder to start a journal. I want to remember this feeling. I've never been so happy in my life. Maybe our grandchildren will listen to this one day.

First I should explain about why this love is so precious to me. My name is Wilhelmina, but I've been called Meena my whole life. Kids at school tried calling me Willa-Meanie for a while, but I was so shy that the nickname never stuck.

I should explain that my mother suffered from schizophrenia. The things she told me about the world gave me serious problems with reality. I don't always know what's normal and what isn't. It wasn't until I got to school that I learned from the other kids that the CIA can't watch you through your television—at least not so far. She didn't trust telephones, radios or TVs, and she wasn't so sure where else bugs might have been planted in our place. Maybe it's just as well my mother didn't live to read the news about the government wiretapping innocent people's phones. A lot of her paranoid fantasies have happened in real life.

What it boils down to for me is that I try to keep an open mind. Just because something sounds crazy, I never dismiss it out of hand.

When I first met Hal I started to believe I could have a normal life. He's an amazing man—tall, handsome, sophisticated and madly in love with me. Hal's love and affection made me feel so good. Today, when he proposed, I couldn't believe how happy I felt.

Except that he also told me that he believed in vampires, and he confessed that he wanted to become one of them himself. Most girls would have said "You are crazy—goodbye." But I've seen insanity up close when I was growing up, and this was different.

Hal is older and more educated than I am and he says he's seen these things. He offered repeatedly to prove that the vampire exists, but so far I'm too afraid to go see. Maybe he does have a vampire in a shed in his backyard. Or maybe it's like my mother believing that the government planted listening devices in the toaster. I don't know if I'm more afraid that Hal is crazy like my mom, or that he's not crazy and there really are vampires.

I love Hal and I don't want to lose him. I don't dare demand it now, but I'm hoping when we're married, he'll be able to give it up. Maybe he needs medication. I've lost too many people. My mom's mental illness led to her suicide. She left me behind and I've never been able to fill the void.

I feel so lucky to have found my therapist, Kristin. She's about the age my mom would have been and she listens without judging. And she's never said she didn't believe me, even when I told her about the vampires.

CHAPTER 3

KRISTIN MARLOWE'S TYPED NOTES
AUGUST 4ᵀᴴ

FOR SEVERAL MONTHS MY CLIENT, Wilhelmina—Mina—has come in twice a week to talk about her fears of being stalked by vampires who wanted to make her undead. I don't believe in vampires. But something was scaring the hell out of Mina. Her terror came along with her into my consulting room with a presence strong enough to make my own throat tense up. So the last thing I expected was for Mina to come in and start off the session with a shy smile and the words, "I'm engaged!"

I smiled back and almost said "Congratulations," but stopped myself, kept the smile and retreated into my therapist role. "Tell me about it."

She lowered her voice. "He wants to become one of *them.*"

"So how are you feeling about that?"

Translation into normal English would be—where the hell did THAT come from? Mina hadn't mentioned meeting someone new. Her only friends seemed to be these vampire types that both attracted and scared her so much. Marrying the thing that terrified her made no sense. So why was she doing it?

We weren't close to discovering what "vampire" meant to Mina. In the first few sessions she mentioned a schizophrenic mother who killed herself when Mina was fourteen. Her father was physically abusive, and she had moved out as soon as she finished high school and supported herself ever since.

Mina had dealt with a great deal of suffering in her twenty-three years, and just as she began to talk about it she had switched gears and

13

started talking about vampires. We'd been on that topic for six months now. Maybe that was the only way she could approach her family history. She said the men in the group were attractive, but she talked about the vampire women's bodies at length. Was that her anxiety about her own body, or was she secretly attracted to the women?

Many questions and so far no answers.

"He's amazing. I love him so much." She began to smile, and her face took on a just-got-engaged glow, the fear vanishing for once.

"Yes? Go on." I smiled back and nodded encouragingly, noting the "he" and shuffled the latent lesbian theory to the back of the pack.

Why she was so drawn to this group of people? Could they truly be dangerous? Her fear and isolation worried me. I kept wanting to make a joke to break down some of the tension. But that was my own way to deal with anxiety, not hers. She needed me to pay attention, to listen for clues.

Mina crouched on the edge of the sofa nearest me, as if for protection against invisible enemies. She didn't seem to belong to the Goth or vampire-fan subculture. No pale make up, visible tattoos, dark lipstick or antique black clothing—at least not when I saw her. Of course she did come to her therapy directly from her administrative assistant job at a business school in the Financial District.

She seemed pathetically grateful when I took her delusion seriously. She showed no signs of paranoia beyond her conviction that she was both drawn to and threatened by a clutch of vampires. I looked up the plural.

I found it sad when she praised the beauty of the thin women in the vampire group as compared to her own voluptuous figure. Mina could not accept how lushly attractive she was. She had glossy brown hair and blue eyes. I did mention that no matter what vampires may think, her sort of hourglass figure is greatly admired by many men of the human persuasion.

It wouldn't be ethical to talk about my own life to her, but I wish I could have told Mina that even though I'm in my 40s with streaks of gray in my hair and rounded hips and belly, way larger than this culture's ideal, I managed to attract a handsome man nearly fifteen years younger. Sometimes I wanted to bring my boyfriend in and show him off and say, "See, it's possible. Some men do enjoy a woman with an abundant figure." *Zaftig* was the word my lover used when conducting an appreciative inventory.

But Mina surprised me with her positive news. She leaned close enough to whisper, glancing around as if someone might overhear her. "The vampires still frighten me, but I'm so much in love, so proud to be getting married."

"What's he like?"

Mina sat back on the sofa and stared, unseeing, at some of the fanciful prints I'd framed on the walls. "He's tall and athletic, but he likes my body the way it is. He says I'm *zaftig*."

I laughed. "Ah. Do you know what that word means?"

"Juicy," she said with a blush, and we both laughed.

"He's very passionate." She laughed again, blushing even more. It was the first time she had laughed since we began our sessions. I scribbled briefly on my tablet. "He's smart and funny. He was born and raised here, but he went to school back East. He's got a great job but he can't talk about much because it involves some government stuff. It takes him abroad sometimes."

Several red flags popped up about the fiancé in that statement. The "great job" shouldn't be mysterious. Mina admitted to problems sometimes telling reality from illusion. Could this man be lying to her about the government job? I noted questions to deal with later.

The smile faded and Mina tensed, leaning forward again. "The only thing that frightens me is that he wants so badly to be one of them. The vampires, I mean. I'm not sure if he wants power, or if he just wants to be immortal. He's an older man. He's thirty-five."

I sat back just a little, partly to keep from smiling more, remembering my own twenties when thirty-five had seemed impossibly old to me. Now, in my late forties, it seems impossibly young. Scratch that. I happened to be dating—well, sleeping with—a thirty-five-year-old man, so I couldn't call it impossibly young.

"His name is Henry Roy." She smiled, happy to say his name.

It became very hard to breathe in my office at that moment. Henry Roy was the name of my own thirty-five-year-old lover. Everyone called him Hal.

"Everyone calls him Hal," Mina said.

CHAPTER 4

HAL ROY'S SPOKEN NOTES
SILVER FLASH DRIVE/VOICE RECORDER
UNDATED

I CAME TO LIVE IN MY AUNT'S HOUSE by the ocean when I was fifteen and in a state of shock from my parents' death in a plane crash. Aunt Reba wanted to be kind to me, but she was constitutionally unable to pay attention for more than sixty seconds to anything except herself. Whenever she remembered me she would look up from her *Chronicle* and say, "Poor Hal, you must be sad. I'm sorry that you don't have any friends here in the city to play with. Look, Nordstrom's is having a spring shoe sale!"

They'd taken me out of school and the semester was nearly over, so I was at loose ends.

I gravitated to the back yard. It sloped down toward a collapsing fence through which you could see the long drop to the coast road and beyond that, the ocean. The ideal place to smoke cigarettes and drink the odd beer or whatever I could steal from my aunt. My excuse was Aunt Reba never gave me any cash. Even when I asked for bus fare she managed to forget before she gave it to me. I didn't need much money because I didn't know anyone in San Francisco to help me obtain the drugs that had been so readily available at my prep school.

The shed challenged me because it was locked up so tight. There wasn't a window or a crack or a loose board you could pry out to even look in. I hammered at the windows with a rock, but I couldn't even dent the metal that reinforced them. Barely even chipped off a little of the old green paint.

The summer fogs off the ocean turned the garden into a strange, cemetery-like place. I stayed out of my aunt's way and got my own meals. She didn't seem to notice. But I watched the shed when she wasn't around and discovered one night that the padlock had been opened and hung in the hasp. The shed was empty except for some dusty lawn tools stored there, including a huge, empty box. Sudden, inexplicable terror grabbed me and squeezed the curiosity right out of me. I didn't stick around to find out more.

The next day I casually walked around the shed and found it sealed up tight, the padlock solidly closed.

I had to find out what was in there.

CHAPTER 5

MINA MURRAY'S JOURNAL, RED DIGITAL VOICE RECORDER AUGUST 4TH

I DON'T KNOW IF KRISTIN BELIEVES ME about the vampires, but I trust her and talking to her helps. She makes me feel safe in a way no one has since my mother died. Therapists aren't supposed to talk about themselves, but she did say that her mother had died young like mine did. I feel like she understands me.

Hal is like a star to me. I loved him from the first time he spoke to me. He's so brilliant and funny and sexy. Knowing he's chosen me, even though I'm not educated or thin or sophisticated, makes me feel happy. I don't feel secure, though. Not even since he proposed. It's the vampire thing. He didn't start to talk about it or introduce me to his vampire-crazy friends until after we fell in love. He trusts me, and I have to trust him.

Hal seems to be waiting for me to see something—I just don't know what. Maybe he's the one who should be in therapy, but he'd never go. If only Hal would at least talk to Kristin. He could use some of her wisdom. I worry about what he's doing with those vampires, and she could help me protect him. I don't know what I would do if I didn't have Kristin.

CHAPTER 6

KRISTIN MARLOWE'S TYPED NOTES
AUGUST 4ᵀᴴ CONTINUED

I WAS GOING TO HAVE TO REFER MINA to another therapist. Talk about a conflict of interest! I somehow got through the session and I walked her through the garden and out onto Clement Street. I usually walk guests in and out, just to double check that the gate is closed and firmly locked. We live in a nice neighborhood, but it's also a big city.

The next time I talked with Mina she was going to be very angry.

I drew in several deep breaths of cold, damp air, hoping to clear my head. I closed the wooden gate and stood with my back against it for a moment. The gate was set into the eight-foot-tall wooden fence that ran from the corner of Vi's house right on the sidewalk on Clement Street. No front yards in this part of San Francisco. Every square foot of land was precious. Vi's front door was three steps up from the pavement.

I wouldn't say anything till I confirmed it with Hal. But my gut told me Mina's fiancé was my Hal. She had shyly showed me the exotic blue diamond engagement ring Hal had found for her in some Eastern European capital, and as I leaned forward to look, I noted that I had been touching the antique amethyst necklace Hal had brought back for me from his last trip. I dropped my hand as if the stones had turned red-hot. Damn it, Hal!

Now my hands were shaking. I wondered if I could make it through the next hour, the next client—and even though it was a quarter till the appointed hour he rang the buzzer.

"Hi Kris, I'm early."

Luther Kemper was the absolute worst client to follow Mina's announcement. In his mid-sixties, casually conservative, with an immaculately barbered gray beard, he may have been recommended to me because of my writing about loving one's body at all sizes. He had married an opera singer, fifteen years older. In recent years she had lost interest in sex and he was looking for romance, without the inconvenience and expense of getting a divorce. I asked if he wanted a referral to a sex therapist. He said no thanks, but he kept coming to therapy—probably to complain. The term hasn't made it into any diagnostic manual, but essentially Luther was a whiner.

I sat down and took notes to make myself focus while Luther described his latest personal ad offering a no-strings relationship to a spectacularly unimpressed female population.

CHAPTER 7

MINA MURRAY'S JOURNAL
RED DIGITAL VOICE RECORDER
AUGUST 4ᵀᴴ CONTINUED

RIGHT AFTER MY SESSION WITH KRISTIN I went over to Hal's place. He lives in an old, creepy house on a cliff overlooking the ocean.

He was supposed to meet me there. I was early, but I had a key. Unfortunately so did Hal's friends, Lucy and Ned. Lucy was one of the reasons I hadn't moved into the house. The other reason was the shed behind the house.

"Hal went out, said he'd be back soon," Lucy said as opened the door. She was wearing nothing but sandals and an ankle bracelet. The wood floor must be cold or she'd have ditched the sandals. She didn't even bother to hide behind the door. Would she sign for courier package deliveries that way? Probably.

She was the palest blonde I had ever seen, very slender, with light green eyes, blue veins visible under her thin skin. At first I wondered if she was trying to seduce me, or steal Hal from me in front of everyone. Then I realized that Lucy only paid attention to other people when she wanted something from them. The rest of the time she amused herself by shocking anyone she could. Lately that had been me.

Ned wasn't so bad. As usual he sat on the sofa in Hal's front room. Sometimes he sketched on a little pad. Today he bent over a comically wafer-sized laptop computer. Ned was a very big, hairy guy. His headphones disappeared into a mop of wiry black hair. He had gentle blue eyes, very pale skin and a thick beard that ran up the sides of his face to meet his sideburns. As he tapped away on the keyboard, a jagged line on the screen indicated the audio tracks he was playing that we could not hear.

He wore jeans and a black T-shirt with purple-and-red calligraphy. "What's Atrocity Museum?"

He shifted the headphones away from one ear. "My band."

"I thought it was Recreational Paranoia."

"You remembered!" He seemed surprised and touched that anyone would. "I changed it."

I examined the T-shirt again. "I think I like the new one better."

Ned smiled serenely, nodded and resettled the headphones.

Hal called Ned's band "Dork Shadows," even to his face. Ned didn't seem to care. But he never invited us to hear his band play any gigs, and I never met any other band members. I wondered if the band even existed outside of his audio files.

Ned did look up to watch Lucy embrace me and hold my face an inch from hers so I could look into her pale green eyes.

"You look uncomfortable, Mina." Lucy looked down at her slender body, firm, small breasts, narrow waist, hips and thighs, and a slight trace of nearly invisibly pale pubic hair. She laughed. "I'll put on clothes just for you. Ned doesn't mind if I'm naked, do you, Ned?"

Ned looked up and smiled slightly. "Suit yourself," he said. "Or don't." He smiled at his own pun and turned back to the computer.

"Mina, you're missing out on more fun with Hal by being such a stick-up-the-butt." Lucy grabbed a black turtleneck from the sofa and pulled it over her head. I was absurdly grateful that she had discarded her clothes here rather than in Hal's bedroom.

The twinge of jealousy hit me like an actual knife-stabbing pain. When Hal asked me to marry him, he promised I would be the only woman in his life. I asked about Lucy. He swore that there was nothing between him and Lucy except a yearning for this vampire blood that they shared with Ned and a few other vampire-obsessed people who followed Hal around and went out to the shed behind the house. I didn't ask details about what happened there. Just looking at the place seized my chest with dread.

I glanced back at Ned. He raised his shaggy head from staring the screen. He watched and seldom spoke. He had been in high school with Hal. Hal told me he came from a prominent family and his full name was Edward J. Harker Poins, but he just seemed quiet and shy.

Lucy wriggled into her tight jeans. She was so slender that she made me feel clumsy and huge, watching her squeeze her thin frame into tiny jeans that wouldn't have fit over one of my legs. She slipped out of her sandals and pulled on black leather boots.

Her pale eyes looked luminous in the dusk. "It's going to happen. Hal's come up with a plan to make us into vampires," she said. "Hal is going to move the casket out of the shed and threaten to leave it out in the sun if the vampire doesn't bring us over. Direct sun kills them, you know." Her voice was thick was excitement.

"Um." Hal was smarter than I could ever be in so many ways, but this didn't seem to make sense. "If you kill the vampire how can it give you what you want?"

Lucy stopped and looked at me and then waved her hand to dismiss me. "It will work. It's got to work."

"What if you just piss it off?"

"That won't happen." She said it so quickly that I wondered if Lucy would admit to being afraid, even to herself.

"I'd be scared."

"Come on, let's go look. You wouldn't be scared if you saw him in daylight. We keep the door closed because sunlight could kill him. But he just looks like a regular dead body until sunset."

"Looking at a regular dead body out in the shed. Tempting, but no thanks."

"This may be your last chance if Hal moves the box."

"I hope he does move it. It creeps me out."

"Where's my cloak?" Lucy rummaged through Hal's hall closet, tossing coats out onto the hall floor. "He's going to have a big showdown tonight. Hal won't let any of us come while he talks to the vampire. He said it was personal. But we're going to come later. This could be the night we all become vampires. Get Hal to bring you along. Or you could pretend to sleep and then go watch them talk. I wish I could."

She dug through the pile of clothes she'd dumped on the floor. "Here it is." She pulled a velvet cloak over her shoulders and fastened it at her throat. Is it cold outside now? I haven't been out since noon."

"Yeah, it's cold." Had she been there naked with Hal most of the afternoon? Probably. I got a sinking feeling in my gut.

The door slammed as Lucy went out. Ned came over and started hanging coats back in the closet. I helped him. "Doesn't anybody else have to work around here?" I asked.

"Lucy's got a trust fund. I do freelance graphics," Ned said.

"Oh, sorry, I meant no offense."

"None taken." The last coat hung, Ned returned to his computer and I went to the back of the flat and looked out the bay window as Lucy's black-clad frame appeared in the yard below. She turned back to see me in the window and stuck her tongue out at me. Then she advanced on the grungy old shed, her lean body bending into the wind that came up off the ocean. She disappeared into the shed, shutting the door carefully behind her.

The windows had been painted the same green as the wood. Was that to screen out daylight?

A weathered, plain wood fence separated the yard from the open space of the park next to it and ran just a few feet from the back of the shed. More bushes and wild geraniums grew up to cover the half-tumbled down section of fence that faced the ocean. One night I saw a man in a huge overcoat crawling like a giant spider out of those bushes.

After we get married, I plan to seriously ask Hal to get the fence fixed. I feel nervous enough spending the night in the house. If Hal was moving his vampire out of there, I hoped he did it as soon as possible.

CHAPTER 8

KRISTIN MARLOWE'S TYPED NOTES
AUGUST 4TH CONTINUED

LUTHER FINISHED HIS HOUR OF WHINING and left. I had no more clients scheduled for the day, and I desperately needed to talk to someone or at the least walk off some of my anger. My friend Larry Segovia lived about 10 blocks away on Lake Street. As a therapist, and an unattached gay man in his 40s, he understood about boyfriend troubles. Larry didn't work Mondays, and he never minded company. If he wasn't home, the walk out in the fresh air wouldn't hurt me.

Larry's door was opened by a cheerful-looking man about my own age and Larry's. I was surprised because so many of Larry's friends were younger. This man was not handsome, but commanding, with unruly gray streaked dark hair cut short but starting to curl already. Startlingly black eyebrows framed penetrating green eyes with sparks of hazel. What really caught my attention was the mischievous quirk of his mouth, as if he were just about to tell a great secret. I liked and trusted him instinctively without knowing why.

Of course, I'd been wrong before. Witness my reaction to Hal. But something about this man drew a pang of attraction from me that was welcome in that it dulled the pain of Hal's betrayal. Larry's friend was most likely gay, but I felt better just knowing there were still attractive men in the world. Oops, I was staring.

"Oh, sorry, I was looking for Larry," I blurted out.

"He's just gone out to run an errand." He moved aside. "Want to come in and wait? I'm house sitting when Larry goes to Edinburgh next week."

Suddenly I felt like an idiot. "I'm not a client, I'm a therapist too. I should have called, but—"

Some of my inner turmoil must have crossed my face, because the stranger leaned forward. "Seriously, why not come in and wait? Larry should be back any minute. Something about picking up his dry cleaning."

I followed him in, introducing myself.

"I'm Abraham Van Helsing," he said over his shoulder, leading the way down the hall. "But please call me Bram. Abe just doesn't suit me. Honest Abe Van Helsing sounds like an accordion-playing used car salesman."

I laughed and felt a little better.

We went into the little front parlor of Larry's Victorian flat. "I'll be house sitting when he takes off tomorrow for that conference in Edinburgh. Did Larry warn you about me?"

"No, this is kind of a spur-of-the-moment visit. He didn't mention you."

"I don't know if I should be reassured or insulted."

"Um, are you the new boyfriend?"

"Nope. The old friend from college." He settled on the sofa. "Still, you'd think he'd say something about me. He can't have that that many friends who're researching vampire cults."

I stopped halfway in the middle of sitting in Larry's burgundy-colored wing chair. "Did you say vampire cults?"

Bram smiled with a bit of mischief in his eyes. "I didn't mean to shock you."

"No, it's just that I have a young client who's fixated on vampires, and she said something that bothered me today."

"If you ever need to talk about it I'm always glad to discuss vampires."

"Wait a minute." I suddenly put the name and the subject together. "Wasn't there a Professor Van Helsing in *Dracula?*"

"There was. That was fiction, but my grandpa from Hungary didn't find it amusing. He was a trade unionist. But as a kid when I found Abraham Van Helsing in *Dracula*, I got interested in the culture. It's a pretty good stand-in for whatever you're afraid of. In the 1930s it was sinister Europeans like Bela Lugosi in the old movies. Lately vampires and blood-drinking are a metaphor for sex." Bram settled back on the sofa. "Who knows? Even if it were my calling to hunt vampires, there would be the small problem that there really aren't any, so I have to make do."

"What are you researching now?"

"I've written a few books on the so-called 'real' vampires, the history of the belief in the old country. Now I'm interviewing kids who are drawn to vampire cults. If you ever want to feel old, try interviewing a few dozen teenagers and twenty-year-olds."

I laughed. "The client who is into vampires is twenty-three."

"There you go. Graduates of Ann Rice University."

"What's that?"

"People who've read every book, seen every movie. Some even do the RPGs."

"Sorry, you've lapsed into Greek again."

He laughed. "Role Playing Games based on vampires. So far it's all wishful thinking. But show me a real live vampire and I'll get out the stakes and silver bullets and go to town."

"Or go to jail—you might have some trouble explaining the dead body."

"Oh, the legends all say that the body disintegrates into dust once it's properly destroyed. So convenient."

I just managed a wan smile. "I wish I could have talked to you earlier. But for reasons that have nothing to do with vampires, I'm going to have to refer this client to another therapist. That's part of what I need to talk to Larry about."

"Well, I'll be in town for two weeks, so if there's anything a certified vampire expert can help with, let me know."

"They have certificates for that sort of thing?"

"I'm self-certified." He smiled and patted me on the hand. "Sorry, I can see you've had a rough day. But Larry will be back and have you sorted out in no time."

"He has a way of doing that. Larry really saved my sanity during the months after my husband died."

"He's a good 'un."

"Are you talking about me, Bram? Hi, Kris."

Larry came bustling in. He was short, olive-skinned and brown-eyed. As long as I'd known him he had cut his hair close to his head to minimize a receding hairline, and he looked younger than his forty-some years. His smile always lit up a room. Just seeing him gave me a psychic jumpstart.

"I'll make a discreet exit here. I've been inflicting my family history on Kris, complete with its mythical vampire tradition."

"That whole stake-in-the-heart of the older male has always sounded distinctly Freudian to me," Larry said

Bram laughed and got up to go. "I promise not to bring back any vampires from my interview."

Larry draped his dry cleaning over a chair and came over to give me a hug.

After hugging Larry hello, it seemed natural to hug Bram goodbye. "I'm glad to have met you, Bram, and thanks for the vampire insights."

"Hey, who you gonna call?"

"You bust ghosts as well?"

"No, I specialize."

"Okay, I will definitely call you if I run into any vampires."

"Please do."

I waited till I heard the outside door close before I turned to Larry. "Hal just got engaged to one of my clients."

"Oh, Kris." Larry gave me another hug and then leaned back on the sofa and rubbed his hands over his eyes. "I thought I'd heard everything. How did he meet her?"

"I have no idea."

"What are you going to do? Aside from shooting Hal."

"I haven't decided whether to tell her. I probably should. I do know I've got to refer her to another therapist." I sighed. "Most of the people I know will know about me and Hal."

He shrugged. "You and Hal really are too good not to talk about. Older woman, younger man, reversing the usual gender clichés. Intriguing hints of Oedipal issues."

"I didn't really mind when they gossiped about us being together. But now—I feel like a fool—an old fool."

He sighed. "As a middle-aged gay man, I wouldn't know anything about that. If you think your client will accept a referral, I can send you a list of good local therapists who don't know you."

"Thank you." Larry's address book was legendary, and he gathered affection and admiration wherever he went. "I don't look forward to telling her."

Larry sighed. "You need to let her know that she's engaged to a guy whose screwing around, and there may be others. I'd get tested—seriously."

"You're right. I hadn't even thought of that."

"She's going to hate you. She may not want to take a referral from you, but I'll email you a list anyway. Anything about her that would narrow the field of potential referrals?"

"Body image around her weight."

"Just like almost every woman and gay man in America."

"Vampires figure on her list of fears."

"Now there's a coincidence. No wonder you were chatting so cozily with Bram." He patted me on the shoulder. "You're not ready to joke about it yet, are you?"

"Not yet. I left a message on Hal's voice mail, but we still need to have that last conversation."

Larry shook his head as he walked me out to the door. "I wonder how he was going to tell you about his engagement. Perhaps slipping a wedding invitation under your pillow. You're going to get through this, Kris. Call me any time. Look at the bright side—at least you weren't sleeping with one of your patients."

"Thanks, that makes me feel so much better."

Oddly, it did.

CHAPTER 9

HAL ROY'S SPOKEN NOTES
SILVER FLASH DRIVE/VOICE RECORDER
AUGUST 4TH

MEETING MINA GAVE ME THE COURAGE to think I could take control of the situation. Now she's going to marry me and I think she'll keep me on an even keel even when I gain the power I need.

Dad was a diplomat and Mom was one of those diplomatic wives who did whatever it took to help Dad. The bottom line is I need a wife who can help me with my work. Mina is all of that.

Wandering the night with Jack has given me a taste for robust, intoxicating women, and I keep putting off ending the affair with Kris. She's warm and funny, sexy and exhilarating, but she could never be part of the life I want to make, the power I need to find. She's too old, too big, and maybe even too smart to be an ambitious man's wife. If Kris really thought about it, maybe she might figure out for herself that our affair never had a future. After all, I never gave her a key to my place, told her about Jack or introduced her to my friends.

It's different with Mina. I want her to be a part of all of it.

Mina's perfect—beautiful, voluptuous but elegant, and sensible. Maybe too sensible.

She might save me, if I can just hold onto her. I tried to explain about Jack, and she refused to meet him. But she didn't run away either, even after I told her what I wanted. My only hope is that she can love me enough to see me through the change.

CHAPTER 10

KRISTIN MARLOWE'S TYPED NOTES
AUGUST 4ᵀᴴ CONTINUED

ON THE WAY HOME I checked my voicemail—nothing from Hal.

I walked through the garden where a violent *snip-snip* sound led me to Violet wielding garden shears on some hydrangea bushes. Vi was short and wiry with a wild mop of mostly gray curls and sharp green eyes behind wire-rimmed glasses. She and her ex-husband bought the house with its garden and cottage in the 1960s, when such things were possible. When they divorced, she got the house. They had painted it blue, and Vi planted morning glories, blue hydrangeas and a small vegetable garden. She lived in the house, rented the cottage to me, and did a bit of bookkeeping for hire to make ends meet. Some of Vi's vampire books had been published and brought her a little money. Her other passion was cats, but the cats don't bring in any money at all.

When she wasn't attacking a keyboard or chopping at things in the garden Vi had an energetic way of pouring out the most amazing ideas. Even people who wanted to dismiss her were mesmerized once she began to talk.

"So how's *Vampire Wedding* coming?" I asked.

Vi waved the shears in greeting. "The course of undead love did ne'er run smooth." She bent back down to lop off a dead branch—she was brutal with her pruning, and her plants flourished. "But look who I'm talking to—the woman with a young stud for company."

"Not anymore." I sighed and sat on the stone bench. "I just found out Hal is engaged to someone almost literally half my age."

Vi stopped in mid slice and straightened up to look at me. "Kris, I'm so sorry."

"But not surprised."

"No. That doesn't make him less of a bastard." She turned back and lopped off a few more branches before she set her clippers down and came to sit beside me. "When did you find out?"

"Earlier today. I'm still in shock."

"That's why I stick to fictional romance. Much less painful, and you can kill or maim the dirty rotten scoundrels at will. Would you like me to kill him for you—fictionally speaking?"

"Thanks—that would be lovely, if you can work him into the book."

"This book is nearly done, but I'll make it a point to arrange a bloody death for someone suspiciously like Hal in the next book. I'm going to the store this morning—do you want anything? Ice cream, chicken soup, hard liquor?"

"No, thanks. I'm just disappointed in love, not stricken with a cold."

"You should still keep warm. When you're all stressed out, you're vulnerable to germs."

After Violet left I logged onto eBay and indulged in some therapeutic Windows shopping. It soothed me to search for the speckled Bob White pattern of my mother's china—a very modest pattern with a little bird mother and chick.

My own mother had a set of much used dishes like that, and I inherited a few chipped pieces that I'm too afraid of breaking to use. Looking at images of strange 1950s relish dishes shaped like boomerangs and deviled egg plates with little hollows for each egg comforted me.

My mother had been like the brown, speckled birds painted on the dishes, with modest feathers and a bright, fast-moving energy about her. I only had one picture of her—in a silver frame, on a table just inside my line of vision as I sat at the computer. The rest had been lost in a fire at my parents' house, along with all the china, photo albums—everything material. I kept meaning to have the picture duplicated, but I didn't like to have it out of my sight. I knew it was irrational, but I feared it might be damaged or lost, and then I would have no image of her at all.

I marked a few online bargains to be watched, but I never bought anything. What's the point? My mother had the whole set and it couldn't save her.

In a flash of anger and rebellion, I abandoned all pretense of shopping and moved over to search out a few online dating sites and put up a profile. *Gay or not, Larry's houseguest got your motor going*, I told myself. Computer dating hadn't worked for me when I tried it after Mark died. I hastily posted the ad and logged off the computer. Too soon. Technically Hal and I hadn't even had the obligatory "we're breaking up" discussion, and even though I'd warmed up to Bram Van Helsing, if my perfect soul mate had knocked on my door that very moment, I'd have told him to shove off.

HAL HAD BEEN A GUILTY PLEASURE for me, and now I was paying for it.

I met Hal at a hearing in the neighborhood over tree cutting in one of the parks. He was highly distracting, sitting one seat away, tall and lean with brown hair and eyes and a mischievous face. Cute, but way too young. I put him out of my mind and concentrated on the tree debate—which involved picketing and shouting matches. People take their trees very seriously in San Francisco. The arguments grew heated and the egos were so titanic that I almost wished I could have brought some popcorn and a cold drink to sit back and better enjoy the drama.

In one corner, the All Trees Are Good faction that used the word "murder" to refer to the removal of any tree. In the other corner the Native Plant Restorationists, who wanted to root out every eucalyptus in the city and send the pieces back to Australia as bags of wood chips.

Halfway through the debate, Hal leaned over the empty chair between us, his leather-clad shoulder touching mine, and whispered, "Some people need to cut down on their shade-grown, eco-friendly, family-farmed coffee intake."

I smothered a laugh that provoked disapproving stares from others around us. Our eyes met. He leaned toward me again, eyes slightly closed as if savoring my perfume. I could smell his leather jacket and a complicated musky aftershave. I took in the depth of his brown eyes, pale complexion and artfully rumpled hair, so dark brown it was nearly black. I sat back in my chair, breathless, overcome by the kind of instant, simple lust I hadn't felt in years. Too young. Don't be a fool.

I forced myself to turn away. But when I sneaked a glance at him, he was looking at me. Did he wink? Did I imagine that?

I ducked out of the meeting with the first wave of escapees, half afraid he would follow and half afraid he wouldn't. He was right behind me. When the early exit crowd crammed into the elevator ahead of us, he tapped my shoulder. "I know where the stairs are. Come on."

He didn't look back. Of course I followed, admiring the view—blue jeans, and that black leather jacket. A bad boy, dangerous but somehow sophisticated. He held the Exit door open for me but stood close enough that I had to brush past him. He walked down the stairs with slow steps, as if teasing me to watch him as I followed. On the next landing he stopped so suddenly that I ran into him. He turned back and put his hand on my arm in a gesture that might have been concern for my footing. Or something more intimate.

"Sorry." His hand on my elbow kept me from backing away, but I didn't want to move.

Wildly inappropriate, my internal shrink shouted at me. But my blood was pounding in my ears loud enough to drown out any thought of common sense.

His face was close to mine, with those deep brown eyes a few inches away. "I know this is out of line, but you are such a goddess, I would like to get to know you better. Any chance of that?"

My body answered for me with a tremendous sigh of longing that startled me and caused him to nearly smile, but he kept his face solemn, so close to mine. "If you say 'no,' I promise I won't bother you again."

But he knew.

I took another breath, barely trusting myself to whisper, "I'd like that."

"You'd like me not to bother you, or you'd like to get to know me better?"

"Now you're teasing me."

We both smiled. I took a deep breath. "Don't let go of me. For some reason my knees feet a little weak just now." No one had had this strong of an effect on me since the day I met my husband.

"Okay." He put his arms around me in a chaste bear hug. Just a hug. It felt good, affectionate. It wasn't only sex but human contact I'd been starved for. The smell of the leather coat, a very faint whiff of sweat under the aftershave, something else my mind was too lost to classify. I felt warm all over. Lust or an early hot flash? Both?

A man and woman brushed past us on the stairwell, and everything suddenly congealed to remind me how much younger he was. I tried to pull back in confusion.

He didn't let me break away. I looked into those dark eyes. "What's your name?" I asked.

"Hal. Short for Henry. My father was the fourth in a long line of stuffy Henries. It didn't fit me, so I've been called Hal from a very early age." He smiled. Devastating. "What's your name?"

"Kristin Marlowe."

"Kristin Marlowe." He murmured as if he were tasting the flavor of it. "When can I see you again?" He explained that he was staying with an aunt in the city on a leave of absence from a job with the State Department.

A warning bell went off in my head. He was lying about something, but I didn't want to know. I told myself it could never last. In the expert opinion of my friends, most of whom were shrinks, I was crazy. But I could tell some of them also envied me.

NOW IT WAS OVER. Ended in my predictable humiliation—dumped for a younger woman.

I went to bed, totally drained and hurting, half expecting to toss and turn for hours. But exhaustion did its work and I slept, and did not wake until Hal slipped into the room.

CHAPTER II

MINA MURRAY'S JOURNAL
RED DIGITAL VOICE RECORDER
AUGUST 5TH

HAL GOT UP SO STEALTHILY IN THE DARK that I could tell he was trying not to wake me. I pretended to sleep. The minute the door closed behind him, I sat up and looked at the clock. Two-thirty. I got up and got dressed too. I watched from the window to see if he would go down to the shed in the back yard. He did. He came back out again a moment later with his motorcycle.

I ran downstairs and grabbed Lucy's trail bike from the inside hallway. She left it there behind the stairs, although she usually drove her car. By the time I quietly opened the door he was in the street, starting his engine. He never looked back and didn't seem to notice me pedaling about a block behind him.

I'd ridden a trail bike in high school and Lucy's bike was just like the one gathering dust in my dad's garage. They were right—it does come back to you.

I wasn't wearing any of the reflective gear Lucy wore when she rode at night. If there was any traffic out there, I would have been invisible. But even when he turned onto Geary, Hal and I were the only traffic on the road. The noise of the motorcycle covered the quiet sound of the pedals and creak of the frame. I half expected to lose him when he speeded up on Geary. But he only went about 18 blocks to 30th Avenue, turned left, then right, and parked on Clement Street.

I coasted to a stop, still a block away. I couldn't believe where he was going, but there was no mistaking it. I went through the doorway next to the house every week. But I rang the bell so Kristin could buzz me

in. Hal had a key. He had a key to my therapist's house.
   The door slammed shut. Hal never noticed me.

CHAPTER 12

KRISTIN MARLOWE'S TYPED NOTES AUGUST 5TH

I WOKE UP WHEN HAL CAME IN. The red digits on the clock showed nearly three a.m. He left the light off. For a few seconds my body thrilled with anticipation as he stood there, peeling off his clothes with his usual speed and no doubt his usual grace, though it was too dark to see. Then the truth crashed down on me.

"Hal?"

"Yes, baby."

"When were you going to tell me about Mina?"

He stopped in the middle of taking off his pants, dimly visible in the darkened room, standing on one leg. Then he pulled his pants back on and sat on the bed.

Naked from the waist up, only a few feet away. I could have sworn I could smell Mina's White Musk perfume on him.

"I never meant to hurt you."

"So you knew I was treating Mina?"

"Yes."

"And you two are getting married?"

"Yes."

I turned on the light, wanting to see his face, until I did see it. He stared down at the carpet, as if measuring the distance to where he had dropped his shoes.

I took a deep breath. "How long have you been seeing her?"

"Six months."

Hurt and rage flared up, and made me reckless. "Did you know that she thinks you're—" I stopped myself in time.

"Thinks I'm what?" Now he did meet my eyes. His expression of contented bemusement made me want to slap him.

"Never mind." I could have bit my tongue for saying even that much. But I couldn't stop looking at Hal. I had to hold back. My body seemed to have a will of its own, leaning toward him, wanting to reach out to him and beg him to stay.

His eyes were too dark in the lamplight, unreadable. "You must know better than anyone that Mina gets some strange ideas."

I didn't say anything. When he said Mina's name, I felt myself grow deadly still.

"Are you going to keep her as a patient?"

"I'm not going to discuss it with you."

He reached out his hand, as if he wanted to touch me. Our eyes locked for several seconds. I couldn't look away—or move. His hand fell back down to his side. He stood, retrieved his shoes and socks from the floor and sat on the chair at the foot of the bed to put them on. He picked up his shirt last of all, and buttoned it up again. I hated him. Yet in that moment all I could think was that I would never be able to touch him again.

Then he was gone. I heard the front door close. I got up, put on a robe and went out into the hall. I wasn't going to be sleeping anytime soon.

CHAPTER 13

MINA MURRAY'S JOURNAL
RED DIGITAL VOICE RECORDER
AUGUST 5TH CONTINUED

SOMEHOW I RODE THE BIKE BACK TO HAL'S without crashing it, crying all the way. It's a wonder I didn't run off the road.

I wheeled the bike back behind the stairwell and went up the red stone stairs to Hal's apartment. In the bedroom I jammed the few things I kept there into my tote bag. Then I stood in front of the mirror above the antique dresser and took off the engagement ring he had given me. I left it in on top of the dresser. It seemed so lonely in the middle of the bare wood. I pulled a silk scarf out of my bag and folded it and put it under the ring as if to keep it warm, I guess. I didn't leave a note. I didn't know what to say.

Closing the door, I realized I would probably never come back here again. I walked down the red stairs and through the shadows of the foyer. At least I wouldn't miss this creepy place.

I got as far as the sidewalk in front of the house and stopped, stood still, and wondered where I should go. I hadn't given up my own apartment, even though I'd been spending most nights with Hal. But that would be the first place he would look. I didn't want to talk to Hal right now. I didn't want to see anyone. I hated everyone.

I started to cry again, walking along the unpaved path that bordered the park to get my car. Something rustled in the bushes. Before I could think to run, hands in the shadows reached out to grab me.

CHAPTER 14

KRISTIN MARLOWE'S TYPED NOTES
AUGUST 5TH

HAL HAD LEFT HIS COPY OF THE KEYS to the gate and my cottage on the small table in the hallway, just inside the front door. I grabbed them and threw them against the wall. Barely restrained myself from throwing the table as well.

Rage turned to tears, and I walked through the small cottage crying. Finally I sat in the kitchenette staring at the wall, trying not to think. My mind had started running the whole thing through over and over and getting more upset with each minute.

I got up and wandered into the front room. Hal's key ring lay on the floor where it had fallen after I threw it against the wall. I went to pick it up. That was when the absence of the silver framed picture hit me like a hammer.

The bastard had taken the picture of my mother.

Why would Hal do such a thing? But it had been there. I had glanced at it earlier in the evening when I was on the computer. Now it was missing. The pain of betrayal merged with a rising tide of rage.

I looked down at the key ring in my hand. My two keys were there and so was another. He had never given me the key to his house while we were dating. Could this be it?

CHAPTER 15

MINA MURRAY'S JOURNAL, RED DIGITAL VOICE RECORDER, AUGUST 5TH, CONTINUED

THE STRONG ARMS THAT HELD ME GENTLY turned me around. "Mina? Are you okay?"

"Ned! What are you doing here?'"

"I was supposed to meet Lucy, but I think I have once again been stood up. I was going to check to see if she was visiting—um, you know—the shed."

My tear-congested voice sounded like a child with a cold. "Lucy said Hal was kicking it out, the thing in the shed."

Ned gave an exasperated snort. "Right! Hal is the center of the universe. He told me to show up after this big confrontation thing he was doing to get his way. Then typical Hal, he's a no show. Lucy fell all over herself to get me here, then she didn't even bother to tell me it was cancelled."

At the mention of Hal tears began to roll down my cheeks. I could feel my chin quiver and I held back a sob.

Ned seemed to really see me for the first time. He bent down to look into my face. "You're shaking. You were leaving the house. Are you okay?"

"I don't know." I started to sob.

"Oh, please don't." He hugged me and patted me on the back, then let me go. I put my hands over my face.

"Here, let me take your bag. Come with me. I'll show you something."

I hung back.

"It's not like that, Mina. Look, it's me, Ned. I'm Hal's best friend, and you must have guessed I'm in love with Lucy."

"You are?" I stopped crying in surprise.

"God help me, I am. You can trust me." He slung my bag over his shoulder and grasped my hand. "Come on. Let's go someplace where it's not so cold. Maybe I can make you laugh, or at least smile."

"Unlikely."

"You'd be surprised."

I let him lead me.

Ned had parked his moped in Hal's back yard and I didn't want to go near the place again, so I let him drive my car. I stopped crying on the way over to his apartment, a tiny studio south of Market.

Ned's place astonished me. Small, uncluttered and scrupulously clean. A big screen Macintosh computer and a dozen unidentified pieces of audio and video hardware were wired up and stacked on plain wood bookcases next to a tilted drafting table with a goose-necked lamp over it. He switched the lamp on, illuminating a piece of paper with a comic strip in progress on the board. Completed strips signed by Ned were pinned up to the wall.

"I didn't know you did cartooning."

"There's a lot about me you don't know. That's the Abominable Snowman at School." The hairy creature wore a sweatshirt that said Yeti U. With wild eyes and a goofy grin, it did bear a certain resemblance to Ned, right down to the sheepish expression.

"There's a smile, that's better," Ned said, coming up behind me. I tensed, half expecting him to touch me, but he stayed about a foot away. I relaxed a little. "Would you like a drink?"

"Yes, thanks."

"You'd better save your thanks till you see what I've got to offer."

I followed him into the small galley kitchen—just a sink and stove, with a counter separating it from the rest of the room. He looked in his tiny fridge. "I have vodka, and we could also split a cream soda."

"Okay." I would have said yes to cough syrup at that point if it had alcohol in it.

He pulled a bottle of vodka out of the kitchen cabinet. Before he could open it, the phone rang. He froze. We both looked at the phone. It rang again.

"I don't have to answer it—it's nearly dawn, after all."

Ned's answering machine took the call and then we heard Hal's voice. "She's gone, man. Mina's missing." Ned crossed the small space in two strides, grabbed the receiver. "Hal, slow down. What do you mean, missing?" He raised his eyebrows at me.

I waved my hands to warn him, and shook my head, placing a finger on my lips in the universal "don't tell" gesture.

"Okay, so she's not at home. Doesn't she have family in town, her dad or—? No, I didn't know she was scared of him." He mouthed the word "sorry" to me. "She probably went to a friend's place, man. Yeah, check in the morning, it's nearly dawn. No, you can't come over here."

I stood up and went to get my purse and coat.

Ned held up a hand for me to wait. "Because I have company, that's why. No one you know."

I sighed and sat down again.

Ned gestured to me that he was winding up the conversation. "I couldn't stick around your backyard all night, Hal, waiting for your big vampire scene—which evidently didn't come off. Oh, so now you tell me that if you harm the old guy you lose your trust fund. He knows it was just an idle threat. At least you entertained Lucy for a night, that's more than I can usually do. Don't worry about Mina, she's the most level-headed person I know."

I looked at Ned in astonishment. He nodded and mouthed, *You are.*

"She probably just wanted some time off from your relentless charm," he said into the phone. "Seriously, I can't talk any more. I have a guest." He paused and ran his hands through his already wildly wind-blown hair. "Get some sleep, man. I'll see you tomorrow."

He put the phone down and came to sit across from me. He picked up the bottle of vodka and put it down again. "He said you left and took all your stuff with you."

"That's because found out he was cheating on me with my shrink. I followed him."

Ned whistled. "Hal's doing your shrink? Are you sure?"

"He had a key to her place. He went in at 2:00 a.m." I started to cry again. He scooted over close on the sofa and put his arms around me. I cried into his T-shirt. It smelled freshly laundered. "I'm getting your shirt wet."

"Go ahead. I don't mind."

"Do you have any tissues?"

"I'll go look." He got up and went into the other room and came back with a roll of toilet paper. That made me laugh. He stood next to me, hovering over the sofa while I mopped my face and nose.

He shifted awkwardly from foot to foot, but his eyes showed kindness. He didn't come back to sit with me. But he didn't move further away either. Looking up at him, for the first time I saw the two scarcely healed, raised welts on the side of his neck.

"My god, Ned, what happened to your neck?"

"I thought you knew." He put his hand up to touch the marks, and then stopped himself. "They're real, Mina. It's a vampire bite mark. I'd have thought you'd seen them on Lucy, she's got them all over."

"I try not to look when Lucy's wandering around nude. Hal doesn't have anything like that. I would have noticed."

Ned smiled with a strange sadness. "Hal doesn't have any because the vampire that lives in the shed refused to drink from him or any of us. Something about soiling the nest." He sat down on the sofa.

I pressed against the opposite arm of the sofa, ready to get up and run. "I didn't know they were so picky. So how did you get...bit?" I gestured to his neck.

"Lucy and I found another vampire." He seemed to be searching my face for a clue as to how I would take the news. "It's very hard to hook up with them. The other vampire we found likes Lucy and me, but he won't touch Hal, some kind of turf thing. It drives Hal crazy."

I leaned back against the sofa cushions. "Oh, god. I was hoping it was just a game Hal would get tired of."

"Sorry. I shouldn't burden you with it."

"I want to know all of it—I need to know."

"You want some of this vodka?" He looked over toward the cupboard. "I've got some jelly glasses."

My need for a drink had evaporated. "No thanks."

Ned unscrewed the vodka bottle, took a drink, recapped it and put it on the table. He took a deep breath and turned to me. "I'm not sure you understand the depth of Hal's ambition."

"I know he wants to be able to have an impact, to really change things."

"That's right. With his education and connections he's been able to score some pretty impressive overseas assignments for someone his age. But he's just a junior errand boy. It could be twenty years or never before he gets any real say. What he wants from the vampires is a shortcut to power."

"Is it possible?"

"Who knows?" He shrugged. "The vampires aren't telling. But Hal is convinced he can make it work for him."

"And you go along with it because—?"

"You know Hal. He's fun to hang out with. The rest of us just got sucked in. To coin a phrase." He laughed at his pun. I didn't.

"How can Hal change things if he can never go anywhere in the daylight?"

Ned laughed. "Okay. I didn't see that coming. Hal always says you're the most pragmatic person he's ever met. His idea is to exercise power outside of the system."

I made a skeptical face. "By drinking blood?"

Ned leaned forward and a yearning expression came over his face. I moved away from him on the sofa without even meaning to.

"The blood just starts the energy flow. It's the life force they take," he whispered hoarsely. "And it feels good, Mina. So good. When they take some of yours, you get some of theirs. Hal thinks he can control people and get things done that way."

"But you say he hasn't had a vampire bite him, so how does he know?"

"Oh, we told him what it was like." Now Ned looked a little smug. It probably didn't often happen that he had something Hal wanted but couldn't get. "Hal may be right. It's pretty powerful."

"Except the other vampire also refuses to turn any of you into vampires."

"Yeah, so far. That's the problem."

"Did you ever think maybe they can't turn you into a vampire? Maybe you have to be born with it."

Ned froze for a moment, startled. He never had thought of that. I don't know why it even occurred to me.

"You're right, we need to know a lot more," Ned said hurriedly. "That's why Hal is looking for the others—if they can't take us over, maybe we can work with them."

Nice save, Ned, I thought, but didn't say it. For once I wasn't scared—I was angry at Hal for not thinking this through.

"So far all we know is that there are others," Ned said. "But the two vampires we have met refuse to discuss them."

"So what do you get out of this?"

He shrugged. "Maybe I'm hooked on the excitement."

"And you're in love with Lucy."

He looked away. "Oh, you heard me say that. I thought you might have been too upset. I'd be a fool if I was, wouldn't I?"

"I'll take that for a 'yes.'"

"I can't help myself. She's worse than Hal. She's totally obsessed with becoming a vampire."

I buried my face in my hands. "Oh, god. Can't everyone just stop it?"

"That's a good question, Mina. I'm not sure we can stop anymore."

CHAPTER 16

KRISTIN MARLOWE'S TYPED NOTES
AUGUST 5ᵀᴴ

A LITTLE AFTER DAWN I HEARD VI in the tiny garden outside my kitchen window. I pulled on a sweater over my T-shirt and sweatpants and went out.

She held up a hand. "Wait just a minute. Don't scare the ferals." A Himalayan cat, longhaired and blue-eyed with Siamese dark mask and paws, wound back and forth around Vi's shins with demanding meows while a venerable old Maine Coon cat came out of the bushes and crouched gravely as she dumped a can of food in a bowl for him. Now she talked so softly, I couldn't tell if it was to me or the cats. "I met these ladies in Safeway buying bulk cat food." Vi put the bowl down in front of the Himalayan.

"Did they initiate you into their ancient society of cat ladies with the secret handshake and discount coupons?"

"Cat people are not by nature joiners. But one of them did tell me about a 24-can special. She said the canned food is so good, she'd eat it herself."

"This gives us all hope for our old age."

The battle-scarred old Maine Coon cat had polished off his bowl in record time and stretched and settled down for a post-meal grooming, while the Himalayan returned to rubbing his cheeks against Vi's calves. "There you go, kits, you'll live for another day," she said to them.

I was used to Vi alternately addressing me and whatever cat she happened to be talking to. "Both these guys were somebody's pets," she said softly to me. "Blue-eyes here begs for attention, but if I put my hand down to try to touch him, he bites. I've got a corner in hell

48

marked out for his former owners."

She gathered her bathrobe around her. "That's enough for now," she said to the cats. "I don't put out more than they can eat. No sense encouraging the raccoons to come around."

She didn't turn to go back in. "I heard Hal's motorcycle in the middle of the night."

"He dropped in. We broke up and he stole my mother's photograph on his way out the door."

"Wow."

"I thought I knew him." I sat on the stone bench. "God, this bench is cold."

"Yeah." She didn't sit down, but came over to stand next to me.

"First my client is going on about vampires, now she tells me she's engaged to Hal and he wants to become a vampire?"

"Hal?" Her face lit with professional interest.

I put my hand on my forehead, against a headache that was just beginning to throb. "I shouldn't have said that. She's my client. She deserves confidentiality. God, she doesn't know even know yet that he's cheating on both of us. What a mess."

"But—" The "V" word had snagged Vi's attention. "She said he was a vampire?"

"Wants to be a vampire."

"Oh. That. Hal sounds a little old for the Goth scene."

"Bram Van Helsing said it's like a youth cult."

"You spoke to Abraham Van Helsing?"

"He said everyone calls him Bram. He's staying with Larry."

Vi took a second to process this and another thought arose. "Bram Van Helsing is gay?"

"Most of Larry's houseguests are. You know Van Helsing?"

"I've never met him. I thought it was a pen name, but he's a major authority on vampire lore."

I raised my face with sudden determination. "Hal left me a key and I think it's his house key. I'm going to go over to get my mother's photo back."

"Want me to go with you?"

"No, thanks. I need to do this alone. If I meet Hal, I might have a few more things to say to him. Either way, I'm mad enough not to care."

Violet smiled. "Call if you need anything. Bail, wooden stakes, anything at all. If Hal really does hang out with vampires, they'll be asleep in daylight. So just get out of there by dusk."

CHAPTER 17

KRISTIN MARLOWE'S TYPED NOTES
AUGUST 5TH CONTINUED

MY LAST CLIENT APPOINTMENT ENDED late in the afternoon and I headed for Hal's house. I could have walked the distance in half an hour, but I took my car in case I needed a quick getaway. I had only been there once, late at night after drinks at The Cliff House nearby. In daylight it was even more dramatic the way the trees of Sutro Heights Park suddenly gave way to a cliff-side view of the ocean as I drew near the house.

The flat ocean stretched an opalescent pearl color under the late afternoon haze. Wind shook the branches of the trees surrounding the house. A wind-scoured, pale green house, three stories tall, divided into three flats. A big hole gaped in the exterior wall on the third floor. Probably dry rot. No wonder Hal closed off the top floor.

Standing on the front steps, I started to put my key in the lock, but the door was jerked inward before I could put my key in the lock. A stooped, elderly woman stood in the doorway, her wrinkled face contorted and flushed with rage. Hal's aunt's caretaker. She spit some verbal venom at me and told me not to go in the shed.

But she let me slip past her. Why would I go in the shed anyway?

I don't know why I shivered.

While the afternoon faded into evening outside I searched Hal's apartment. Looked over the photos on the wall—memories of a childhood spent in transit.

Hal as a beautiful youngster. I felt a pang of tenderness for his dark-haired, eager, youthful image, then the anger rose up in my throat to choke me. He has his pictures, why did he have to take mine? Plaques and honors of the parents that died before their son graduated high school. Recent souvenirs from Istanbul, Sarajevo and Kabul. I looked first on every table, mantelpiece and even the kitchen counter. No sign of my mother's picture.

A board creaked and I jumped, landing on another board that creaked even louder. I laughed uneasily, telling myself that if Mina or Hal or anyone showed up I had every right to demand my mother's picture back.

I went through all the drawers, putting everything back the way it had been. My heart was hammering so hard I could feel the blood pounding in my head. I had to force myself to concentrate and look.

I looked everywhere he might have stashed a framed photo. Then I realized the sun was setting. Time to go.

I let myself out of the flat empty-handed. Still frustrated, I kept the key, thinking that it might open one of the other locked doors. I went up to the next landing, but the stairs were blocked with a wrought iron gate. I didn't even try the key, because the space was crammed to the gate and stacked to the ceiling with odds and ends of furniture. The gate appeared to be the only thing keeping them from tumbling down the short flight of stairs to the landing in front of Hal's apartment. Everything visible up there was liberally coated in dust undisturbed by any new additions.

The old building and the fading light outside wore away at my nerve. I walked down to the foyer, and on past the ground floor apartment where Hal's aunt had lived. I couldn't see Hal putting my mother's picture in there with the old lady and her hostile caretaker.

So, the shed in the back yard was the very last remotely possible hiding place. I went down the hall bathed in red light of the sunset. A few minutes later I was standing in the shed under the glare of the electric light bulb, watching the lid rise on a crate that should have been empty.

CHAPTER 18

KRISTIN MARLOWE'S TYPED NOTES
AUGUST 5TH CONTINUED

A PUDGY HAND FOLLOWED BY A LARGE, rounded arm appeared in the gap, raising the lid until it rested against the wall and revealing a huge, white-bearded man. He sat up, still coughing.

I watched, frozen in shock.

The man was old, fat and also broad-shouldered, with unruly white hair and beard. Santa Claus? Not quite.

His face seemed startlingly pale when paired with the reddened cheeks and nose of a serious drinker. He wore an ancient, old-fashioned long underwear shirt that might have been World War II army surplus. He gave one last wracking cough, then took a deep breath. He turned to regard me with eyes that were bleary but bright blue, not bloodshot. No shaking from alcohol withdrawal, as some drinkers have on arising. No, he was totally still, his eyes sharp and piercing as the eyes of a hawk, but with a most unhawk-like twinkle.

Turn and run. But I stood frozen. Not so much terrified as stunned, like a small mammal suddenly confronted with a large snake.

"A vision of womanliness," he said in a thick, English accent. Even with all my public television viewing I couldn't place its location in the British Isles. Definitely not a BBC announcer generic English accent. Not a Scottish burr, or an Irish lilt. Not Eliza Doolittle Cockney or Liverpool Beatles either. Maybe a little closer to the Yorkshire accents on that series about the country veterinarian. It could have been Welsh. Everything I know about Welsh accents I learned from actors playing Fluellen in Shakespeare's *Henry the Fifth*.

"You can't be a dream. It's dusk and I'm awake." The exotic flavor of the words and his deep rumbling voice didn't fit at all with a crate in a garage, yet he seemed perfectly at home. "Fair mistress, what name shall I call you?"

"I'm Kristin," I managed to say. "And you are?"

He cleared his throat. "Jack Falstaff with my familiars, John with my brothers and sisters, and Sir John with all Europe. At your service, my lady."

CHAPTER 19

HAL ROY'S SPOKEN NOTES
SILVER FLASH DRIVE/VOICE RECORDER
UNDATED

THE MYSTERY OF THE SHED CONSUMED ME. I set out my own surveillance patrol, keeping in the shadows and the bushes so no one would see me watching. The only person who came in the back yard was my aunt, and she went straight for the shed without looking right or left. She removed the padlock and went inside, leaving the door slightly open. I crept closer, but didn't dare risk getting close enough to look in. The sounds I heard then startled me.

Some time later she emerged and made her way unsteadily up to the house. Almost immediately after that a huge bear of a man came out and glanced around. I drew back into the bushes and tried not to breathe. For a moment he seemed to look right at me and chuckle. Then he walked to the end of the yard and, with unexpected speed and agility, elbowed his way into the bushes.

I mentally marked the spot he went though to check later, but never found any signs of any gap in the bushes, let alone an opening big enough for such a big man.

Nothing more happened for a few hours. Eventually I got cold even in my sleeping bag, and stiff and sore from lying on the ground waiting. I went inside. When I checked the next morning, the padlock was back in place.

I usually ate lunch with my aunt. This involved nothing more complex than opening cans and buttering bread, but we both did that at the same table at the same time. I cleared my throat to get her attention away from her magazine for a moment and asked her why the shed was locked in the daytime but not at night.

Aunt Reba looked at me full on for several seconds. Her hand went to her throat, always covered by a turtleneck sweater. She played with a short gold chain that hung around her neck. I had never noticed before that the key on the chain was not an ornamental jeweled pendant, but a small steel padlock key.

"My—special guest stays there," she finally said. "I open the door at night so he can get out, and I close and lock it in the morning to protect him. He's got a kind of medical condition. It would kill him if he saw the sun. I'm telling you this, because he is a responsibility you will eventually inherit."

"Is he like a crazy relative or something?" I asked, trying to put this together with the sounds I'd heard coming from the shed. They didn't sound like any family I'd want to know about.

"Not a relative." For a moment Aunt Reba almost shuddered, but I couldn't tell from what. "I'll introduce you tonight. But Hal—"

"Yes?"

"This has to remain secret between us. If you reveal his existence to anyone, or if you harm him in any way, I will see to it that you never inherit a penny under my will, and if you think my lawyer can't do that, think again."

"Yes, ma'am—I mean, no ma'am, whatever you say." I was fifteen and I had no idea what she was talking about.

THAT NIGHT MY AUNT TOLD ME to wait in the living room of the ground floor flat while she went into what was then her bedroom upstairs with a huge, shadowy figure in what looked like the world's oldest greatcoat.

They stayed up there for about half an hour and the sounds filtering down seemed even louder than the ones from the shed. Then my aunt came down with a dreamy expression on her face, leading a huge, fat old man with brilliant blue eyes, pink cheeks. He was wiping his hand across his mouth when he came out. For a moment I thought I saw blood on his lip, but that seemed unlikely.

"This is Jack."

The old man made a surprisingly fluid, old-fashioned bow.

"Jack?"

"Just remember this, Hal—you take care of Jack, he will take care of you." She gave him a little shove toward me and ended up almost losing her own footing. He caught her around the waist and held her up. She giggled like a naughty toddler.

My face must have shown my shock. The old man steered Aunt Reba over to a chair and gently set her down in it. Then he came over to stand before me. "So it's Hal, is it?"

I nodded.

"Can you drive, young Hal?" He had a deep, commanding voice with a strong British accent.

"I've got my learner's permit, but I haven't been able to take lessons yet. My Dad used to let me drive the golf cart when we played golf."

Mentioning my dad brought an unexpected sob to my throat. I had been trying not to think of my parents.

"Mistress Reba, may we have your keys?" Jack leaned close to her. She stared at him with a dazed smile and nodded.

"Lad, would you fetch her purse?" Jack raised an eyebrow at me, completely certain I would know where she kept her purse. I brought it to my aunt and she fumbled her car keys out and handed them to me.

"Mark how we ask permission, lad, before we take what we need. There may be tolls to pay—have you enough coins?"

"Coins?"

"Money, lad. We may need to ask your lovely aunt for more."

"I've got some."

My aunt was now clutching her purse with a death grip. Did she know that the money in my pocket had come from her wallet?

Jack nodded. "Well enough, then. We bid you farewell, my lovely Reba. Come, Hal. I'll show you sights that I'll warrant you've never seen, even though you're born and bred here."

What teenaged boy could resist that?

THAT NIGHT WAS A RIDE that went further into pure debauchery than I could have imagined possible. I was hooked.

When it got close to dawn I followed his and Aunt Reba's instructions and locked him in the shed.

It took a few nights for me to understand just what Jack was. The first time I asked him, he laughed and said, "There are more things in heaven and earth, Horatio, than are dreamt of in your philosophy."

"Who's Horatio?" I had to ask.

Another fit of laughter. "We may meet him up at Land's End, or mayhap at Devil Slide to the south. Let us see what the night will bring."

CHAPTER 20

KRISTIN MARLOWE'S TYPED NOTES
AUGUST 5ᵀᴴ CONTINUED

"SIR JOHN—SORRY—I DIDN'T CATCH your last name?" I had, I just didn't believe it.

He examined me with eyes that were bloodshot but showed no sign of yellowing from the jaundice of liver disease. He seemed to come to some kind of decision. "The Bard dubbed me Falstaff, and many know that name. But in your fair city most call me Sir John. I was born John and won my knighthood on the field of battle."

Falstaff did seem appropriate to his age and girth. But he had picked an unusual figure to impersonate, or fixate on—not Napoleon or Elvis—but Shakespeare's Falstaff, a character from literature!

No harm in talking to him. Had there ever been a journal article on delusions of being a fictional character? I would look it up as soon as I got to my computer. A flicker of self-interest ran through me at the thought of writing a journal article on this subject. I must have showed it in some way because he leaned toward me.

I tensed up, remembering the months when I worked in a full-fledged mental hospital. You thought you could tell the dangerous ones, but you could make a fatal mistake. I knew a psychiatric nurse who guessed wrong. The patient she misjudged had always been so quiet—right up until he nearly fractured her spine.

This man bowed in such a courtly way that all my misgivings melted away and I took his outstretched hand. He bent over my knuckles to kiss them in that European fashion that always causes consternation in American women. He released my hand and stayed a safe arm's length away. I relaxed a little.

Despite his hair sticking up in all directions, and his track suit pants with the stripe along the side that he clearly had slept in, he smelled faintly of pine shavings with perhaps a hint of wood smoke, newly cut grass, and a faint, not unpleasant, overtone of fresh mushrooms.

The man in the box began to cough again—at length. "Beg pardon. The dust. A quintessence of dust, as the poet would have it."

"Right, from *Hamlet*. Are you an actor who played Falstaff on stage?" I started to edge backwards towards the door, but I didn't dare look back to check my progress.

"One man in his time plays many parts," he said with a chuckle that became a cough.

I stopped backing up. "That's from *As You Like It.*"

"Indeed. Remarkable. Few in this age find time to read the Bard. A gifted gentleman. His homage caught my attention, as well it might. I have had centuries to study him, since our chance meeting when he studied me."

I ignored the part about meeting Shakespeare. He seemed harmless. A deluded lover of theater. "Have you been staying here?" I gestured to the shed around me.

"Since it was new. Now, like myself, the old building's sadly fallen off."

I blinked. Delusional or flat out lying, of course. The shed looked as old as the house itself, which must have been built in the 1930s. He would have had to be in his eighties to have been living here that long. His hair and beard were white, his cheeks and nose mottled red, but for all his coughing and groaning he moved with a fluid grace that didn't advertise advanced age.

"Surely you weren't born here." His strong English accent sounded genuine.

"No, the old girl in the main house brought me over here when she was young, poor gal. Hold on a moment. Mistress Reba?" He raised his head, nostrils flared as if scenting the air, head tilted as if listening. "A sea change. She's gone from here. Must have taken her off while I slept the daylight away."

"The nurse said they're changing the locks."

"The nurse! A nun in deed, if not profession. All in black with vinegar for blood."

I laughed and nodded. An odd turn of speech, but it did describe her well. "You might want to get your stuff out first."

"And so I must." His eyes narrowed as he focused on me.

Oops. I took another step backwards with one hand behind me to feel the door knob. "Do you need me to call someone for you?"

"No."

"Any family in the area?"

"All dead. Long dead."

"Have you tried the Veterans Hospital just up the hill? They have resources. Are you a veteran?"

He gave me a rueful smile. "Yes. But that was in another country."

"And besides, the wench is dead." I finished the quote without thinking.

He examined me again carefully. "Not only the Bard. You also know Chris Marlowe."

"I am Kris Marlowe," I said, again without thinking. Damn. I hadn't meant to give him my whole name.

"That cannot be. Christopher Marlowe was a man, and dead 400 years."

"No, my name is Kristin Marlowe."

"Ah." He lurched forward and stood with difficulty, hanging onto the edge of the box. He held out his hand to me. "Pray you help me get out of this box then, Mistress Kit? Just a hand from you for leverage."

Against my better judgment I went over next to the box and held out my hand, which he gripped strongly. He clambered up and out of the box, still holding it.

"I'm sorry, sir—" I let go of his hand.

"A thousand thanks. Your servant, ma'am." He sketched a bow, short-circuited when he staggered sideways and had to grab the edge of the box to stay upright. This brought on another coughing fit.

"Would you like some water? I've got bottled water in the car."

"Water!" he gasped between coughs. "Would you kill me, girl?" He shook his head, "Thank you, but no."

I noticed a faint twitch go through him at the word "car." Uh-oh, he was going to hitch a ride. I decided to see if I could make a dent in his delusion. "I remember now. In the plays, Falstaff drinks sack."

"Sack and sugar, so he did, and so did I once." He sighed so gustily that the light bulb on the string above us shifted, casting huge shadows.

Maybe he had quit drinking. From his looks he should have reeked of it, but there was no scent of liquor around him. "By your speech you must be English—"

"Yes, as you say now, I am an export of that sceptered isle, the other Eden." He turned his piercing blue eyes on me. "Shall we go, then?"

"Oh, I'm sorry. I just realized that if you're English, the Veterans Administration here wouldn't be able to help you, unless you've served in the United States military."

Sir John bent over the open crate and hauled out an enormous great-coat that looked as if it had survived the Battle of Waterloo. He put the coat on with surprising agility, closed the lid of the crate without so much as a creak. Then he turned to examine me with entirely too much interest. "You wouldn't have a basement or even a dark corner of a shed—" he gestured eloquently to the space around him, "for an old solider to lay down a bedroll for a day or an evening."

"No, I'm sorry, uh, Sir John," I sighed. "Maybe the VA hospital could give you some British contact information or referral to some agencies."

He looked at me expectantly. He already knew I was going to help him. Damn my co-dependent nature, this was beyond stupid and into dangerous. Maybe I was still angry enough at Hal and the world to do something crazy. But the old guy did not appear dangerous and he was more than a little charming. I felt sorry for him about to lose his shed crash pad.

"All right. Come on. It's not far. "

"Let us to this hospital. The touch a plump and rosy young nurse or three would revive me in no time." He saw my scowl and swift-ly amended. "Even a few words with some other old soldiers would steady the nerves."

Other old soldiers with bottles in paper bags? He took my arm and I did not protest. Again that piney, foresty smell.

I didn't have a sense of violence about him, but I did remove my arm from his grip and kept just out of reach as we walked toward the car. He paused outside the car as if needing an invitation. I opened the door and said "Here you go," feeling like a fool, but something about his presence dispelled fear and inspired amusement. His bulk was enough that it took some maneuvering to get him into the passenger seat. But I had purposely bought a reasonably roomy VW Beetle because of my own size. Sir John didn't try to buckle the seat belt, and I wasn't about to reach over to help him fasten it.

It was only a few blocks and a few hills to the Fort Miley VA Hospital. I knew the route intimately. My late husband had been in and out of it several times in his last years.

I paused at the main entrance on Clement Street. "The hospital is right up there."

Sir John gave a disheartened sigh. "That's a long march uphill for an old man at night. Not fond of hills. Less altitude, more breath, I say. Are you sure you wouldn't have a place for me to sleep?"

I sighed. "I'll drive up the hill and drop you in front of the hospital." At the top of the hill, I stopped for the stop sign before driving into the drop off area. No visible pedestrians. A cab was just pulling away and a Muni bus waited at the terminal just beyond, doors open, motor off, the driver not visible.

Sir John suddenly reached out, grabbed my neck and pulled me across the seat.

"Hey!" was all I could say before I felt a sharp stab of pain just below my chin. *My god, he must have a knife.* I leaned forward onto the horn, but I didn't hear it sound. I was pinned in by the steering wheel in front of me and his body holding me by the neck cutting off breath and any scream for help.

My last thought was *Kris, you fool—you should have run when you had the chance.* But instead of fear, I felt overwhelmed with an almost pleasurable, drowsy tugging at my mind, like a drug, pulling me down into dark oblivion. Then nothing.

CHAPTER 21

HAL ROY'S SPOKEN NOTES
SILVER FLASH DRIVE/VOICE RECORDER
UNDATED

JACK WAS A HARD HABIT TO BREAK. Aunt Reba didn't want to try. As I heard the story later, she had installed him in the old house to begin with, but moved him out to the shed when they quarreled.

After a summer of wild rambles with Jack, I went off to boarding school, then to college. I tried to patch together a suitable life for myself, but I couldn't stay away from Jack.

Every time I left San Francisco my life seemed to slow down. I didn't start to live again until I stood outside the shed ready to open the padlock, help Jack out of his coffin, open a bottle of wine and delve between the thighs of the ladies who gravitated to him. My only fear was that I would arrive and find he was gone. I deputized Ned and Lucy to keep an eye on him in case my aunt could not. When I came back he was there and waiting for me.

We talked into the night, serious conversation wrapped in laughter, and punctuated by Jack's own style of orgy. He asked about my education, and I told him. He grasped it all and turned it back to me as a joke. He had read so much over the centuries, but he never seemed to have had the urge to master any serious course of study—not that it was book learning that drew me to him.

I could never take him all in—just when I expected him to be a lowlife rogue, he would turn philosopher on me. His easy grasp of every world he entered hinted at a mastery of secret knowledge that I wanted more and more. When he told me it was dangerous, I knew I had to have it.

I only told a few people about Jack. Ned and Lucy because I had known them since high school, but no other friends at school or girl-friends. This was one thing I could not share. They all would have thought I was insane. Even if I had brought them here to show them—well, I couldn't trust anyone that much. After college it was either going to be grad school or the army for me. I went with a graduate program in international politics and United States foreign policy.

"I served as a page to a great lord," Sir John said. "Got my education in his service, and my knighthood on the battle field. One must needs be a knight in those benighted times. But you must be a scholar." He patted my shoulder. "Let's have a brave debauch to send you off to battle the books."

CHAPTER 22

KRISTIN MARLOWE'S TYPED NOTES
AUGUST 5TH CONTINUED

I OPENED MY EYES TO FIND MYSELF behind the wheel. The only sound was the engine of the car. A glance at the gearshift showed it in Park. I recognized one of the remoter parking lots at the edge of the Fort Miley VA Hospital grounds. I had no memory of how I drove here or when I stopped the car. I took a deep breath and realized I felt good. Beyond good. Obscenely good, relaxed and drained of tension, as if I'd just come from a session with Hal and hours of lovemaking.

"How goes it with you, lady?" a deep rumbling voice asked near my ear.

I turned and gasped to see the round face of the white-haired, white-bearded stranger in the passenger seat.

"Mistress Kit."

It all came back in a rush—Hal's house, the shed. Sir John—who was now looking at me with an unreadable expression. His voice radiated kindly concern, but there was a kind of self-congratulation on his face that made my heart sink. He certainly looked better, as if he had shaken off the effects of a hangover.

"You jumped on me!"

"I bent over you. You fainted."

"I've never fainted in my life."

"No? You did seem to rally."

I felt distanced from my body, as if I were floating just slightly above it. Considering the odd setting, I should not have felt this way. A faint trickle of fear invaded my euphoria. "What did you do to me?"

"I swear I took no liberty with your person." He laid one plump hand across his heart. "Look to your clothing, my lady—not a button undone, not a fold misplaced."

Embarrassed, I looked down and put up a hand to feel how my blouse seemed to have been buttoned up to the top button. Odd. I never do that.

"The last thing I remember was the stop sign just before the admissions entrance. How did we get here?"

"You drove through there, out here, and then—I know not what overcame you."

"Let's go back to the entrance."

I had to turn the car around. It was pointing toward the dark trees and bushes of Land's End that separated the VA from the ocean and San Francisco Bay.

I pulled through to the Admissions area drive-through under the hospital that I remembered so well from Mark's stays here. The wards loomed back into the darkness of the hospital night—a slower pace than daytime, but never totally sleeping. A taxicab pulled in ahead of the car, and a middle-aged man on crutches climbed out slowly. I looked at the dashboard clock and found it was eight p.m. It felt much later.

I fumbled a few bills out of my purse and pressed them into Sir John's hand. "You have to go now. You can follow that guy who just got out of the cab. There's an information desk in there."

Sir John took the bills, and stuffed them somewhere up inside that huge coat. "Most kind, my lady. Fare thee well." He made a production of getting out of the car, and even bowed dramatically. Nice touch— one last gasp of Shakespearean fantasy.

I drove away feeling saddened. He would probably end up sleeping in the park with a bottle I'd given him the money to buy. But I felt I had to do something, and I needed him out of the car.

It wasn't until I got home, unbuttoned my collar and looked in the mirror that I saw the two puncture marks on my neck.

CHAPTER 23

SIR JOHN FALSTAFF'S WORDS
ON BLACK DIGITAL RECORDER, UNDATED

I AM LITTLE BETTER THAN A MAN TRAPPED in amber—and what a prodigious stone it would take to hold the man in full.

Time to reset that stone.

I whisper in the dark into this small black lump, like a weightless stone, and it whispers back my words. Hal gave it me to learn my secrets while I slept. As if I did not know how to hide it from the daylight and from him. If they could hear this smooth stone repeating my words back to me, the folk I knew where I was born would burn me as a witch, if not as a vampire first. If I can elude their clutches for centuries, can I not sidestep this nosy pup? If I whispered my secrets to anyone who asked I would not have lived a hundred years past my first death.

"Minions of the moon, under whose light we steal," the Bard said of us. He meant robbing purses by moonlight, but I steal dearer than that. A famous glutton I may have been—I sup no more on roasted fowl, no more stave off the cold with sack sherry, cakes and ale. Cruel, is not? A man of famous appetites now lapping up small drops of blood. I drain a taste of life from several in an eve, killing none and yet making a meal.

The belly that I forged in life still leads the way like the prow of a ship, identical to the day I died these many—ahem! I shall not say how many centuries ago.

I could haunt this bustling hospital for many a night if necessity did not demand I move my coffin. First, a visit to my lady Reba. Easily tracked by the bloodhound I've become. Her scent's a luminous road to where she is. Someone under these harsh lights will gladly drive me to her, and never remember the journey.

Poor Reba, once so young and wild. Sipping her life was like drinking bolts of lighting. Now near the end. She must be old—indeed, she has no choice. Her mind's long gone. I'd never bring her over to share undeath with me. But I might take her last breath. Where she is now, if she had her wits she might beg me to do so. Or she might be glad if I just drop in from time to time to take a little blood and leave a little pleasure. For her. And mayhap the night nurse as well.

Can I do that and make a jest of this, my long half-life? I can. And mortals gladly pay a small piece of life for the rare entertainment I can offer.

Young Hal has plans to root me out of my earth, and now his shed's a risky place. So to gather my forces and find a likely wine cellar, windowless closet or basement, where an old man might store a casket and sleep the daylight hours. Times change, tunes change. The old fox needs a new den.

CHAPTER 24

KRISTIN MARLOWE'S TYPED NOTES
AUGUST 6TH

I WOKE UP LATE AND RUSHED TO GET READY for my first client, followed by a day so full of interruptions and unexpected demands that I had no time to think about the two marks on my neck covered by a blouse with a high collar. It was already dark when I stood on Vi's back steps and knocked on her kitchen door holding a box of pastries from a bakery down the street.

When she answered the door Vi was in such a state of rare excitement that she could barely stand still.

"Oh, thanks, wonderful! Put it on the counter and come through to the front room—you have to see this." She led the way through the hall.

"My lady, your presence honors us." Sir John's smiling presence made the air shimmer with anticipation that I totally mistrusted. He half rose and sketched a bow, then settled back into the big wing chair next to the tall bookcases that framed the fireplace. The huge greatcoat I'd seen him wear was draped over the back of the sofa.

"How did you get in here?"

He smiled, inclined his head toward Vi.

"Kit, this is so exciting." She waved a spiral notebook at me.

"Oh, God." I felt the blood stirring inside me as if I were blushing all over, yet there was also a chill down my spine. Vi's front room, where I had stood a hundred times, seemed strange and alien. Even my own psychology reference books in the bookcase opposite Vi's vampire books looked alien, as if I were seeing them through someone else's eyes.

Vi sat down on the sofa and leaned toward the wing chair. "Sir John has been telling me about his life as a vampire. He met the real Henry the Fourth and the Fifth, and Christopher Marlowe. Shakespeare's Falstaff is based on him. This is so exciting."

I sat next to her on the sofa. "Violet, are you crazy?"

She smiled even more broadly. "I think the jury is out on that one."

"This is so unwise. You don't know this man."

"I know." Vi waved her notebook. "That's why I'm interviewing him."

I turned to Sir John. "How did you find this place?"

Ignoring my hostile tone, Sir John leaned back in his chair.

"My sojourn in the ranks of the undead, young madam, has sharpened my senses immensely." He stretched with a show of massive arms and belly. "Once I had your perfume in here—" he tapped his reddened nose—"'twas a simple matter to track you to this place. As soon as I arose this eve, I came here looking for you and found our lovely hostess on the steps. She invited me in. She even found a place for my luggage in a spare room. In return I promised I would a tale to her unfold of the tragical life and undeath of poor Jack Falstaff. A man deprived. A man who loves roast fowl and sack, condemned to a life without either."

He heaved a sigh that I could have sworn stirred the curtains. "Food, I miss mightily. But sack! No sack, no reason to live."

"Uh, excuse us a minute. Violet, come here." I pulled her out into the hallway. "What's this sack he keeps talking about?"

"It's sherry. I looked it up. "

"The man is mentally ill."

"I can hear every word, most clearly, ladies," Sir John called from the front room.

I stuck my head back in the door. "All right, Sir John. You must know that you can't abuse Vi's hospitality much longer. Amuse yourself with some books or something and we'll be back in just a minute." This time we went all the way to the kitchen, testing the theory that maybe he wouldn't hear us back here. "Vi, everyone knows that Falstaff is a literary character. He wasn't even alive."

"Vampires are mythical too. So what?"

"Two myths don't make a reality. A literary creation can't become real enough to sit in your living room, and vampires don't exist. Can't you see you're being conned? He's either deluded, or an actor playing a part, or both."

Every objection I raised increased Vi's enthusiasm. "If he's acting he's better than any Falstaff I've seen on stage. If I can only keep him around long enough to go to the Ren Faire, he'll be a major hit. He's got some wonderful stories to tell. I think they'll make a terrific book."

"He could be dangerous, Vi. Come in here." I motioned her over. "I didn't want to show you this. But I think he assaulted me."

"He was violent?" Her expression dimmed a little. "What do you mean *you think* he assaulted you?"

"I went into some sort of a trance when I gave him a ride to the VA, and I woke up with this on my neck." I held the hair back so she could see the marks on my neck.

"Wow that is so cool!" Her voice was tinged with awe. "Maybe he really is a vampire."

"Violet!"

"I'll watch him. Okay? I'm a night person anyway, and I'll just stay up tonight with him. In the daytime he'll either sleep or die."

"Yes, well, what if he doesn't do either? He could be on drugs or manic—some people with mania don't sleep for days."

"Well, we should know by dawn. If he's a real vampire, he'll go to earth. Except—"

"Except what?"

"Except I'm out of cat food and I really do have to go out for just an hour or so to do my shopping. If I'm going to watch him and get his stories for the next week or more, I'll need to get a bunch of groceries."

"Why don't you let him help you?"

"Look at how he's dressed."

"So get him some clothing."

"I was hoping you'd do that. He says he has money, but I need some help—you're more assertive—"

I sighed. "Oh, all right."

CHAPTER 25

KRISTIN MARLOWE'S TYPED NOTES
AUGUST 6TH CONTINUED

VI WENT TO GET HER COAT. I came back to the front room to find Sir John standing by a bookshelf holding an open volume, shifting from foot to foot, and muttering under his breath. "Look at this!"

It was a copy of *The Basic Writings of Sigmund Freud*.

"This is Freud, he was a physician in the early years of the 19th century—"

"I know who he was, Mistress Kit!" His voice rumbled in deep base tones of rage. "A man couldn't venture out of his coffin in the past century without hearing the name. But here I see the arrant knave slanders me."

He moved a pudgy finger down the page as he read. "...the fat knight, Sir John Falstaff, is based on economized contempt and indignation. To be sure, we recognize in him the unworthy glutton and fashionably dressed swindler." He threw back his head and roared, "'Glutton!' he calls me. Swindler! Fashionably dressed, I grant you—when pocket permits. But how would he know a swindler, unless he himself was one?"

"I had a colleague who called him 'Sigmund Fraud.'"

Sir John started to laugh. "A brother swindler!" He tossed the book down, open, on the table, and subsided into the armchair, arms and legs spread wide with a gesture that conjured up a youth who was considerably fitter and carried a sword.

I ventured close enough to pick up the book and eluded his cheerful grab.

"Sir John!"

"Begging your pardon, madam. The ladies need more wooing, while a man stands, like a hungry vampire outside the door, begging invitation to enter." He hung his head in mock contrition. "I await your pleasure, madam."

Vi was right, the man had an advanced degree in Renaissance Faire behavior. It was alarming how easy it was to fall into the illusion that he was a time traveler from Elizabethan England.

I picked up the book, and examined the page he had been reading. "My recollection is that Freud did end up liking you, Sir John."

"Indeed?" For all the bluster in his voice the big man had subsided. He raised his eyebrows as if challenging the long-dead analyst. "The man recants his slander after heaping insults on my good name?"

I took the book and looked little further down, "Here it is. 'Sir John's own humor really emanates from the superiority of an ego which neither his physical nor his moral defects can rob of its joviality and security.'"

"Physical and morally defective. But jovial! This is damning with faint praise indeed." His voice was a low growl.

"For Freud that was pretty close to a valentine."

"I'd call him out for a duel," Sir John muttered. "If I knew where he lived."

"He's been dead a long time, Sir John. Unless he's become a vampire somewhere."

"Not he. Not the type."

"You're probably right. I'm sure Freud would have preferred death to considering that there might be a reality in what he thought of as superstition." As I said it, I wondered if it was Freud or myself I was describing.

Vi waved as she went out the door on her grocery errand.

Sir John stood and bowed goodbye. He turned to me. "So, wench, shall we to supper?"

I stepped back and put my hand up to guard my throat instinctively. "I thought vampires couldn't eat solid food."

"Nor can we. Come, Mistress Kit, there's a way round many a locked door. Who calls me glutton? Let us go to the banquet hall or tavern, you eat and the smallest sip of your substance will last me the night."

"I take it I get to pay the bill as well?"

He laughed, "So you do. So you do, indeed." He dug into the pocket of those awful striped track suit pants and pulled out a much-worn velvet bag, opened it up and dug out a handful of odd looking coins, mostly dark with age and strangely lumpy looking. One of them, I noted, had been cut in half. He selected three and motioned for me to put out my hand. He pressed two dark coins into my palm with a solemn expression.

They seemed very old and crudely minted. "I've never seen a coin like this."

"That is a groat. Worth much more now."

I pointed to the face stamped in metal. "The man on there looks like you."

He bent to look and I smelled his strange, scent. "Ah, that is Great Harry, the eighth by that name."

"Henry the Eighth of England?"

He nodded. "The same."

I examined the other. "This one says, *Dum Spiro Spero.*"

"Meaning—'While I breathe, I hope.'" He snaked the other arm around my waist to pull me close. "The third coin could be had, my lady, if you could be had."

His hands were cold, and I felt a rush of fear. Then as if my skin reached out for his touch, a drowsy, sensual warmth stole over me. This must have been what happened in the car. I tried to pull away, but he held me fast.

"Let me go."

For a moment we stood almost nose to nose, then I saw the coin he held up just out of reach. I laughed. "That third coin is an Eisenhower dollar, you cheapskate. Let's go to dinner."

He released me so quickly that I nearly stumbled.

"So it's not a rumor that vampires—?" The question was half out before I realized how unwise the question was.

"What rumor would that be?" He smiled as if he knew what I had been about to ask.

"Never mind." Had I really been so unwise as to think of questioning him about whether vampires had sex? I put the two coins he gave me in my pocket. They could have been fake, or rare and valuable enough to repay me for the money I was surely about to spend on him in high-priced, twenty-first century San Francisco.

I looked him in the eye. "I won't let you drink my blood."

"No need of that, fair one. Take me to where people eat and drink, and I will do the rest."

I sighed. "Do you have anything else to wear?"

He glanced down at his outfit. "Not this?"

"Not for a nice restaurant."

"Mistress Reba brought in a seamstress to clothe me in style. Then she took back the splendid garments in a fit of rage, and exiled me from the house. No need for fine clothes in the garden shed." He raised his eyes mournfully to the ceiling.

"I'm not going to ask what you did to provoke her."

"You wound me. I only trifled when invited." His pantomime of reaching up under a skirt added a few fluttery details that infuriated me, partly because they also aroused me against my will. He cast me a sly look that compounded my anger. "She took my finery away to keep me from the clutches of her lady friends." Sir John looked at me sideways, then down at the floor as if meditating on the past. "Surely none would seek me out in the garden shed, clad only in these sorry garments."

"Uh-huh."

"Or so she thought." He raised his blue eyes, chuckled a little, and then sighed. "Time has taken its toll with those fine ladies. They no longer go out of nights and climb through hedges, even for such a large reward."

"So none of your women visitors ever brought you any new clothes?"

"They had things in mind that did not require clothing." His deep voice was wickedness distilled. The mere sound of it snapped my senses open like popcorn hit by hot oil.

"The store should be open for another hour or so. Let's go." I hoped the fresh air would bring me to my senses.

CHAPTER 26

IT WAS AFTER RUSH HOUR and the downtown area had cleared out enough that we found a parking place on Mission Street near the store. Sir John gravitated toward the velour and spandex, nattering on about trunk and hose. First one, then three, then every clerk in the store and a couple of customers swarmed around him with suggestions. Before I knew what was happening he was led off to a dressing room. His laughter rang out so loud that one or two men wandered in off the street, craning their necks to see what was going on. A crowd formed outside the fitting rooms as clerks went in and out, whispering, laughing and passing in garments for him to try on. A few crowded in with him.

At last he burst out of the dressing room, followed by clerks carrying clothing for him. One had bagged his used shirt and pants and handed it to me at arm's length with an accusing stare, as his clothing was my fault. "You may want to burn these." He turned back to Sir John. "We found some much better things for him."

Another clerk handed me the greatcoat in a separate bag. He leaned forward and said in a low voice, "I'd have this cleaned very carefully. It's an antique." He handed me a slip of paper with a name on it. "This is my friend at the De Young Museum who does textiles. I think this coat may be valuable."

While one staff member was ringing up the purchases, another thrust a card into Sir John's hands. "Come visit us in Guerneville, Jack. The bears would eat you up with a spoon." A small crowd gathered around the register.

"Would you make me bait for bears?" Sir John chuckled. "I have hunted stag."

All the men laughed. "It is a stag party," the boldest clerk said, shooting me a brief look. "But I think the bears would hunt you."

Sir John paused. Everyone waited. "Perhaps we could take turns."

This won him general laughter and some applause. A small parade of clerks and customers came up, exchanged a word or two, and tucked business cards in Sir John's pocket—usually the front pants pocket.

Sir John received the attention with smiling, nodding cordiality. He waved to the crowd that gathered at the windows to watch him go. While we put the bags in the trunk, I checked out his new clothing.

They had chosen his outfit well. He now wore a blue suit and pale blue shirt with a maroon, gold and green tie and dark green suspenders that brought out green notes in his blue eyes. To replace the greatcoat they had selected a stylish black raincoat. "They call it microfiber." He held out the sleeve for me to see the fabric as we got into the car. "I've heard of those micro things," he said. "Invisible, they say. But I see this cloth well enough."

"Did you know that the bears they're inviting you to visit are men who love big men—preferably hairy, bearded men?"

"Big hearty men, you say?" He took out the cards and examined them with interest. "Ruddy men, who drink ale and eat sausages?"

I turned to stare at him.

He roared with laughter. "Mistress Kit, you look thunderstruck."

"So you've been to bear events?" I tried to envision Falstaff at a gay hot tub party with a bunch of bearded gay men—and found it not that hard to imagine.

"Bare, you say? As in 'Back and side go bare, go bare, Both foot and hand go cold; But, belly, God send thee good ale enough, Whether it be new or old'—that sort of bare?"

"I've heard that poem before."

"William Stevenson, a rare malt worm he was." He chuckled. "No, Mistress Kit, I take your meaning. But some things were not invented this year." He put the cards back in his pocket. "Or this century."

We went to my favorite seafood grill on Lombard Street. It was mid evening and we had to wait in line until a table became available. Sir John studied the menu when the line took us up to the window where it was posted. "No suckling pig."

"I'm a fishaterian—"

"You're what?"

"Well, it's very close to a vegetarian—I don't eat meat, just fish."

He sighed. "I'll warrant the learned doctors have been at work here. Unnatural, I call it. Here now, roast pork. That's a natural food."

A couple of other people in the line laughed. His deep voice and laugh opened up a hush, and everyone looked toward Sir John.

A woman in the line behind us leaned forward to touch his shoulder. "They do an excellent stuffed pork chop here."

"Do they indeed? Many thanks, kind lady." He turned his attention to her with such heat that her eyes widened, already beginning to be intoxicated by his voice and presence. She was a buxom brown-haired, brown-eyed woman in her late thirties, dressed in red, with impressive cleavage.

"With that, perhaps a fine port wine. Wait, here's dry sack sherry on the list." His voice sank intimately toward her, as if he had reached back to wrap her up in velvet.

"I think I may have some of that myself tonight," she said, favoring him with a naughty smile as we moved up in the line.

"Lucky the man to taste it on your lips."

The two other women in her party were giggling now. The *maitre d'* told us our table was ready.

Sir John nodded to him and turned back to gaze at the woman in red.

"Behave yourself, Sir John."

"Yes, madam."

Much as I hated babysitting the old guy, I still felt raw from Hal's betrayal, and the prospect of being publicly abandoned for another woman hurt. Now he was winking at the woman in red. Maybe she'd like to keep his coffin in her apartment. I was beginning to realize why Reba had confiscated his better clothing—he was mischief incarnate. I took a deep breath. I had to get him fed and back to Vi's. She would be angry if I let him wander off.

"I am not ordering pork," I whispered to him as we were escorted to our table.

"Nor would I ask that, with you being a fish terrine."

"That's fishaterian."

"Indeed. Would you not consider sipping a cup of ale, so I could drink it in your kisses?"

I took a deep breath and reminded myself to watch him. Whatever he was, he had to eat something—or did he? I doubted that real vampires chowed down on stuffed pork chops with or without sherry. Real vampires. My God, what was happening to my sense of reality?

Sir John might have been getting to me a little, because I did order the ale. I told myself it went with the fish plate. The waiter turned to Sir John.

Sir John shook his head. "Alas, nothing."

"We have several excellent diet entrees—low fat, low carb, low calorie, if you are watching your weight."

"No, lad, I leave it to the ladies to watch my weight."

The waiter favored me with a carefully neutral look, tinged with disapproval. A controlling woman who wasn't exactly so thin herself—where did she get off eating and drinking in front of her poor, fat, starving companion?

While I ate, Sir John looked around the room and favored me with his observations about our fellow diners. This couple was quarrelling, that one was counting the minutes till they could go home and do the deed. I will grant that he had the good grace to keep his voice low.

"That woman had just been serviced mightily." He tilted his head subtly toward the table near the window. "But not by the man who sits with her."

"How can you tell that?"

He tapped his nose. "Since I was drafted into service as a creature of the night, I catch the odor of friction—of any sort." He laughed uproariously at his own joke, drawing the attention of everyone in the restaurant. His laughter was like a rich, rare wave of pleasure. I could feel it blanket my skin, and the healing wound where he had bit me tingled as if it had grown extra nerves.

"I've made many a meal of quarrels. When one leaves, I sit by to hold the other's hand." His voice was soft, but every word vibrated my whole body.

I tried not to look at him, for fear I'd end up once again pierced by his fangs in the front seat of my own car—or worse yet, right there in the restaurant. But he was funny. I was torn—social embarrassment, lust and hilarity cycled through me. Just when I thought I could stand it no longer, Sir John fell silent.

He stood up. The woman in red was saluting him over her glass— probably dry sack sherry. Sir John bowed to me. "A moment's pardon. That hot wench in red has finished her sack and pork chop. I must speak to her."

He made his way to the table where the woman was dining with her two friends. He bowed, whispered in her ear, and stood over her for a moment. Then he settled into the empty chair next to the woman in red. Her two friends were as charmed as she was. Sir John made a point of touching her hand and sniffing her wine glass, although he shook his head when she offered him a sip.

I to force myself to concentrate on my sole, although I was too distracted to pay close attention to it. Had there been a hush when Sir John switched tables, or did I just imagine it? I willed everyone to return to their conversations. Gradually the noise rose to its usual level and I let myself look again.

The seats Sir John and the woman in red had been occupying were empty. The two girlfriends were whispering and casting looks toward the back of the restaurant

Above the conversation, I heard a faint, but rising sound. A rhythmic moaning and incoherent cries. The volume was increasing. I set down my fork, threw my napkin on the table, and headed for the restrooms. This time everyone turned to stare and laugh as moans of ecstatic communion filtered through the restaurant. As I got closer to the ladies room, the sounds got louder. A woman's higher tones moaning incoherent words, in concert with a rhythmic thumping sound that I preferred not to identify.

Under it all an occasional deep bass note of Sir John's voice carried out into the room.

Then the woman commenced to screaming.

CHAPTER 27

KRISTIN MARLOWE'S TYPED NOTES
AUGUST 6TH CONTINUED

THE MANAGER GOT TO THE LADIES' ROOM DOOR a moment
after I did.

"Is there a problem?"

I rattled the doorknob. "I believe that my gentleman friend is in
there with another customer. Can you bring me the check and my
jacket from the table? I'd really prefer to pay without going back in
there." I tilted my head toward the dining room behind me.

He nodded sympathetically. "Would you like some help in removing the gentleman? I can call for—?"

"It's all right. I think he'll go peaceably." I had no idea if this was
true.

He nodded, went back down the hall, whispered something urgently to a hovering waiter and disappeared around the corner toward the
kitchen.

"Sir John!" I called through the door. "Sir John, come out of there
immediately. We have to go now."

The waiter returned to hovered near me.

"He'll be right out." I shook the handle and pounded firmly on the
door. "Sir John, come out of there this instant!"

"Got to hand it to the Brits, eh?" the waiter smiled. "They do like
their liquor, and the accent's like catnip to the ladies." His smile died
when he saw my expression. "The manager is coming with a key, and
some help to get him out to the car."

The manager came bustling down the hall with two tall, burly men in white jackets. Muscle from the kitchen staff. The manager brandished a key, but before he could use it the door flew open and we were all forced back up the narrow hallway as Sir John emerged, hastily adjusting his waistband and suspenders. His shirt was half untucked and one suspender was slipping, but a quick look assured me that he was zipped up in the trouser department.

The manager stared at him in horror as Sir John licked what appeared to be blood from his lips. "Is the lady—?"

But the woman in red came slipping dreamily past Sir John, the manager and me. She didn't show any visible wounds. She ran her arm along Sir John's shoulder as if they were in mid-tango. When he had her at arm's length, he bent and kissed her hand, and whispered against the skin "You'll forget me when I am gone," in a soft voice so deep I could feel it along my own skin.

"Never."

"Forget me when I am gone," he said again. "Unless I find you again, forget me." It was a command.

She nodded and turned to wander back to her table, amid the buzz of conversation, which had resumed as soon as her screaming stopped. As she dropped back into her chair she said, "I have no idea what happened, but I feel wonderful." She sat looking dreamily into the distance as her friends plied her with questions.

The waiter appeared with our coats and my purse. The hall was crowded with restaurant staff.

"The rear entrance is just behind you." The manager was blocking us from going back into the dining area. "Please go out that way."

"Whenever possible, my lad. Whenever possible." Something about the magic of the old reprobate's voice seemed to soothe the manager.

"No charge for the meal. Just go," he said as he shoved us out the door. "And don't come back."

Sir John followed me back to the car. Once in the passenger seat he leaned back and sighed contentedly. "Excellent good pork chop and sack. I tasted secondhand."

"That used to be my favorite restaurant. Now I can't go back there."

"More's the pity." His cheeks had gone from that waxen pale to flushed.

"You drank that girl's blood?"

"Now, Kris, 'tis my vocation, Kris. It's no sin for a man to labor in his vocation."

"But I didn't see any mark on her."

His voice sank to a low growl. "There are veins I can tap, Mistress Kit, if a woman be willing, deep down in places that leave no mark to the inquiring world." He pulled a pair of purple silk panties out of his pocket and dangled them from one plump hand. "No match to the dress, but a pretty souvenir."

"Put those away!"

He laughed, sending a thrill to places I wasn't about to acknowledge and a dizzying sense that my life was spinning out of control.

CHAPTER 28

KRISTIN MARLOWE'S TYPED NOTES
AUGUST 6ᵀᴴ CONTINUED

VIOLET MET US AT THE FRONT DOOR to her house with an air of suppressed merriment. "I have a surprise for Sir John."

"Can it wait just a minute? Will you excuse us?"

Sir John nodded graciously. Radiating good will and cheerfulness, he went, humming a melody I'd never heard, to sit in the front room.

I pulled Vi into the kitchen and told her what had happened at the restaurant. "He could be dangerous, Vi." When I got to the part about pulling the pair of panties out of his pocket, Vi started to laugh. "So he didn't eat a thing?" she asked

"Unless the lady in red slipped him a pork chop in the ladies room."

"More likely he slipped her—"

"Vi!"

But her eyes were shining. I had never seen my friend so happy. "You say vampires are fictional and Sir John Falstaff is a fictional creation, but fiction has to be based on some kind of reality."

"Not necessarily, it could be—"

"Yeah, yeah, superstition, misinterpretation of other illnesses, blah-blah-blah. But you saw him before he went out to dinner—he was pale and he came back all pink and rosy. Did he drink someone's blood?"

"I didn't see him do that. Maybe he's just a horny old con man," I concluded.

"I'm sure he's all that too." Vi didn't look in the least discouraged. "But Falstaff was a rogue too, wasn't he? In the plays, I mean?"

"Maybe he's a gifted actor who turned to crime because it's hard for fat actors to get the good roles. This Falstaff and vampire yarn could be part of some elaborate con. Maybe he's working his way through the Ashland Shakespeare Festival mailing list."

"Hey, you found him. How was he to know you'd wander into Hal's garden shed?"

"Good point. Just don't let him near your wallet or your credit card info."

"Don't worry, Kit, he's just as good material for me if he is a con man. Come on, I brought him a can of Falstaff beer. Let's see what he says about that."

I sighed. "All right." I didn't want to leave her alone with him.

CHAPTER 29

KRISTIN MARLOWE'S TYPED NOTES
AUGUST 5ᵀᴴ CONTINUED

SIR JOHN LOVED THAT THEY HAD NAMED A BEER after him. He didn't seem disappointed when Vi explained that we couldn't drink it since it came from a bartender's collection. He said all his hunger and thirst had been satisfied at the restaurant.

I hadn't ruled out an elaborate con game, and he might have partners in crime. I held all possibilities open while Vi brought out her old fashioned tape recorder and a box of fresh cassettes.

Sir John talked for hours. The man could spin a wild tale. He talked of medieval warfare and of royal intrigue. After several hours even Vi, who was recording it and madly scribbling on a pad of paper, stopped and shook her hand. "I've got writers cramp and I'm going to run out of tape soon."

"I've got clients tomorrow. Shouldn't we all get some rest?" I needed to get some sleep, but I was afraid to leave them alone together.

"Wait, just a few more questions." Vi turned to Sir John. "If you're Falstaff, then maybe you're really Sir John Oldcastle?"

"Ah, you've heard of him?" Sir John's face was suddenly guarded.

"I haven't." I looked from Vi to Sir John. "Who's that?"

Vi's passion for vampires was exceeded only by her passion for Shakespeare. "Oldcastle was a friend of Henry the Fifth, although he ended up getting burned at the stake for his religious views. The legend is that Shakespeare got in trouble with Oldcastle's descendents for portraying him as a drunken lowlife. So he had to change the name and make a statement about how he didn't mean it in the play."

"Wait a minute, Shakespeare was what? 1600. Wasn't Henry the

Fifth—" I turned to Vi—"A couple of centuries earlier?"

She nodded, "More or less, around 1400." She leaned forward. "So were you Sir John Oldcastle?"

He winked. "I have had many names. Over many years. The best way to live a half-life is with discretion. My hostess at the Boar's Head Tavern put me in Arthur's bosom, but I have found myself in many a softer bosom since. Women, Mistress Kit! My downfall and my salvation."

"You're not answering Vi's question," I said.

But Sir John was off on a tangent and Vi wasn't pressing the question. "Passed along like a guilty secret," he said with a gesture like flowing water. "Mistress Reba found me on a visit to a friend in Yorkshire, and grew enamored of my embrace."

"You turned her into a vampire?" Vi was fascinated.

"I did not."

"But you could have?" she asked.

"That's best not spoken of."

"That woman you fed off in the restaurant—" I didn't want to bring myself into this inquiry. "Will she become a vampire?"

"That is no simple matter of a tryst on the tiles. She knows not where to seek me out—I can find her if I need to." He tapped his nose. "As I sought you."

"My God." I got a sick feeling in my stomach. "Vi, can I speak to you a minute?"

"No need to hide. I hear every word spoken in these walls, and can predict your future words. You will say—banish Jack." He rose and put a hand to his heart in playful martyrdom. "Drive him from your gate." He waved his arms dramatically and stood as if to go.

"Don't be silly, Sir John, you can stay." Vi stood up too, and took his arm.

"Banish plump Jack, banish all the world!" He was really getting into it, with self pity so blatant that it did have an edge of satire.

"Come on, Sir John. Let's just agree to one rule—no biting me or Kit or anyone in my house without an invitation," Vi said with a flirtatious glance. "Can you agree to that?"

"You have my word on it." Sir John bowed and sat back down.

Vi had suddenly started calling me Kit. For ten years she called me

Kris, and after a few hours with this man she now called me Kit. I sighed and shook my head, but the historical details set Vi off on a new round of questions and Sir John began to describe a colorful odyssey across Europe, packed up like luggage and passed from one rich patron to another over several generations.

Vi changed the tape. At some point I fell asleep.

"Help! Quick." I awoke to a hoarse rumble of urgency in Sir John's voice, then he loomed over me pulling at my hand

I sat up with a start. The house was filled with a predawn gray light. I got to my feet, unsteady with very little sleep. Sir John pulled me into the room where the guest bed had been pushed against the far wall and his huge crate now took up most of the floor space. His rough, round face looked gray in the light. He was pawing urgently at the Venetian blinds, which were partly open. His breath came hoarse and quickly. Could he be having a heart attack? Did vampires—I couldn't finish the thought.

"Are you ill? Should we call a doctor?"

"Doctors? No." He coughed again and took a deep, raspy breath. "Each dawn I die. Direct sun will kill me past repair. Pray you close the shutters."

My muddled brain finally registered that he couldn't work the blinds. I lowered them and closed them so that the room fell into a deeper gloom.

Sir John took a deep shuddering breath. Bars of predawn light filtered through the blinds as the sun began to rise. There was a faint hissing sound. A cloud of dust particles rose off him like smoke where the light struck his skin. He backed away from the window and threw the lid of his crate open with a tremendous crash.

"That should wake Vi," I said.

With one swift motion he hauled a massive length of battered black velvet from the box. Sir John clambered in with surprising agility and seized the lid in one hand. He pointed with his free hand to the huge pile of velvet on the floor next to the box. He was wheezing now. His voice came out halfway between a croak and a groan. "Cover the box straightaway. Block all the light, I pray you."

He lay back down and the box lid fell with a heavy thud.

"Kris?" I looked around to see Vi behind me, rubbing her eyes.

"Vi! Help me!" I yelled. "Please!" came a muffled cry from within the box.

The hissing sound grew louder, and what looked like dust particles were shooting out of the box.

I grabbed the velvet cloth and started to drag it over the box, Vi helped and we had the box completely draped in the black velvet in a few seconds. A faint sigh that might have been "Thank-ee" came from within the box, and then the whole thing shook with such a rattle that the floor trembled. For a moment I thought of an earthquake, but the Venetian blinds hung still and the china cat statues on the window sill didn't move. Stronger light filtered through the blinds now, in a bar pattern on the draped casket, which sat totally silent.

CHAPTER 30

KRISTIN MARLOWE'S TYPED NOTES
AUGUST 7TH

VI AND I LOOKED AT EACH OTHER and without a word turned and left the room. We ended up in her kitchen leaning over the stove as if some dangerous force could overhear our conversation.

"Do you think he's okay in there? I didn't see any air holes," she whispered.

"Oh, my God! We should look." I started back toward the bedroom and Vi followed behind. The house was so quiet that I could hear the antique clock on the living room mantel ticking two rooms away.

We looked at each other and at the crate sitting still under the black velvet drape.

"I don't want to do this," Vi said. "Except—"

I took a deep breath, slipped a hand under the drape, and seized the lid. "Hold the cover out, so no direct sunlight gets—um—gets on him."

She took the drape and held it up while I raised the lid, which was heavier than it looked, half expecting a sudden convulsive leap out of the box or a repetition of the shuddering. But all was silent. No sound. No breath.

I ducked under the drape and the lid, and saw Sir John's lifeless body. Gingerly, I reached into the box. I put my hand on his chest, startled by how stiff his body felt. He had been living and breathing less than five minutes ago. This was no yogic breath control trick. His flesh was hard as wood. I pressed my fingers to his neck, seeking a pulse. Cold and rigid. I jerked my hand out and leaped back, letting the lid fall down with a terrific crash.

Vi jumped back and dropped the cloth. For a few seconds my head and shoulders were smothered in dark velvet. I scrambled out from under it.

"Damn it!"

"What did you feel?"

"He's not breathing. His chest and neck feel as hard as this box." I started to rap the wood, but realized I half expected an answering rap from inside. I just didn't think I could bear that.

"Admit it, Kit. He's a vampire," Vi said.

"Stop calling me Kit. Maybe he just died and got unusually fast rigor mortis." I was trying to be logical, but my brain was too tired for the exercise.

"In less than five minutes? Maybe in Antarctica with the freezing temperature. I don't know."

"Come on, let's straighten out the drape, so no sun gets in," I sighed. "Vi, do you think we should prop the coffin lid open a little under the drape. Just in case he is breathing very slowly, like those yoga guys. That way he can get some oxygen?"

"Okay, just stay there."

Vi came back with a large book. Of course it was *The Complete Works of William Shakespeare*. That cheered me up a little. She held the velvet drape out while I ducked under. She helped me lift the lid, and I held it while she set the book securely on the corner to hold it up. There was no repeat of the dust particles shooting out of the box, so I guess the light didn't get in.

"Let's get some coffee, okay?" Vi's eagerness seemed to have vanished along with Sir John's life. Sitting at the kitchen table, waiting for the water to boil, she rubbed her face. "Maybe I made a mistake. Suddenly having a corpse in the spare bedroom is creeping me out."

"What do you want to do?"

"I just don't know."

"You're the vampire expert. What happens now?"

"Well, in fiction, the vampire sleeps—or actually dies—all day and rises at dusk. But I don't know anything about real vampires. Up until last night I truly thought there was no such thing. I thought Sir John would make some excuse and leave."

"Maybe the fiction is based on some kind of reality that we 've just encountered. We should call Bram Van Helsing. He's the expert and he's at Larry's."

It was still too early, but I was too exhausted to care. I made the call, got Larry's machine, apologized for the early hour. "I'm trying to reach Bram Van Helsing. If you could tell him I really need his help. I don't know if he remembers our conversation the other day. Seriously, I have an emergency of a vampirical nature."

A voice came on the phone immediately. "Hi, Kris, it's Bram, and I'm screening Larry's calls. He's already at the conference in Edinburgh. So what's this vampire crisis?"

"I don't expect you to believe it, but I'm hoping you can come and take a look and give us some advice. We have a guest here in her house who says he's a vampire, and he appears to have gone into the most deathlike cataleptic state I've ever seen immediately at dawn. I know this sounds bizarre, but after talking to him and observing him, I really do worry that calling for medical assistance might injure or kill him."

"That is interesting." Bram sounded enthusiastic, or maybe he just hadn't been up all night. "Some vampire fans have tremendously strong beliefs. Also he could have porphyria. People with that disease really do get third-degree burns from the sun."

"Would you recognize that if you saw it? Is it too much to ask you to come and take a look at him? My friend Vi and I have been up talking to him all night and we're in no condition to be objective."

"Sure, I'd be glad to take a look. I have some interviews, but not till afternoon. Shall I bring my holy water, stake and crucifix?"

I sighed. "Bring whatever you think makes sense. We're totally puzzled."

He paused for long enough that I realized he was joking. Of course he would think we were being hysterical or deluded.

"Seriously, Kris. Give me the directions and I'll be right over. I *will* bring my cell phone and a can of Mace—I'm licensed to use it. Oh, and Kris—"

"Yes."

"Do you have coffee? Otherwise I'll bring some. At dawn, with cata-tonic vampires on the premises, the beverage of choice is coffee—the stronger the better."

"We'll have it ready."

"I'm on my way."

Vi brewed her strongest coffee, and we brought a carafe and cups into the front room to wait for Bram. Staring at the tape recorder and box of full cassettes, I wondered if Vi was thinking what I was. We were either in deep trouble with the law or we had both simultaneously gone insane. The third alternative was that it was all true, and that one was hard to believe in the cold light of dawn.

The doorbell rang. Both of us jumped as if shocked by electricity.

CHAPTER 31

HAL ROY'S SPOKEN NOTES
SILVER FLASH DRIVE/VOICE RECORDER
AUGUST 7TH

THE WEEK KEPT GETTING WORSE AND WORSE. Breaking up with Kris hurt. But having Mina find out about her at the worst possible moment pulled away the ground I'd been standing on. Then Jack had laughed at my threat to expose him to sunlight. He knew all about Aunt Reba's estate planning to protect him. Then he was gone. Casket and all—if you want to call that monstrous huge wooden box a casket.

The only sign that he'd been in the shed for seventy years was a big, slightly sunken square on the cement floor where the crate had stood. I couldn't believe he would just leave like that. Where could he go? His rich old lady friends were like Aunt Reba, too feeble to take him in.

Who could he go? You couldn't put him in a studio apartment or Lucy would have taken him in a heartbeat—even if I gave her hell and Jack refused to make her a vampire, she would have been glad to have him just for the leverage.

There had to be others. Damn it, for all I knew the other vampires had a coffin relocation program. He purposely blocked me from entrance to the vampire world. He was probably laughing at me now for all my vain threats to try to get him to cooperate. Let him laugh. Now I had no way to find Jack.

But I intended to find the others, one way or another.

CHAPTER 32

KRISTIN MARLOWE'S TYPED NOTES
AUGUST 7TH

VI SAT THROUGH THE DOORBELL AS IF she was too tired to stand, so I went to let Bram in. I felt an unexpected surge of relief to see him on the doorstep, looking as whimsically gallant as he had in Larry's parlor. "You are a really good person to help us," I said as I led him down the hall.

"I'm the lucky one," he said with a smile. "If you've got a real vampire, it's the opportunity of a lifetime for me."

Vi greeted Bram so quietly that her voice was barely audible. "I've got all your books."

"Thank you, I'm flattered."

"*The Natural History of the Undead* is my favorite. It's there." She pointed to the floor-to-ceiling bookshelves on either side of her old fashioned fireplace, and subsided into exhausted silence.

"Ah, the fact books and the so-called-fact books." Bram smiled at both of us. Vi didn't seem to notice. We I exchanged a glance over Vi's head.

"We had a rough night," I said. I poured him some coffee, which he drank black as he looked around Vi's sunny front room, the window looking out over Clement Street.

He put down his coffee cup and went over to examine the shelves. "Vampires on one side, psychology on the other," he said. "That's an intriguing split."

"The psych books are mine and Vi writes vampire novels. You may have seen them—Violet Semmelweis." I gestured to the row of books.

"Forgive me if I haven't read them. I think I have heard of you, but

I'm concentrating on the interviews I'm doing. There's so much vampire fiction that I can't begin to keep up with it all."

Vi waved her hand wearily. "Don't worry about it. You're not really the target audience for vampire romance."

Bram came back but didn't sit down. "Thanks for the coffee. I'm awake now and ready for vampire action. Oops. What have we here?"

"My roommates," Vi said with a smile as her long-haired tuxedo cat, Ariel, came out of hiding with his short, twisty Manx tail waving back and forth like a flag. The orange-striped cat, Sly, joined him, walked up to Bram, and sniffed his pants leg.

"Hey, I haven't seen your cats all night, Vi. Do you think they hid while Sir John was awake?"

"Sir John?" Bram asked.

"Our vampire guest." I felt flustered. "Aside from being a vampire, he says he's Sir John Falstaff and that Shakespeare modeled the character after him."

Bram laughed. "Multi-delusional, I like the guy already. But you say the cats didn't."

Vi nodded. "I think he wasn't a cat person. But they seem to like you." Vi introduced each cat.

Bram leaned down to politely offer an outstretched hand, which each duly sniffed, He also nodded when I pointed out the shaggy tail sticking out from the armchair, where Hamlet thought he was safely hidden. "Er, how many cats do you have?"

"Well, there are the three you see at least some part of, and two that are invisible."

"Um." He tilted his head skeptically. "These invisible cats. Are they here now?"

Violet laughed. "They're a feral mother and daughter. They hide in the closet or under the bed. They don't trust strangers. Hell, they don't trust me very much—yet."

Bram must be a pretty good interviewer, because Vi seemed to be reviving from her exhaustion. "What are the names of the cats that are hiding? Or do feral cats have names?"

"They know some words like 'food" and "N-O.' But just for my own sake I call the feral mom Lady Macbeth and her daughter Juliet. Lady Macbeth hisses when I try to get near her, and Juliet is very shy and hides behind her mother."

"Hasn't met her Romeo, I guess."

"Being spayed, she's not out there looking."

There was a pause and Bram instinctively broke in—which was good, because Vi was about to start explaining about the deceased felines whose ashes and pictures lined the mantelpiece—all of them black cats, and from the pictures they could almost have been the same cat, although the ashes testified otherwise.

"So where is this vampire?"

"He's in the guest bedroom." Vi led the way and we followed her into the dimly lit room that was almost completely filled with the bed and the huge crate next to it.

"He said that the sunlight burned him through the blinds, and all this dust started rising when the dawn hit him. He asked us to drape this over his casket." I cautiously picked up the edge of the heavy material.

"Maybe if we hung that cloth over the curtain rod to block the light," Bram suggested.

"Makes sense," I said.

It took all three of us to haul the cloth up and heft it over the valence above the window. The room got darker. "If he starts doing that disintegration thing again, we'll drop it right back over the box again."

Bram raised the lid and stared down at Sir John's impassive, unbreathing corpse. He reached in and felt for a pulse. He shook his head. There was a faint hiss and visible particles began to rise from the box like a dust storm.

"It's the light—put the lid down!" I yelled.

Bram let the lid fall, and we all hastily pulled the drape down and put it back over the case.

Bram backed away a few feet. "And you say he was alive until dawn?"

"Very much so."

"If I came back at dusk, you're saying he would rise?"

"That's what he did the first time I saw him," I said. "Unless we've damaged him by letting the light get to him. Maybe we shouldn't have taken the drape off."

Vi shook her head at me and turned to Bram. "She's co-dependent even with vampires. Did he get enough blood? Perhaps she should help him pick out a better coffin."

"Vi!" I started to laugh. "Let's just remember who invited him to store his coffin here."

Bram laughed too. "Is there somewhere around here where we could have breakfast while you tell me the whole story from the beginning?"

Half an hour later we were sitting at a table in a place on Geary that had home fries and good coffee and telling Bram the whole story. I did edit my romantic woes with Hal to make me sound a little less pitiful. After the part about how he died at dawn and was stiff as a board five minutes later, all of us sat in silence.

"I've been studying this for nearly twenty years, and up until an hour ago I would have said that this existed only in people's fantasies," Bram said. "I want to see this guy when he gets up."

"Oh, we want you there too," I said.

Vi nodded. "Please."

Bram looked at us solemnly. "You aren't expecting me to put a stake through this man's heart, are you?"

"No, no!" Vi and I were horrified.

"We like him," Vi said.

"But we don't know what to do about him," I added.

"Whatever it is, it doesn't fit with any single syndrome." Bram took out a small metal case with a notebook and pencil and made a list. "First of all he was red-faced and he didn't have any of the symptoms of porphyria—people with that have to stay out of direct sun, but they get burned, not disintegrated. As far as the full-fledged rigor, there is a cadaveric spasm. When someone dies violently, struggling, it depletes the oxygen in the muscles and they contract instantly, rather than taking two to eight hours for rigor."

"There was that shuddering of the whole crate," I mused. "He might have been dying violently."

"I'll definitely come back this evening just before dusk."

"You won't tell anyone though, please!"

"Are you kidding? I wouldn't pass up this opportunity for the world. Let me give you my cell phone in case your guy wakes up during the day. Most distracting." He winked at me. "I probably won't be much use in the interviews I have to do today."

I put his cell number on speed dial on my phone and we all sat silent for a moment. Bram looked from me to Vi and back again. "We should all consider what we'll do if the old guy doesn't rise this evening. What if he just he stays dead?"

"Yeah," I said. "I'm not sure what I'm hoping for."

"Kris!" Vi said, "I like Sir John."

"Yeah, but he's literally a bloodsucker, and that makes us his dinner." I held up a hand. "I'm too tired to argue. But thanks, Bram, for giving us your expert opinion."

He smiled that crooked smile. "An opinion based on no real experience. But I'm very interested to see what happens tonight."

Bram walked back toward Larry's place. Vi went up the steps from Clement Street to her front door. Bram did bring a rational mind to this situation. That was sorely needed.

"Vi, are you sure you want to sleep with him in the next bedroom?"

She looked down at me from her front porch. "I'm so tired, I'm asleep on my feet already."

"Keep the phone near you and call if anything weird wakes you up."

"I think we're safe during daylight. If we're not, screw it. I've got to sleep."

I had to get some rest before my first client arrived at one o'clock.

My message light was blinking and I played back a call from Mina, firing me as her therapist and telling me never to try to contact her again. I couldn't blame her. I felt awful, but too tired to let myself contemplate it further.

It wasn't until I was standing in front of the bathroom mirror washing up that I realized I hadn't told Bram about the bite marks on my neck. How could I leave that out?

CHAPTER 33
MINA MURRAY'S DIGITAL JOURNAL
AUGUST 7TH

HAL LEFT A DOZEN VOICEMAIL MESSAGES on my phone at work and home. I counted. He knocked on my door, but I didn't answer. I found flowers and an apology card outside the door later. I managed to avoid him for two days. The second day I hung around the office till nearly six, hoping to avoid him. But Hal was waiting outside the building when I finally did leave for the day.

"We have to talk, Mina. Why did you just leave me with no word? I found the ring on the dresser. Why did you break up with me? What's wrong?"

"I followed you to Kristin's place that night."

That stopped him. He stared at me—those brown eyes that I had trusted so deeply. "Why?"

"Maybe because I thought you were doing something behind my back. And guess what? You were. You were cheating on me with my own therapist. That is so, so sick. I told her that when I fired her."

"Mina, I need to talk to talk to you." Homeward bound Financial District people flowed around us—not the full flood of rush hour. Hal flinched as a man brushed past him and muttered in annoyance. "Would you please come for a drink or some dinner?"

I didn't say anything. I'd never heard Hal this upset before. For some reason it made me feel calmer.

"Mina, I swear to you I meant to break it off with Kris as soon as I met you."

I turned away. "But you just never got around to it. Bullshit. You just didn't expect to get caught."

He moved to block me from leaving. "Please, don't go. Listen to me. I need you so badly. You're the only person who can save me from this. Just give me a chance to explain."

People walking past on the sidewalk slowed down as they passed by, glancing our way.

"I can't imagine what you could say that would make me forgive you."

Hal lowered his voice and moved closer to whisper. "We can't talk about it here. That thing in the shed that you were so afraid of—it's gone."

I was confused. "Where did it go? Lucy said you were going to threaten to kick it out?"

"You wanted it gone. It's gone." Hal pulled me over close to the building, out of the flow of foot traffic, and knelt down on the sidewalk in front of me, keeping hold of my hand. "I swear to you, Mina, the moment I first laid eyes on you, I loved you. Remember how I came up to you on the sidewalk. It was right outside of Kris's gate?"

"Of course I remember the first time we met." I started to cry. "You're saying you were on your way to see Kristin?"

"I was on the way to spend the rest of my life with you—I just didn't know it yet. I didn't know she was your therapist. But Mina, I fell in love with you that moment. From the first time I saw you, it's always been you."

A huge shadow fell over us. It was the security guard from the building. His name was Rafe. He always flirted with me. He'd probably enjoy telling Hal to get lost. "Is this guy bothering you, Mina?"

I looked down at Hal. His eyes were pleading. Somehow having the power to get him in trouble with Rafe made me feel better. I sighed. "No, Rafe, it's okay. But thanks for paying attention."

"Just doing my job." He gave Hal a hard look. "Let me know if you need help." Rafe went back into the building, but I could see him hovering near the glass door.

"Let's go somewhere quiet to talk," Hal said softly, getting to his feet. "I really need you. I'm all alone now and I don't know where to turn."

He was hard to resist when he begged. I made him get up and we went to dinner. The least I could do was let him explain.

CHAPTER 34

KRISTIN MARLOWE'S TYPED NOTES
AUGUST 7ᵀᴴ CONTINUED

WHEN I GOT BACK HOME I LAY DOWN TO NAP and woke up, shuddering after less than an hour. Fear and exhaustion kept me in a daze. So I got up and took a container of yogurt over to the computer to check my email. Someone had answered my personal ad. Right. Romance. I closed the email program without reading it. I didn't delete it, though. Maybe tomorrow I'd feel like reading it. If our little experiment with Sir John didn't land us in jail or worse. Bram had a good point about preparing our strategy in case Sir John did not arise at dusk. Policemen take a dim view of unidentified corpses lying around the apartment all day. I'd have to amend the ad—*Accused murderess, former licensed psychologist seeks soul mate.*

I went looking online for information about this Oldcastle person Vi mentioned as Shakespeare's model for Falstaff. I printed up the relevant parts and put them in a folder. The historical record didn't offer any answers that I could see, no connections with vampires.

If it hadn't been for Sir John's death and instant rigor mortis, I might have imagined that he was simply a very well-informed English history buff who was operating an elaborate con or possibly living out a delusion. But there was no denying what happened in Vi's back bedroom at dawn. That froze my theories cold.

Then my first client arrived and the rest of the afternoon was spent drinking coffee and forcing myself to stay awake and pay attention to other people's problems.

Vi called in late afternoon and we had soup and sandwiches together. She was so excited about Sir John that it scared me. She didn't seem to see any down side.

"He's a treasure trove of stories," she said. "I could get half a dozen books from the stories he's told me so far."

"I just wonder how safe it is."

"He's harmless, can't you see?"

"I'm not so sure about that."

Bram showed up at around sunset, bringing a black bag and a small tape recorder.

"What's in the bag?"

"I brought my vampire killing kit." The way he ducked his head when he said it telegraphed his embarrassment. "You know, with the stake and holy water and all."

"Maybe you should put that away. He'll be awake—"

Too late, a strident coughing announced Sir John's arising.

CHAPTER 35

SIR JOHN FALSTAFF'S WORDS
ON BLACK DIGITAL RECORDER, UNDATED

TIMES I AWOKE AWASH IN BLOOD and slaughter and thought I was back in battle. But it was just mine hosts. They fed on blood, pain, life force and death. My natural gift to charm fascinated them. They could not learn from me, and everything I learned from them took longer, flavored by their cruel sport. Once I dug out the truth beneath their games I had the lesson and could make my own way.

A hundred years to perfect the illusion of life. To come and go invisible, unnoted and untouched by creatures that stalk the undead. A hundred years to learn debauchery by proxy. A chance encounter in a tavern and I find myself maligned as a glutton, coward and a drunkard. I who have not tasted ale firsthand in nigh 600 years.

But now, the drape pulled aside, I greet a new dusk and the ladies have a male companion.

"Good evening, Mistress Kit and my Hostess Violet. Some new blood, I see."

"I'll be damned." the man says.

"I hope not so, but you must better know the state of your own soul." The man has many a gray hair on his head, yet I can taste his awe.

"I saw you dead, stiff and unbreathing in the coffin this morning."

"If you look in my coffin after dawn, that is what you must expect to see. Now, after dusk, you see me live and breathe and hasten out into the world to break my day long fast."

They know not how they tempt me with their blood running rich, so close to the surface, and I just risen from the grave to feed.

CHAPTER 36

KRISTIN MARLOWE'S TYPED NOTES
AUGUST 5TH CONTINUED

BRAM LOOKED STUNNED AFTER EXCHANGING a few words with Sir John.

The old rogue clambered out of his box. He leaned against the edge and coughed a few more times. "Pardon, gentles all. I lost a bit of substance to the sun and breathed in my own dust on rising. And who are you, sir?"

"I am Bram Van Helsing."

Sir John stopped in mid cough. "A branch from the famous vampire hunter's tree?"

"Only in fiction."

"Ah. Fiction—that holds the mirror up to nature."

"That reminds me—you have a reflection." Vi pointed to a mirror in the twilit room. It reflected all four of us. "They say vampires don't show up in mirrors." She took her notebook and small pen out of her pocket.

"A mere myth." He coughed again, "Some lose ourselves, and then become well nigh invisible. 'Tis a long road for the undead." He pointed at the black bag Bram carried. "What have you there?"

"Uh, it's a vampire kit." Involuntarily Bram moved it further away from Sir John.

"Vampire kit." The tilt of Sir John's head expressed his skepticism. "You mean a vampire-killing kit, do you not? Show me."

Glancing at me, Bram opened the black case, laying it flat on the bedside table. We all gathered round to examine it. In separate compartments it held a stake over two feet long with a wicked metal tip, a wooden crucifix, a few labeled bottles, and a small derringer pistol with what looked like silver bullets.

Sir John laughed.

Bram reached for the stake, but Sir John snatched it out of the box quicker than I would have thought possible.

"Hey!"

"This, sir, could do some damage." Sir John dropped the stake into his pocket and patted it. "Can't have it falling into the wrong hands."

"So it worries you, does it?" Bram's voice was tight.

Sir John ignored him and bent over the case, his nose close to the crucifix and vials marked *Garlic* and *Holy Water.*

"It's a replica of an antique kit that sold on eBay for $12,000." Bram's voice betrayed his anger. "The real kit was made in the early 1900s when Bram Stoker's *Dracula* was popular."

Sir John picked up the crucifix without cringing, and held the vial marked *Holy Water* up to the light.

Curiosity overcame Bram's irritation. "I thought vampires couldn't handle holy objects."

"So they say. But so you see." Sir John put the cross down in the case and held up one of the bottles. "Where did you get the holy water?"

"That came from eBay too."

"Holy water comes from a font, not a bay."

"This eBay is more of an electronic marketplace."

Sir John shook his head mournfully. "Holy water bought and sold in the marketplace."

Vi scribbled notes, leaning forward to catch everything, utterly fascinated.

"Do you believe in this?" Sir John reached out and tapped the vial of water against Bram's nose. All of us jumped, and Bram stepped back out of reach a second too late. "I see. Water from this eBay you speak of inspires no awe."

Vi and I laughed. Bram's face grew red.

Sir John pointed to the crucifix without a hint of his usual twinkle. "This cross. Do you have faith in this?"

"Um—" We looked at one another. Clearly none of us were seriously involved in any religion.

"I see you do not. You probably have more faith in the garlic. But

I use it to perfume the blood of those I drink from. I am no threat to your life." His voice sank to an eerie whisper, "There are things. Right outside your window, if you had the eyes to see them. Things undreamed of that frighten even vampires. Ponder this—what do you believe in? What can protect you?" He picked up the derringer gingerly between his thumb and forefinger. He didn't touch the bullets, though.

Bram recovered enough to ask. "What about silver bullets?"

"Better. Pricey. Invest in some. These are silver plate. If you want to at least slow down a vampire, get thicker plate. But there are those who stop at none of these toys. Never invite any of the Others in."

"Others?" I asked.

"Never mind." His stomach rumbled loudly. "Just don't invite anyone, or any unknown thing, into your home."

"Sir John—" Vi held up her hand as if in class. "I've been meaning to ask you—"

"Can a man break his fast before the inquisition?"

Vi's smile dimmed. "Do you have to go out?"

"I must feed and soon."

"Could I offer you a snack here?"

"Violet!" I was shocked.

"Indeed?" Sir John examined her with interest. His voice, already deep, seemed to go down another octave.

"Vi, that's a bad idea. Sir John, isn't that some kind of violation of hospitality?"

"If my hostess freely offers—" He raised his bushy white eyebrows with such entreaty that it was very hard not to laugh.

"Come on, Kit, he drank your blood. Why should you have all the fun?"

"Fun! It was terrifying."

"You wound me, madam. I had the distinct impression you enjoyed our interlude."

"He drank your blood?" Bram looked from me to Sir John and back to me again.

"Yes." I held my collar aside.

Bram came close and examined the scar. "Wow."

"He jumped me with no warning. I didn't know what happened till I got home and saw the mark."

Sir John turned to me. "I never drink without permission."

"You never asked me. You just, blanked out my mind and—you know—?

"This lady bid me enter her small car—" Sir John took a step back and seemed to cast back in his memory. His deep rumbling voice was hypnotic. As he described it, I found my memory of the event had grown fuzzy. Surely I never offered him my blood. "We sat so close we almost touched. Famished and faint with hunger, as I am now—" He held up a hand. "A sip, I took a sip. I do confess it."

"So he drank your blood without your consent?" Bram's hand hovered around the scar on my neck. My hand went to pull up my collar to cover it.

"I'd hardly agree to it." My voice sounded strange to me. "I had no idea that such a thing was possible. I never offered him anything but a ride up to the VA."

"Madam, I trespassed, but 'twas your beauty that drove me to it, and the closeness of your lovely neck." Sir John bowed his head. "But you know I have not touched my hostess or yourself since being here."

"That is true." I admitted.

"It's hard to separate the fiction from your reality." Bram's eyes were on Sir John. "If you drink their blood, will it turn them into vampires?"

"That is no such easy matter." Sir John looked away as if to avoid the subject.

Vi's eyes were shining. "Come on, he drank blood from Kit, and she didn't turn into a vampire." She moved very close to Sir John, like a flirtatious toddler. "Will drinking my blood give you the strength to go on and answer our questions?"

"Yes." His voice deepened to the point where I could feel the vibrations in the pit of my stomach. "I will be yours to command the whole night long."

"Come on, let's go in the front room." She took his hand and led him there. Bram and I followed, leaving the vampire kit open on the table in the room with the casket.

Once we reached the front room, Sir John drew Vi into a corner next to the fireplace and put his arms around her in an embrace that slightly lifted her feet off the ground. He held her as lightly as if she were a small bird rather than a full bodied woman. I wanted to look away, but I couldn't seem to move.

Sir John turned his massive back to us so that Vi seemed to disappear into his embrace. We could not see how he was piercing her neck. There might have been a faint sucking sound, but Vi's breathing changed. First she took in deep, sighing breaths, then quickened into short, panting gasps. There was no other sound in the room.

A breath near my ear made me turn to find myself looking directly into Bram's eyes. Green with streaks of yellow. His nearness made my breath catch, and I noticed he seemed short of breath as well. A wave of heat washed over both of us. Pulses of lust radiated from Sir John and Vi.

No more able to resist than a flower can resist seeking the sun, we stood together, managing not to embrace by sheer force of will.

Bram took my chin in his hand and turned my head till he could look into my eyes. Then he ran his hand over the small scars on my neck and my knees got as weak as if he had touched me much more deeply. "He did that to you?"

"He must have," I sighed. "Frankly, I don't remember what happened, but I didn't invite him. I think he hypnotized me. Then the next night when he came to Vi's, I took him to a restaurant and a woman sneaked off with him to the restroom."

"Really?" Bram chuckled a little, I could feel his whole body respond to the idea. He looked down at me. "He did that to a woman in a restaurant?"

"Well, she was definitely willing and eager. She made a lot more noise than Vi. And whatever he did to her appeared to involve removing her panties, because he had them in his pocket when we got to the car."

I glanced over at Sir John, and looked away immediately when I saw how Vi was moving slowly, ecstatically, in his embrace. I turned back, looking up into Bram's eyes.

"And your panties, were they missing when you got home?"

I laughed a little giddily, then for some reason I remembered Sir John talking about drinking men's as well as women's. Lust was here, and I was totally confused. "I'm sorry. All this sensuality, I think it's a vampire thing. I realize that you're—one of Larry's friends."

"Yes." Bram reached out a tentative hand and touched my hair, then he froze. "What?" Anger rose up to replace the lust in his eyes—well, not entirely. "Because I stayed at Larry's house you thought I was gay?"

"Uh—"

He turned aside with a harsh bark of laughter. The tide of passion receded for a moment. "I can't believe this. In supposedly enlightened San Francisco."

Now I was blushing from embarrassment. "Bram, I apologize. In my situation, a widowed older fat woman, it's safest to assume that attractive men in a gay setting are gay, until proven otherwise."

The "attractive" part brought him back to look at me. "So you want proof, eh?"

"I just got rejected pretty brutally," I whispered.

"I'm not about to reject you." He took my hand and led me over to the sofa. We sat down together, trying mightily to ignore the moans and sighs coming from the other end of the room.

Bram pulled me close enough to kiss, but instead he murmured, "This is the worst day of my life. I've always wanted to meet a real vampire—not that I thought they existed—well, not since age 12 or so. But I finally meet one and he laughs at my vampire kit."

For a moment we just sat breathing and looking into each other's eyes. He reached out and stroked my hair. "Now I meet a woman who arouses me on every level and you say you think I'm gay. Open your eyes and look. You must be able to tell that I really like you. All you had to do is call—at an ungodly hour, I might say—and I came running."

"I liked you from the moment I saw you." I put a hand on his arm in apology, somehow couldn't make myself move it, enjoying the feel of him through his shirt. "Oh. I think it's a pretty good night."

"It's improving by the minute." He slipped both arms around me and pulled me close in a passionate kiss. No flirting. No circling around to building up anticipation. Even young impetuous Hal and I had teased back and forth for a little while before jumping on each other.

But sensuality hung in the air like incense smoke, and the entire room seemed to be raw and throbbing with lust. Bram and I began caressing and kissing each other as if we had been waiting months for the opportunity. Our kisses grew deeper and more intense until a scream from the other side of the room made both of us break away and look over.

Vi struggled out of Sir John's embrace, not reluctantly, but dreamily, as he lifted his face away from her neck and cast blank eyes over us. The expression on Vi's face was dreamy and dazed. Two small puncture wounds glittered on her neck like rubies. I looked away as Sir John leaned down to lick the last drop of blood from the rapidly closing wound.

Sir John kept his arm around Violet and walked her over to the sofa where Bram and I were still entwined. His cheeks were pink and he looked strong, while her skin was noticeably paler and she half staggered. He held her on her feet. She had a big goofy grin on her face.

I broke away from Bram to lean close to her. "Are you okay?" I turned to Sir John. "Did you take much blood?"

"The blood's a mere condiment. Salt and pepper to the life force that's my main meal. And a lovely meal she gave me."

I felt like kicking him, but Vi was blinking as if happily drunk. "What's wrong with her?"

"Something in this—" he touched a finger to what I now saw was a sharp fang, hidden under his white moustache and beard—"Gives the pleasure that you see." He nodded at Vi.

I guided Vi to sit at the end of the sofa. Bram moved to the other end, so I could sit in the middle.

Sir John stretched and moved to sit in the wing chair. He hooked a boot around the ottoman, pulled it close, propped up his feet and leaned back to survey us with contentment. "Questions? Ask them."

I glanced at Vi, who was just surfacing from her trance. Bram didn't say anything either. So I started. "Who ARE you?"

CHAPTER 37

KRISTIN MARLOWE'S TYPED NOTES
AUGUST 5TH CONTINUED

HE LAUGHED. "YOU THINK I AM not Sir John Falstaff?"

Vi roused herself enough to say, "You can't be Falstaff, he's a fictional character." She sighed, half wistfully and half contentedly.

"But Falstaff was modeled on Sir John Oldcastle, who was a real historical figure," I said, primed by a day of research on the net. "But his descendents made a big fuss, so Shakespeare changed the name and put in a line to say it wasn't Oldcastle."

"Oldcastle died a martyr." Sir John tapped his chest. "This is not the man." But his bright blue eyes had lost a bit of sparkle on hearing the surname.

"A direct quote from the end of *Henry the Fourth, Part Two,*" Violet beamed. She seemed to be coming round again. "Lawyers give writers the same advice about avoiding slander to this very day. Like—'The characters in this book don't resemble anyone, and least of all my rat of an ex-husband. Not in the slightest. Nuh-uh. Nope.'"

"Okay," I continued, "There were witnesses to Sir John Oldcastle's death. He was burned in front of a crowd in St. Giles Field in 1417. I found a picture of it on the net."

"A picture?" Bram's voice was skeptical.

"Well, a reproduction of a woodcut. Want to see?"

"Yes," Vi and Bram both said.

Sir John's face, which had grown ruddy with Vi's blood, paled visibly. "Do not bid me remember my end."

"Does the picture bother you?"

"Do as you wish." But he turned his face away as I went to get my folder. I brought it back to the sofa and sat down between Vi and Bram. Sir John stared at the empty fireplace as I opened the folder.

We all looked at the woodcut. "It's not a likeness to you," Bram said to Sir John, who refused to look.

"It's also not very gory," Vi said, "compared to modern day pictures."

"Like a line drawing," I agreed. "Or a really grisly coloring book with no crayons."

The woodcut depicted simple, grim figures. Men in hats, puff-sleeved antique jackets, and knee breeches surrounded a man a lot thinner than Sir John, bound hand and feet, who dangled suspended from a chain, fixed to a cross-beam so low that his feet and legs nearly touched the wood of the fire. A few men stood watching in the background. A hat and jacket, perhaps the dying man's clothing, occupied the foreground.

"Why burning?" Bram touched the outlines of flames in the picture. "Isn't that the typical punishment for a witch?"

"Maybe that was about the heresy," I said. "Oldcastle was a follower of John Wycliffe, who was an early Protestant. See the text under the graphic?"

Bram read it. "It says Wycliffe—and his followers like Oldcastle—were considered heretics because they read the Bible in English."

"They also had some radical ideas about the Catholic Church not owning property and women being allowed to preach. Come to think of it, those ideas are still considered radical in some circles." I said.

"Cool!" Vi said.

There was a faint sound from Sir John. He had his face turned to the fireplace, so I couldn't tell—but my guess was that it was a snort of derision.

"Oldcastle was the first layperson to be martyred in England," I concluded.

"Roasted alive." Sir John's voice was hollow and he still averted his eyes.

I read the paragraph that accompanied it. "It says here—hanged by a chain by the middle, he was consumed by fire, the gallows and all. The gallows must be that wooden thing he's hanging from like a cross-beam. It says while he was burning alive, he prayed for his persecutors and prophesied that he would rise on the third day."

"Like a vampire," Vi exclaimed.

Sir John snorted again. "There's Another that rose on the third day that was no vampire." He was looking at us, but still avoiding the woodcut.

We all looked at each other blankly.

"You call yourselves Christians!" Sir John snorted.

"Well," I said. "I don't belong to any organized religion." I looked at Bram and Vi.

"Me neither—I've always thought of myself as a kind of New Age Druid," said Vi.

"Agnostic," said Bram. "I keep an open mind."

"An open mind can invite much." Sir John's voice rumbled. He shook his head and chuckled grimly, "Agnostic vampire fighter. Most irresolute."

"I'm not really a vampire fighter, Sir John. Until today, I'd have said vampires didn't exist. I'm just fascinated by the idea."

"'Tis in your blood, lad. No shame there." The old man's voice rumbled deep. "But you need to find some faith to arm you, whatever that may be."

"You still haven't answered the question, Sir John." I wasn't going to let him elude it. "Are you saying you are this Oldcastle who was martyred for his faith? Or if not, who are you?"

CHAPTER 38

SIR JOHN FALSTAFF'S WORDS ON BLACK DIGITAL RECORDER, UNDATED

LIKE A LITTER OF HELPLESS PUPS, BUT growing teeth to gnaw at me.

So I told them—as much as anyone could tell such mewling babes.

"You come from a gentler age." I told them. "For all your time's destruction."

If you want to imagine the scene, this Oldcastle, I'll tell you. I know him well as I know myself—no saint, but a soldier, earned his knighthood on the field of battle in his youth. In age, a man of good wit, literate, a gentleman. Yet he read the Bible in English. An act of heresy in that Church-ruled age.

This Oldcastle came to believe that matters of conscience were between man and his Maker without a priest to intervene, that the Church should not own property—are you surprised that they might burn a man at the stake for such views?

They spun rumors of an imaginary plot to kidnap the king, captured Oldcastle and bound him over to be burned at the stake. His king, the noble Henry the Fifth, turned his back on his old friend.

Imagine this Oldcastle, imprisoned in the Tower. In comes a lovely lady, slipping past the guards like a perfumed breeze. Her hair as dark as night and eyes as deep as oceans. Offers him a chance to live rather than die for his faith. Tells him he could live to see the future where his offspring would pay for what they planned to do to him tomorrow. Who would not choose life?

You protest that many saw the man burned alive.

But imagine a creature who could counterfeit young womanhood and slip past guards unnoticed, a creature who could win a man of reason, a man of faith, but also a man of appetites. Could not such a creature cloud the minds of a crowd come out to stand in a field to see a man burned alive? The master-mistress of this dark art could do that and more.

But doubt it not, the man who followed her into undeath did burn, and was reborn before he reached the state of ashes. The first and bitterest of step on the path of undeath was to learn that his new mistress spiced her amusements with the suffering of others. But she kept her promise and he did not die.

The creature he was bound to looked young and beauteous. Yet inside she was old and starved for wit, with no laughter to call her own. She had picked out the man for his sublime wit. The creature watched, and laughed, and it could not bear to let laughter die.

Let's say that man lived, but at a price.

You ask if that price was his soul. Now that soul you speak of, like that elusive thing that they call honor, is invisible. Most difficult to measure.

The man might have wondered afterward if he had made a bargain with the Devil. A fair question. But one with no present answer. I could no more see my soul before my death than I can see it now. 'Tis true I do owe God a death. But until that debt is paid in full, a vampire, like a mortal man, can only wait and wonder.

CHAPTER 39

KRISTIN MARLOWE'S TYPED NOTES
AUGUST 7TH CONTINUED

"HOWEVER I CAME HERE, I FACED DEATH and chose life—even half life. So here I stand and deal with what is in front of me." Sir John bowed as if applause had been offered.

"So you were kept alive to entertain?" I asked.

"Not a pretty fate. But a good wit will make use of anything. If I could turn diseases to commodity, then I could conjure up a smile from a grinning skull and live a season as court jester to an undying ruler. Yet escape fell in my way and I took it. Returned to London, near two centuries after leaving, and found much changed. The Protestants in power, the Catholics hunted, and the Bible read in English. Even so, the name of Sir John Oldcastle was vilified for gluttony and debauching youth. Another immortality stemmed from a chance meeting in a tavern. Tales spun for a balding man with a honey tongue and ink-stained fingers, a poet and player. You know the man."

"Shakespeare," Vi and I both said reverently.

CHAPTER 40

HAL ROY'S SPOKEN NOTES
SILVER FLASH DRIVE/VOICE RECORDER
AUGUST 8TH

JACK CAME OVER ON AN OCEAN LINER in 1939, stowed in the hold, shipped as a load of diplomat's personal property to avoid customs.

Grandfather, who was with the State Department, wanted Reba out of Europe before World War II broke out. She told me she won Jack in a poker game from a countess, but I always wondered if the English-woman who gave him up simply couldn't cope with World War II and Jack at the same time.

The price Reba demanded for going peaceably back to San Francisco was shipment of some crates of household furnishings. Her father asked no questions—if Reba was smuggling, he didn't want to know. The crate around Jack's coffin had a special latch so he could emerge at night to feed, and lock himself in during the days to sleep safely.

Once in New York, Jack's crate was loaded into the baggage compartment of a San Francisco-bound train.

Jack told me Reba installed Jack in her basement at first. Something happened. Neither of them said what, but soon he was exiled to the shed. She reinforced the windows and doors and had a new crate built around his coffin. She padlocked the door at dawn to keep out daytime intruders. Sir John could have gotten out if she forgot to let him loose—he was strong enough to simply break the door. But she always opened the lock to get her daily dose of whatever he gave her when he took her blood.

Whenever I came back, I would wait at dusk to hear him rise from his box. Eventually I brought a few trusted friends, Ned and Lucy, to meet him. He charmed them, as he did everyone. But Sir John did not drink their blood, and he never let us meet any other vampires—except a crazy woman who showed up from time to time. Sir John always stopped whatever we were doing and took her away. He told us all never to go near her, as she might kill one of us as casually as we would kill a fly. Looking at the madness in her face, I could believe it.

Lucy was a big favorite with Sir John. He never admitted it, but she told me later that he took her off to meet another vampire and granted him permission to feed from her. Lucy's eyes got dreamy and she said it was the most intense pleasure she had ever had—and Lucy was a dedicated sensualist.

No matter how often I asked, Sir John refused to introduce me to other vampires. I think Ned went along with Lucy to meet the other vampire, but he refused to discuss it. He knew how crazy it made me that he and Lucy could get something I couldn't.

"I'm sorry I ever introduced you to him," I said to Lucy. She just laughed. "Why can't you take me to see that other vampire?"

"We don't know how to reach him. He finds us, doesn't he, Ned?"

Ned said nothing.

"So the other vampire—it's a man, right?"

Lucy smiled and winked at Ned, who turned away.

"Could you ask him to make you a vampire? Then you could drink my blood."

"Hal, that is so sweet!" Lucy patted me on the cheek. "I'll try to remember." Then she slapped me, just to prove she was unpredictable—she was like a kitten that purred and then bit. "But I do get so distracted when he feeds—it's—"

"Better than sex. You told me that already. What if you refused to let him drink your blood if he didn't make you a vampire?"

Lucy laughed. "What would you do if I refused to have sex with you, Hal?"

"Go somewhere else."

She laughed again. "You do that already, and everybody knows but Mina. Well, this vampire is the same. Besides I don't want him to stop."

"There's a way around this, and I will find it."

"Good, because I want to become a vampire." Lucy stretched out with the total relaxed abandon of a playful kitten. "I think it would be the perfect birthday present, and I'm a Scorpio, so you know my birthday is coming up soon."

PART II
THE DEATH GATE

CHAPTER 41

HAL ROY'S SPOKEN NOTES
SILVER FLASH DRIVE/VOICE RECORDER
AUGUST 12TH

I HAD TO FIND THE OTHERS. But how?

Jack never spoke about other vampires in the city except in whispers to the crazy woman. She might have been a vampire, but I took his advice and stayed away from her. She didn't seem to speak much English, just babbled in a strange dialect that he spoke to her as well, and I could scarcely catch one word in ten. But Jack did tell her to stay away from the others. So there must be some other vampires walking the streets.

You would think after all this time with Jack that I could pick a vampire out of a crowd, but I could not. Jack refused to teach me any such thing. He was blocking me out, and I hated it. I'd already tried watching him for years and he never led me to these other vampires. After Jack moved his crate out of the shed, I was back to watching. Now all I had to watch was the shed.

A few nights later I saw a tall, thin man trying the lock. I approached to within a few feet. He froze without turning around. "He's not there anymore." The man turned. For a moment all I saw was a cadaverous face, then I realized it was my aunt's lawyer. "Mr. Morford."

So he was a vampire. Now that I thought about it, he came to my aunt's house whenever she needed to sign papers, and he always arrived after dark. I assumed that was for my aunt's convenience.

He seemed to be following my calculations with an expression half of hunger and half of anger. "Where is he?"

"When my aunt moved into the rest home, the shed turned up

123

empty. I can open it up and show you."

"Go ahead. Maybe I can find some clue as to his whereabouts."

I brushed past him to open the padlock. Morford moved back farther than he needed to, to let me at it.

From the way he looked at me the few times I had met him before I had assumed he was gay, and now his hungry gaze made me wonder if it was really my blood he wanted. I've never been attracted to other men, but now I consciously moved closer to him, flirting with him. I wanted to become a vampire so badly that he could have asked anything of me. He seemed to guess that.

I opened the door and he slipped past me, carefully not touching me to get in. He looked around, large nostrils flaring, casting around for a scent like a tracking dog.

"Yes." He looked back at me as if he had to remind himself of who I was. Then he closed his eyes and sniffed the air around from a few feet away. My nerve flickered and I took a step backward. A chill settled over me.

Morford chuckled. "Don't be afraid of me, Hal. I am forbidden to touch you. Yet he fed from the woman you slept with not so long ago."

"Lucy!"

He laughed. "No, not Lucy."

"Mina? No!" After protecting her so carefully.

He sniffed again. "No, not the young one—an older woman who lives next to a house with many cats."

"Kris."

"He fed from the woman with the cats as well. Their scents are mingled here, along with the scent of the hauling men who brought his casket out."

"Mr. Morford, when you say you can't touch me, does that mean you can't turn me into—like you and Sir John?" I was afraid to say it. Afraid I had guessed wrong.

He laughed. "By our laws you belong to Sir John, though he never feeds from you."

"You have your own laws?"

He stiffened, offended. "Of course we have our own laws. We are not animals."

"Sorry, I didn't mean that the way it sounded. It's just that Sir John never told me any of this—and neither did my aunt."

"The less you know of this, the safer you are."

"But if Jack won't do it and you aren't allowed to, how can I become one of you?"

Morford shrugged and said nothing.

"Perhaps I should be approaching the others."

"What do you know of the Others?" Morford gave a hiss that was close to a growl. I instinctively shrank back.

"I heard Jack tell his crazy lady friend they were dangerous. You know the woman who looks like a bag lady?"

"A sad case—it's a miracle she still lives." He paused and looked around the yard. He seemed to be seeing something I couldn't see. "Dangerous is too mild a word," he said in a low tone, his eyes darting round again.

"I might know where to find them." I was bluffing.

He laughed, a short, humorless bark. "I tell you they are dangerous and you want to find them." He shook his head. "Where, on the Death Gate? As a human with no vampire venom in your blood, I doubt you could see them if you stood eye to eye with them."

He mused a moment. "Don't tell me, let me guess. You mean to use Lucy. That girl is too wild for this tame town. Has she seen something?"

I just smiled. No sense disclosing my ignorance.

"Never go near the Gate. I would go so far as to say avoid the Bridge because it intersects the Death Gate. Find them and your life will be over. Call for them and you will die—but not to rise again in any way you would wish."

"Thank you for the advice."

"Your aunt's retainer covers advice on a wide range of topics, but I never expected to be talking to you about this. If you should ever be so unfortunate as to see the Others, listen to me—this could save your life. "

"What?"

"Ignore them if you can. Never, ever look into their eyes."

He walked out of the shed. By the time I reached the door, he had vanished into the night.

There are several bridges in the Bay area, but only one that San Franciscans refer to as The Bridge.

CHAPTER 42

HAL ROY'S SPOKEN NOTES
SILVER FLASH DRIVE/VOICE RECORDER,
AUGUST 13TH

IT WAS MIDNIGHT WHEN NED AND I dropped Lucy and her bike near the security gate and drove out onto the Golden Gate Bridge. We pulled over to stop by the East walkway—which was totally illegal. The pedestrian lanes are locked up at nine p.m., but bikers can get buzzed through the security gate and that's what Lucy did. We gave her a head start and planned to meet her in mid span with a story about picking her up if the police swooped down on us, which we half expected. It was windy and freezing above the bitter cold waters of the Bay below. Two or three cars passed in the fast lane. The toll booth attendants were invisible in their stations. There had to be police surveillance cameras on us. If nothing else, they must be watching for people who showed signs of trying to climb over the railings to jump.

I was hoping to contact these vampires quickly and get off the Bridge. But how? Lucy came pedaling up and we put her bike in the car. Still no sign of Bridge security. A car whizzed past us on the southbound side of the Bridge, heading to San Francisco.

"What the hell, here goes," I said. "I invoke the Others. We seek knowledge and power from you." It sounded dumb saying it out loud in the halogen-lit night, with the shudder of the Bridge walkway under our feet and the roar of the wind and water passing through the Golden Gate all around us. I looked at Lucy and Ned and shrugged.

"Come on, Others!" Lucy yelled. Then she spun around like a little kid, ran up one of the orange posts in a skateboarding move, and collapsed on the walkway in a laughing heap.

"Are you all right?" I stepped over to take her arms and help her up.

"Ow, I skinned my knee—look."

Her skirt was short enough that the gash on her knee stood out against her pale skin. "That's a bad cut." I leaned over, Ned came over to examine it too—either the scrape on her knee or how high her skirt hiked up.

Lucy stopped looking at her knee and stared past me as if someone were coming up behind me.

Before I could turn a rush of hot, damp air fell down over us like a breath from a fetid jungle opening up into the middle of the cold, foggy night.

A rush of gray, shark-slippery forms streamed past me to pile onto Lucy. Most of them were smaller than she was, but they filled the air around us, bouncing and floating as if weightless. They converged on Lucy. They swarmed over her in a mass that completely covered her, and seethed thickest around her cut knee.

Lucy screamed and reached out through the mob. I grabbed her hand, but the creatures pulled at her relentlessly, all of them gray-skinned, hairless and staring boldly with unblinking eyes as round and red as bicycle reflectors. A few of them opened mouths full of strangely reddened teeth.

Morford's words came to me. "Don't look at them. Ignore them!" I yelled.

"How can you ignore them?" Ned screamed.

"Don't make eye contact," I yelled. "Let's get Lucy out of here."

"Okay." Ned stood. Lucy's screams were strangely muffled. I couldn't see her face under the seething mass of gray bodies.

Ned thrashed out to thrash at the slippery gray forms swarming over her. They simply floated out of reach and followed us. I felt the same hot, humid wind over my head and I looked up to see the cables and rails and towers of the Bridge covered with glistening gray forms. Floating without wings, they perched lightly on every surface. And they all turned their eyes toward me like a forest of glowing rubies.

"We've got to get out of here." Ned's voice was near my ear.

Lucy had stopped screaming and started laughing hysterically. A huge black sport utility vehicle in the northbound slow lane steered around our parked car and whooshed past. It didn't speed up or slow down. In the haze of fear I realized that the driver couldn't see those things. If he had he would have floored the accelerator and raced off that bridge and not slowed down till he ran out of gas or hit the Oregon border.

It broke the spell enough for me to yell to Ned, "Grab Lucy's other hand."

When Ned and I each took an arm, we could drag Lucy to her feet. The gray, floating shapes flowed off her and trailed along around her. We began to run, stumbling, half-carrying, half dragging Lucy between us. The tide of gray creatures parted to let us through and closed ranks behind us. I didn't have to look back to know they followed us.

CHAPTER 43

THE THINGS COULDN'T SEEM TO GET in the car with us.

I made a suicidal, spectacularly illegal U-turn trashing a couple of the moveable orange cones that functioned as the Bridge's center divider and landing in the southbound lane with a squeal of tires. Miraculously we didn't get broadsided by the midnight Bridge traffic, most of it going faster than forty-five miles per hour. I expected to hear police sirens, but we seemed to be invisible except to the army of floating gray monsters.

They trailed us to the house. Again something stopped them at the door, but they clustered around the windows. I shut all the curtains.

Mina was still mad at me, so it was no problem to let Lucy sleep in my bed.

Ned slept on the sofa till dawn, then left muttering something about deadlines. Later he called to say that by daylight the creatures were nowhere to be seen outside my house. He was gone all day too, which was good, because I got a call to go to Washington. Another contract was opening up.

There wasn't much time. If Sir John didn't have a better idea, I would have to take it. But if he refused to bring us over, maybe Lucy could. She certainly seemed able to get the Others' attention.

Lucy slept all day. Ned came just before sunset and we stood looking at Lucy, sprawled on my bed naked. I cleaned and bandaged the cut on her knee. For all those scary teeth, they hadn't drunk her blood, but she had strange marks all over that leg and on every patch of skin that hadn't been covered—which was a lot considering how short she wore her skirts and how low her necklines.

"You've been sitting looking at her all day."

"Not all day. But from time to time."

"You are such a degenerate. I am so glad you didn't marry my sister, Nell."

"She wouldn't have been open to the vampire life. I never told her. I did tell Mina, and now she's mad at me. Anyway, the marks are getting fainter."

We both leaned forward to examine the worst of the bruises that had blossomed on Lucy's knee, all around where she had scraped it. It was a weird one—gray with overlapping circles of smaller circles.

"It's like a chrysanthemum pattern." Ned leaned close to look.

"I'll leave the flower concepts to you, artist boy. It looks to me like a sucker pattern. Like a bunch of suction cup marks."

"Yeah, I can see that too. But when those creatures were swarming all over her they didn't bite her and drink her blood like the other vampire did."

"Mr. Morford."

"Is that his name? I never knew it. That was one of Sir John's rules."

"He's my aunt's lawyer."

"No wonder Sir John didn't want you to meet him."

"Morford's gay, you know. Did he seduce you?"

"He only drank my blood, no more than that."

"And was it better than sex."

Ned cleared his throat. "Yeah."

"Well, I have to believe you, because Jack is blocking me from that." I realized I was grinding my teeth when I said it.

Ned sighed. "Has Lucy said anything?"

"No. She never quite woke up. The wound was pretty clean already. Her knee healed so quickly. I was worried about some kind of venom in the blood."

"I thought that was the point. Vampire venom. Live forever, all that shit."

"Yeah, but I was thinking of Sir John or some other vampire in his group." I told him what Morford had said me.

"And you didn't mention this before you took us to the Bridge like fools?"

"I thought Morford was trying to scare me away from the other vampires. I just have to find a way in."

"Those things on the Bridge last night won't help."

"No. I don't know what the hell they are." We both stared at Lucy for a minute.

"So they didn't seem to be taking much blood, she's not waking up, and they left those marks on other, exposed parts of her body. Do you think we should take her to a doctor?" Ned's voice was anxious.

"Did you notice that none of the cars that drove past us seemed to even see those creatures?" I asked. "How can we explain what made the marks on her?"

"Maybe they can treat her even if we don't know what made the marks. We have to do something." Ned said with unusual tenacity. Usually he just went along with what I said.

"Look, Ned, I get that you care about her, but I don't think Lucy would want us to look for medical care till we know what's happening. She does have all those vampire bites.

"How do you know what Lucy would want?"

"All right, you perverts, just stop talking about me like I'm not here."

Ned and I both jumped. Lucy had opened her eyes. In the dim light of dusk they glowed faintly red. Her voice was husky with a buzzing kind of quality, as if she was on the edge of laryngitis. "I have had dreams that you would not believe."

"Tell us, Lucy." I sat on the edge of the bed, and after a moment, Ned came and sat on the foot of the bed.

"I was scared when they were all piling on top of me, but once they started feeding on me, it was—well, it was terrifying and then it was glorious."

"Better than the vampire bloodletting?" Ned asked hoarsely.

Lucy turned her face to him. "Way better," she whispered. I could feel a strange throbbing between them, as if the vampire had linked them so intimately even I could feel it.

"So it was different from when Morford took your blood?" I asked, as much jealous as curious.

She stared at me. "Who's Morford?"

"Hal says that's the tall, skinny vampire's name," Ned told her.

"You guys met him when he drank your blood, but he never told you his name?"

Lucy put her hand on my arm. Her hand was very cold and it trembled a little. "Sir John said we couldn't tell anyone, and he hardly even talked to us when he did it—it was really sexy, though. We never knew his name or how to reach him, and we had to keep quiet, or he wouldn't keep taking our blood."

Something about Lucy at that moment radiated power. Either Ned or I would have done anything she asked.

"The other vampire, the one you call Morford, he just took his fill and let go. Those things on the bridge—they would have taken me forever if you hadn't dragged me away. I don't think I would have minded. It was a great way to die." She opened her eyes again and smiled. Her teeth looked a little red too, perhaps a trick of the light. "Look out there."

She pointed toward the window. I had closed the curtains, but not all the way. Usually I don't draw the curtains at all. On the second story no one could see in. My bedroom windows overlooked Sutro Park on two sides and the ocean in the back.

Through the gap in the curtains I could see a horde of the gray creatures massing around the window, huge red eyes staring in hungrily. Lucy tried to get up to go to them. Ned grabbed her to hold her back, and I leaped over and pulled the heavy curtains totally shut.

The room fell into darkness. The only illumination was—My God! Lucy's eyes were glowing red. The irises were almost neon red, and the whites of her eyes were pinkish. Suddenly I was afraid of her. I turned on the bedside lamp.

Lucy subsided back on the bed and Ned sat next to her, leaning against the bedstead. I went back to sit with them.

"So, what's your plan?" Ned folded his arms.

"We need to go to Sir John and give him one last chance to help. Maybe knowing he has competition would move him. If not, there are others who have no such scruples."

None of us mentioned the horde outside.

CHAPTER 44

KRISTIN MARLOWE'S TYPED NOTES
AUGUST 13TH

MY DOORBELL RANG A LITTLE AFTER it got dark. I was more sensitive to the lack of light since Sir John had entered our lives. I didn't want to think about him possibly savoring Vi's blood at this very moment.

I went to the gate. I hadn't been expecting anyone.

It was Hal. Maybe he had come to return my mother's picture. He had brought along a tall, thin man in his thirties with a mass of dark black hair and a full beard, and a thin, very pale blonde woman who might have been any age from fifteen to forty, with pale eyes so visibly bloodshot that they almost seemed red.

"Wait!" Mina came running up the sidewalk behind them.

Hal turned back to face her. "Mina, I was going to call you later!"

"But instead you decided to take all your friends to see Kristin. You said you weren't seeing her anymore." Her voice was harsh with anger.

The last I'd heard from Mina was the irate phone message firing me as her therapist. Then all hell broke loose in the vampire department. I hadn't got back to her, not that she wanted to hear from me, but I should have at least sent a note saying that I was sorry and I hadn't known she was seeing Hal.

"All right, let's take it inside." I opened the gate so everyone could come in off the street into the garden.

"This is Lucy." Hal gestured to the delicate blonde woman, who wavered from one foot to another as if drunk or drugged. The tall, wild-haired young man he introduced as Ned.

Mina stepped in close to Hal. "I was going over to your house to try and patch things up when I saw you taking off with Lucy and Ned—and here you are again."

"We'll have to talk later, Mina, this is an emergency." Hal turned to me. "We need to see Sir John. I know he's here."

Vi must have been watching at the window. Before I could dial my cell phone she came out the back door with Sir John on her heels.

Instinctively everyone turned to Sir John. He nodded politely to each visitor. "Hal, at last I meet your lady, Mina." He bowed deeply. Mina was cowering away from him in a way that made clear she didn't want him to touch even the tips of her fingers.

"What have we here?" Sir John moved close to Lucy. She favored him with a cheerful smile.

Her teeth were pink, as if stained with blood, and he examined her closely. She had an odd rash on her face and neck, even her arms and hands—a pattern of gray circles too sharp for normal bruises. Could she be tattooed on every visible inch of skin?

"Lucy, where have you been?" Sir John asked.

"With the Others."

The word was like a physical blow to Sir John. He turned around to scan the entire yard. "Hal! Young fool, you drew blood and called them. No one else would be so rash."

"Finish her, Jack. If you bring her over, she can bring me and I won't have to go back to the Others."

I had never seen Sir John so solemn. "And you saw the creatures, Hal?"

"Yes."

"Yet no vampire has drunk your blood?"

"No."

"I never thought it possible." He shook his head, "You know so little that you think they will let her go simply because I put my fangs to her?"

"You wouldn't help me, so I tried that another way."

"Brave Hal, to use your girlfriend as bait." Sir John's voice rumbled with contempt.

Mina had been following the argument back and forth like volleys in a tennis match. "So now Lucy's your girlfriend too?" She hit Hal on the arm. "Hal, look at me. You're sleeping with Kris, Lucy—how many girlfriends do you have?"

Sir John turned to her, as if relieved to find something to smile at. "Nay, lambkin, the number is too high. Don't strain yourself with counting."

Mina raised her hand to slap him. She was too far away to connect, but he ducked away and circled back to where Lucy stood.

"What happened to her?" I didn't know what Lucy had been exposed to, but it looked bad.

Hal turned to me with anguish in his eyes. "I didn't know this would happen, Kris. How could I know?"

Lucy stared at Sir John in fascination. "I know you. But—I forget."

"The girl's not right, Hal," Sir John said in a stage whisper.

Lucy took a staggering step to one side. Vi went to catch her and I followed, taking her other arm. We guided her to sit down heavily on the bench a few steps off the gravel path through the garden. Wild-haired Ned followed and sat next to her, putting a protective arm around her shoulders

Sir John turned to Hal. "I cannot fix this. You do her no favor to offer her eternal life. Her mind's a snap away from gone. Then what?"

"You could at least try to make her better." Hal looked around at the rest of us, perhaps seeking allies. Ned, holding the swaying Lucy on the bench, looked as if he were about to cry.

"Suppose I do as you ask?" Sir John said. "The vampire life is not for the frail. The Others would have her at the first dark fall. Indeed, they nearly have her already."

"Couldn't you could teach her to fight them, if you brought her over?"

"Look at her. You see how she is. If she had to live by her wits, she'd be fried in the sun within a week. I learned the hard way not to bring the weak-minded into this half life. Do you think the Others will be so kind? Did you ask them? Did they answer you?"

Hal's bluff faltered. "I don't think they can talk."

"So you have learned that much. You know nothing of them. You think she can make you a vampire—who teaches both of you then?"

A noise in the bushes caught my attention, and the burglar-mask faces of two raccoons appeared briefly, beady eyes intent as they waited for a safe opportunity to attack the two garbage cans next to the gate, and clean up any leftover cat food from the feral cats' bowls.

Then the rustling turned into thrashing in the bushes. A tremendous snarling and squealing erupted nearby.

"That doesn't sound like the raccoons," Vi said uncertainly. She went to the back stairs and hit the light switch for the back yard floodlight. The garden was bathed in a harsh glare.

A crouching, disheveled woman faced off a female raccoon who had tucked her two half-grown pups behind her. The guttural growls came from the woman, not the raccoon.

Then she lifted her head, squinting against the light, and turned toward us. She said something low and guttural that I didn't catch, and strutted over to Sir John with a flirtatious twist to her face.

She wore a long, ragged shift like a nightgown with a man's coat jacket over it. Her feet were bare, her hair a long, tangled mass that might have been red if it were clean. Her face still held some charm under the coating of grim. She seemed a starved street urchin scarcely into her teens, but as she drew closer the light from the house and cottage windows revealed eyes as old as the grave and sharp with madness. We all instinctively moved away from her.

She came close to the bench where Vi stood near Lucy and Ned. Before anyone could say a word, she leaped at Vi and clasped her around the neck, her mouth half buried in Vi's scarf, snarling and biting through the cloth. She snarled again, turning her head to track the mother raccoon, who was taking the opportunity to run for the bushes with two pups tight on her heels.

I took a step toward the woman who was holding Vi, half strangled. She raised her head and for a timeless moment our eyes met. Hers were so dilated that they looked black, hyper alert.

"Doll! Let go!" Sir John's voice boomed a command before he got to her physically. All of us flinched at the sound. The woman let go of Vi so quickly that she stumbled. I stepped up, grabbed Vi's arm and pulled her away. Sir John stepped between us and stood over the now crouching woman. "Where did you sleep last?" His tone was firm but gentle.

The woman's answer, an incomprehensible growl, contained words. Sir John spoke to her in some form of English—an occasional word sounded familiar. But it was a dialect beyond my understanding.

Whatever she said displeased Sir John. He demanded something that must have been, "show me," although I couldn't understand that either. Over his shoulder to us, he said, "Wait," with that same unmistakable command voice.

He followed her, both of them squeezing through the hedge where the raccoon had gone.

We waited, all in shock. I deposited Vi back on the bench next to Lucy, who hadn't seem to register most of what just happened. Ned stood up and moved behind the bench, putting his hands on Lucy's shoulders. He motioned me to sit down with Vi and Lucy. I didn't argue. I perched on the edge of the bench next to Vi, who was shaking.

"Did she bite you?" I whispered.

"No, but she would have if he hadn't stopped her."

Mina put her hands on her hips and marched over to Hal, who looked at the ground.

"That was Doll," Hal said at last. "Sometimes Jack and I would go find her out on the street preying on the homeless. This is the worst I've seen her."

Sir John came back alone several minutes later, looking grim.

"She has a dark hole to hide in when the sun comes up. She stays with a group of men she can feed on. They think they use her, but she only lets them live so she can feed. She's been lifting her skirts and taking men's coins since before your country was a gleam on the horizon of the first exploring sailor."

"You called her Doll. Is she Doll Tearsheet from Shakespeare's *Henry the Fourth* play?" I had to ask.

"The same, or as near as makes no matter." This time he did not smile at my tone of awe, but turned seriously to Hal. "You wonder, young man, why I will not bring you over to this half life. Look at Doll. Six hundred years ago she was a young, contentious girl with a lively laugh and hair like a sunset. No dowry, no husband, too wild for the nunnery. Nothing she could do but whore." He sighed. "Where else would a soldier meet his love, but a bawdy house? Her own wit sparred with mine as few could. We parried words and kisses. We parted. She heard of my death, but when they changed me, I came back for her. I found her dying from disease a needle's worth of your medicine could cure. I saved and damned her in a moment with one kiss."

Mina had come closer to listen. Her eyes glistened with tears. "That is so sad."

"Sad indeed, young Mina. I was so new to this half-death myself, I could not know how endless life could crush a weak mind. The constant change—a new world on your heels, before you truly grasp the last one. Her reason broke. But her body burns on, and she has some low cunning left to scrabble about and live. I would I had let her die. I've no more heart to snuff that candle now than I did when I first relit it. She is my penance. Where I go, I bring her. I look after her as I can. I do not need another such burden on my soul—if soul I still have."

Hal moved closer to get Sir John's attention. "I just need an edge, that's all I want from you. If you give that to me, I won't turn to the others."

"You don't know what you ask, lad. A vampire can go mad—just look at Doll. The Others are pure death for anyone who engages them. Stay away."

Hal seemed not to have heard. "It may be too late for that. Share the blood and power you have. I need it. The job I do, I see what has to be done. I watch the men in charge screw it up, just from arrogance and stupidity. It's not my pay grade to make those decisions, but even if it were, they'd sabotage it. The whole damn system is blind. I need to do it another way. With the right edge I could change the world."

"The gift you ask of me would not solve that riddle."

They looked at each other for a moment, and Hal said, "I already know how things need to be done. All I need is the power to get them done my way. If you can't give it to me, I will go back to the Others. I know how to find them."

"Find them?" Sir John shook his head. "Foolish lad. Look at poor Lucy. The Others are among us already. They haven't followed you yet, but they will," he muttered. "Best to travel by day, if you can. At night—look for a place to hide."

He turned and started out the gate.

"Wait!" Hal caught up with Sir John, and I heard his questioning voice as they walked away. No answer from Sir John.

Ned took Lucy by the hand, nodded politely. "Glad to meet you all. We'd best be going." He followed Sir John and Hal out the gate.

Mina stood looking after them and finally turned to go. "I'm sorry,

Kris," she said. "I'm sorry for everything."

"I am, too," I said. "Call me if you need anything."

She nodded, turned and walked away.

CHAPTER 45

SIR JOHN FALSTAFF'S WORDS
ON BLACK DIGITAL RECORDER, UNDATED

A FEW GROWLS CHASE THE PUP away. Who could look on Doll's fate and want to live a vampire half-life? Six centuries undead. Were she human she would reek, but the unwise man who ventured close enough try to lift that skirt would find she smelled of vampire perfume and new mown hay. Curious creatures, we smell sweet to lure our prey, with a faint flavor of how we died. Doll's death was in a hayloft. My own death smells of wood and smoke and ground cover.

Young Hal has opened the gate to hell. I walk along, preyed upon in the streets and threatened in my daytime refuge.

Danger lurks in the night. Things more fatal to vampires than humans only because we see them and our presence lures them like a deadly spoor. Hungry Ghosts—the city teems with 'em, fragile but fatal to the unwary who walk across their now-unmarked graves without the proper care. And those red-eyed horrors seeping through the Death Gate.

A host of night terrors, yet none I fear more than the dawn.

So now I search the streets without the comfort of safety from the sun. I need to nose out yet another lair, if only briefly. Hmm, briefs may yet deliver me. My fingers find a scrap of purple silk in my pocket, and recall the lips that tasted of sack sherry and a hint of pork chop. Time for a visit to my lady from the restaurant.

CHAPTER 46

A FEW HOURS LATER SIR JOHN RETURNED, accompanied by two men in overalls wheeling a huge dolly.

"I must leave," he said as they loaded up his crate. Vi and I trailed after him.

While the men loaded his coffin, Sir John said softly, "Hal has opened the gate to the Others—I know not how. They speak no words. They never walked as men. They drink the life of those who call them. Most humans cannot see them." He fell silent when the workmen passed by rolling the huge crate down the hall.

We started to follow, but Sir John held us back.

"Where will you go? Will we see you again?" Vi asked.

"If we survive. Because I drank your blood, Vi, and yours, Kit, you may see them."

"We don't even know what they look like."

"Pray you never do. If they come to your window, you will see red eyes. Look away. Ignore them—your attention feeds them. Seal the windows against the night. Invite no one in." He tipped Vi's chin up and looked down into her face. "Leave your curiosity to go hungry for once."

Then he was gone.

Vi set herself to transcribing her notes in a somber mood.

I went home to read client files. It was past midnight when Vi called.

"Kris, do you see something strange in the garden?" I brought the phone to the window with me. The night was dark. At first I saw nothing, but there did seem to be a presence in the garden. I couldn't quite make out any actual figures.

"I don't see anything." The minute I said it there was a kind of rushing toward my window, as if a gust of wind had blown up against it. I jumped back.

"Vi, we should stay away from the windows. I still don't see anything, but that felt like an attack of some kind."

"Good idea."

The next morning the meowing feral cats in the garden woke me. I called Vi and got no answer. I rushed over to her place and found her collapsed on the floor near the window. She was dreadfully pale and I couldn't wake her.

I followed the ambulance to the hospital. I called Larry's place, forgetting that he was in Edinburgh, but Bram Van Helsing answered and came to the hospital to sit with me till we could see Vi.

He got there in time to offer moral support when a doctor told us she was severely anemic and they were transfusing her. She regained consciousness and begged me to go feed all her cats and to come the next day after I had fed them in the morning.

"If she's well enough to obsess over the cats, she'll be home soon," I told Bram.

"She's a very selfless lady."

Bram went with me again the next day, when the resident in charge of Vi's case pulled me aside. A serious young man who looked about sixteen to me, but must have been close to thirty. He looked at the chart in his hands while he spoke.

Fat people make doctors nervous—I've had them crouch against the door when forced to examine me naked, as if my flesh could contaminate them. Fortunately I was clothed and he only had to talk to me about Vi.

"Ms. Semmelweis said she has no next of kin. You're neighbors, right?"

"Friend, neighbor, and tenant. I rent the cottage behind her house."

I felt Bram move closer, so that he was standing next to me.

When he looked up from the chart, the doctor turned to him with obvious relief.

"Do you know anything about the marks on her neck?"

"No." I managed to keep myself from touching the marks on my own neck. Not that it mattered. The doctor was speaking to Bram.

"Well," Bram cleared his throat. "She does have several cats."

"How many?

Ah, the homemade sanity test. Multiple cats with no resident male equals proof positive of crazy-old-ladyhood. Bram looked to me for an answer.

"I've seen three, but she also feeds a couple of strays every day."

The doctor nodded as if this confirmed his worst suspicions. Either he really believed that cats could inflict vampire-style bites on the neck, or he was writing "Older female patient exhibits MCS—Multiple Cat Syndrome—Prognosis Uninteresting" on his chart.

"We'd feel better if we could do more tests and find out what's happening. But she insists on going home. My question is whether she's competent to make that decision."

I adopted a firm tone, just to see if he was capable of acknowledging me. "I'm a clinical psychologist and my professional opinion is that she's sane."

Bram nodded in agreement. "I'm a psychiatrist, and while I don't know her as well as Kris does, from what I've seen of Violet, I'd tend to agree."

The doctor nodded at Bram, with the smile of a man recognizing a colleague. I'd forgotten that as a psychiatrist, Bram was also a medical doctor.

"If you and your wife are going to be around to keep an eye on her, we'll feel better about sending her home. Bring her back in if she has more problems. We may be having this conversation again soon." The doctor snapped the chart shut and bustled off to his next errand.

"Sorry about that," Bram said. "Do you mind?"

"Do I mind the way he treated me like a cranky old lady and you as an equal? There was a time when that stuff bothered me, but in recent years I try to ignore it, and concentrate on getting what I want. "

"Of course that's terrible," he said. "But I meant did you mind how he assumed we were husband and wife?"

"No." I smiled, and he smiled back. "I liked that part. Thanks for sticking up for Vi."

"My pleasure." He took my hand and we walked like that down the hall to tell Vi she'd be coming home soon.

"Seeing my cats will make me feel better," she confided in me. I couldn't refuse her. I told the hospital that I would stay with her and take care of her till she got better.

"Keep her hydrated and make sure she eats," the doctor said. "She could go downhill fast. Bring her back in if she starts to get worse."

Bram helped me walk her to the car and up her front steps when we brought her home. She was very weak.

"Kristin, here's my cell phone and pager number. Call anytime, day or night. I'll be over at Larry's. I can get here in five minutes."

CHAPTER 47

KRISTIN MARLOWE'S TYPED NOTES
AUGUST 19TH CONTINUED

I CHECKED ON VI BETWEEN CLIENTS, but after she drank some of the protein drink the hospital had sent home with her, she slept. I went over at noon to cook her some lunch, but she was still deeply asleep. I kept checking her all afternoon between clients. Finally she roused up a little in the late afternoon and had some soup and more protein drink. I was worried that she would simply go to sleep and never wake up again.

Around sunset I came into the room to see that Vi was up and sitting in a chair. I told her which cats had come out when I fed them. The formerly feral mother and kitten only came out when I wasn't in the room, and ran to hide if they caught me peeking in the door. I managed to sneak a few pictures of them with my cell phone and got a smile out of Vi when I showed her.

I had expected the cats to be piling into bed with her, but even the bold males seemed to be hiding. "I probably smell like the vet's office from all the medical stuff," she said, as if too exhausted to think about it. She ate a tiny bit of rice and chicken casserole and said she would be sleeping soon, but she wanted to sit up a bit.

I made sure she had the cell phone within easy reach, so she could just press a button in case she needed help and was too weak to call out, and I went to the next room to sleep, my cell phone next to the bed.

But it was Vi's voice in next room, strong and loud, that woke me when she called out at three a.m. "Kris, can you see them?"

I sat up, instantly alert, scrambled out of bed and ran into Vi's room. She stood looking out the window in an odd posture, almost as if she was trying to press her face against the glass.

"Stop her!" a voice said so clearly that I looked around expecting to see Sir John next to me.

I rushed to the window and tried to pull her away. "Come on, Vi, turn around."

"Do you see them?"

Looking past Vi, I could indeed see something.

"Look away. Cover her eyes!" Again Sir John's voice in my head.

I turned from the window and put my hands over Vi's eyes. It was hard to shut her eyelids. "Pull her away." Vi resisted when I tried to move her away from the window. But once I turned her head slightly, she slumped against me like a puppet whose string is cut.

I got her arm over my shoulder, put an arm around her waist and half walked, half hauled her over to the bed. I picked up the cell phone from Vi's pillow and hesitated. Somehow dialing 911 didn't seem right. I pressed the button to page Bram. Then I heard Sir John striding through the house. I don't know how Sir John got in, any more than I know how he could speak his thoughts in my mind, but I was very glad to see him.

"The Others are here," he said.

CHAPTER 48

KRISTIN MARLOWE'S TYPED NOTES
AUGUST 20TH

SIR JOHN SAT ON THE BED WITH VI and pulled her up into an embrace. He sank his teeth into her neck hesitantly, as if tasting her. "Cold as stone," he said as if to himself.

Vi moaned faintly.

Sir John shook his head. "Too far gone." He pulled back a moment and looked at her very pale face. "One remedy alone remains." He pushed up his sleeve, took a small dagger from an inside pocket and made a cut along his arm, gritted his teeth and cut a little deeper. "Damn deep veins," he muttered. Blood began to trickle down his arm and he held the wound against Vi's lips.

At first it ran down her chin, but he took his other hand and wiped it up into her mouth. Her lips closed around his finger and she sucked the blood, then she swallowed. Sir John hastily pulled his finger out of her mouth as her whole body jerked in a kind of convulsion. Vi's eyes opened slightly. She looked half dazed and half hungry. She focused on the blood dripping from Sir John's arm. She seized it, licked it from wrist to elbow and put her mouth over the wound.

"There's my girl." He held her up and let her drink for a minute or more. Then he pulled her away and set her back on the pillow.

He pressed on the wound for a moment, and I could see when he took his fingers away that the bleeding had stopped.

Vi stared up at him, breathing shallowly. I stood helpless while Sir John sat pressing the opposite palm against the wound in his arm.

The door bell rang, making me jump, although Sir John and Vi didn't seem to notice.

"That would be Bram," I said, getting up to let him in.

"Nice lad," Sir John said. "Promising." He sighed and leaned back a little. "Always promising." Vi reached out to put her hand lightly on his belly. It was an oddly intimate posture.

I let Bram in and briefly told him what happened. I hadn't got to the part about Vi drinking Sir John's blood, but when we came into the room he was still sitting with his sleeve pushed up. The wound in his arm had nearly healed.

Sir John sighed and half turned away from Vi, who still had her hand resting on his belly. "Have not done that in these 600 years," he said.

"But Vi looked so weak. Will she get better?"

"We must wait and watch."

Bram couldn't stop staring at the wound on Sir John's arm, which was healing right before our eyes, knitting together into a small scar. "She's going to become a vampire, isn't she?"

"That is the best we hope for." Sir John's voice was mild.

"What would be the worst?" Bram asked.

I expected him to say "death." Instead he turned to Bram. "When you came over here, did you see anything strange about the house?"

"No, but I was hurrying."

"Mistress Kit? Did you see what Vi saw outside the window?"

I thought back, "There seemed to be something gray, but you said not to look."

"Wise lady. Those things have sucked away Mistress Vi's life. They may yet pull her into their world—a hell beyond imagining."

He turned to Bram. "You cannot see them. Vampires learn to will them away." He turned to me. "Most in danger are the vampire bitten and newly risen vampires." He rose wearily. "I must go. Mistress Vi will die by dawn, if not before. If she tries to go to the window, hold her down. If she talks, take note of what she says."

I stared numbly at Sir John. "I thought you saved her with the blood you gave her."

He sighed. "Mayhap she will rise in three days. Not all do. I must go. Call this number." He took a metal disk that hung from a cord around his neck, holding it out without giving it to me. I copied down the number down. "They will help you, but Mistress Kit—" he stared at me firmly. "Say nothing of the Others when you make the call. Tell them she was sick unto death, and say what I did, but not why. Be wise, my lady—you and Mistress Violet need their help."

Vi's voice was a faint whisper. Sir John turned back. Bram and I moved close to hear her. "Promise me two things. Take care of my cats."

"Of course I will," I said. "Don't worry, but—"

"Don't cremate my body. My will says to—Don't."

Then she was gone.

"Sooner than I thought. I was just in time." Sir John stopped and turned back in the doorway. "Maybe I did wrong. Time will tell. Keep your eyes to yourself and say as little as possible. Have a care for your own safety, Mistress Kit, and you, sir." He bowed politely and left.

PART III

THE UNDISCOVERED CITY

I SAT WITH BRAM AND THE BODY OF MY FRIEND for a few minutes, too much in shock to speak.

Both of us jumped to hear a scrabbling sound, and a huge, shaggy, black cat came out from under the bed. "Hi, Hamlet," I said softly. "He must have been hiding there the whole time."

Hamlet stared at me wildly and headed for the door, one slow paw at a time, belly low to the carpet. Once he got to the door he turned to stare at Vi. He didn't move closer. He stayed for a moment sniffing the air, then stretched his neck out, hissed at Vi, and slipped out the door. Then Ariel and Sly scrambled out of hiding in the closet and bolted quickly out the door behind him. The feral mother and daughter stayed hidden.

"Oh, God," I said. "That would have broken her heart."

Bram nodded.

I looked down to see I was still clutching the pad of paper where I had written the number on Sir John's medallion. My arms and legs felt like lead as I dialed the phone.

A calm voice answered, "SFUFO?"

UFO? "I beg your pardon?"

The woman's voice grew cautious. "What number did you call?"

I read it back to her. "Sir John told me to call this number."

"Our Sir John Falstaff? That's a very high recommendation. You've reached the San Francisco Undead Fraternal Organization. What is your emergency?"

I took a deep breath. "Sir John was here—My friend, uh—just

died."

I didn't seem to be making much sense, but she said, "I understand. You are not one of us, are you?"

"Um, no, but I think my friend will be."

"Sir John trusted you with this, so we'll send a team right over. Give me your address."

Fifteen minutes later the doorbell rang. Bram looked and told me a San Francisco Police squad car and a large van with "Coroner's Office" on the side had parked in front of the house. "That can't be an official vehicle," Bram said.

"At this point, I'm not so sure we want an official vehicle. We need help."

Bram opened the door and the uniformed policeman and two attendants in black stood awkwardly on the threshold. "You are the one who called our organization?"

"I did," I said.

"We need to come in to help you, but you must invite the three of us and make it specific to us, no one else."

For a minute my mind went blank, but Bram squeezed my shoulder and said, "Officer, you and these two gentlemen may come in."

They filed past us carrying a folded up gurney and we led them back to where Vi's body lay. One of the attendants examined Vi, noting the bite mark and opening her mouth to check for something—fangs?

"If you have some ID for her," the policeman said, "we'll take care of the official paperwork." I noticed that he was very pale and unnaturally still. "The Organization will take care of everything according to her instructions."

"How will you know her instructions?" Bram asked.

The policeman turned to him. "We'll ask her in three days time, when she rises." He smiled with fangs visible. "Did she mention anything she wanted taken care of?"

"The cats. I'll be taking care of the cats."

He smiled, this time with less fang. "That's good of you."

"She asked not to be cremated."

The two attendants stopped in the midst of moving Vi's body onto their gurney, and stared at me in horror.

"Of course not," the policeman said with a shudder. "Our

representative will be in touch about arrangements. The best thing would be to wait before making any announcements to any friends and family until we find out how she wants to deal with her new status. If something goes wrong and she doesn't rise we will bring you official paperwork and a local mortuary we deal with will be in touch. Can you wait three days?"

"I guess."

"Your friend trusts you or we wouldn't be here. The transition is never easy, but it helps a new vampire to have a support system of loyal daylight friends. If you need more information, call the same number tomorrow after dark. We don't work after dawn."

IT WASN'T UNTIL AFTER THEY WHEELED the gurney with Vi's body on it out the door that I sat on the sofa and began to cry. Bram hugged me.

"Do you want me to call Larry?"

"They said not to tell anyone."

"I have to go back to Arizona tomorrow, and I'm worried about you without someone to call on. I wonder if we can tell Larry without going into any details. Did he know Vi or any of her friends?"

"No, he knows my psychology friends, not Vi's friends."

"Larry is the most discreet person I know. We could ask him not to talk to anyone about it."

Larry came right over. Bram sketched out a sudden death scenario that did not include vampires. I was dazed, but relieved not to have to try to explain it.

"She was dead by the time the medics got here." I said.

"It must have been a stroke. I only met her once or twice, but she seemed so energetic. You just never know." Larry offered his place if I needed to get away.

"Or if you want me to stay and sleep on the sofa—you might not want to be alone," Bram said.

I met Bram's eyes. His offer startled me. "Thank you. Both of you, I appreciate it, but I'm going to sleep now."

When they did go Larry hugged me, and when he realized that Bram was hugging me for longer than usual, he discreetly stepped out into the hall to give us a moment. "Thank you for explaining things to

Larry," I whispered.

"I can't think of any rational way to explain what we saw. I only hope we don't regret it."

"Me too. Do you think it was illegal?"

Bram looked at me seriously. "Some things are so far from anything we call reality that it's hard to fit them in that category. If you accept what we've seen in the past week or so, we're going to have to rethink a lot of things. But not tonight."

"I hope you won't get into trouble. I don't know how I can ever repay you for helping us."

"The kissing was nice. Maybe we can try that again soon."

I sighed. "Next time without vampire feeding going on in the corner of the room."

"I have to wind up some things in Arizona tomorrow and get my car. I'll drive back. I need to be here with you for awhile." He gave me a significant look, and I took his hand and found myself kissing that quirky mouth again.

"I'll be back next weekend," he murmured into my neck. "Let me know what happens with Vi, and call anytime if you need anything." We hugged goodbye as if there were some doubts we would ever see each other again.

CHAPTER 50

KRISTIN MARLOWE'S TYPED NOTES
AUGUST 21ST

I WOKE UP NEAR DAWN, STILL ON VI'S SOFA, surrounded by cats. The little tuxedo cat, Ariel, draped over the arm of the sofa just above my head while the orange tabby, Sly, lounged on the back of the sofa. Hamlet had curled around my knees like a shaggy black blanket, snoring softly. I got up and put out the backyard buffet for the ferals, and then came in to feed Vi's cats. They watched me go back to the cottage. Their world had changed too, and that made me even sadder.

I went reached the cottage just before sunrise. The minute I closed the door the phone rang. A resonant male voice said, "Ms. Marlowe, this is Edgar Morford of the law firm of Morford & Bates. We'll be looking after the Semmelweis estate."

"Okay." I suddenly wanted a cup of coffee very badly.

"I'd like to make an appointment for you to come in and take care of the some details on Sunday—say around 9:00 p.m."

"You work on Sundays?" I said, feeling stupid.

"We work after dark. That's our only restriction. We will need a little time after sunset to talk to Ms. Semmelweis before we'll be ready for you."

"Of course. When will I be able to see her?"

"As soon as we've had a chance to explain her situation."

"Mr. Morford, the people I talked to at the number Sir John gave us—the, uh, SFUFO—told us not to tell anyone, but what about official notices and so on?"

"That is always a delicate matter. Some among undead society prefer to maintain a legal claim on life for economic purposes. With the right documentation we can inherit our own estates over and over again. We undead don't age beyond the day we died, so for security reasons we have to reinvent ourselves every three or four decades. Some prefer to make a clean break and start fresh. We won't know what Vi chooses until we've had a chance to interview her. Then we'll provide you with the appropriate documentation."

"Okay. But I'll have to let a few friends know where I'm going."

Morford chuckled. "Most prudent, but have no fear for your safety. I'll send a car for you."

"Oh, that's not necessary."

"I insist. Our offices are well concealed. You'd never find us on your own. I must go, the sun is rising."

"Fine. I have to rest now too." But he had already hung up.

Larry dropped by a little later in the day with a shopping bag full of food.

"It's traditional, Kris," Larry said as he unpacked the bag. "You won't feel like cooking, but you need to eat. Bram took off for Arizona, but he made me promise to look in on you. Are there any relatives coming in? Any funeral planned?"

"I'm going to go through her phone book in the next day or so, but Larry, could you not mention this until I see what's going on with her relatives? Her lawyer called today and I'm going to see him Friday. It might be touchy."

Larry nodded. "I'll do whatever you need, just give me a call. I didn't know Vi well, but she was a great lady. Do you have someone coming over to help out?"

I hated to admit how few friends I did have—none at all who would understand this. After Mark died, the friends we saw as a couple drifted away. In recent years I had settled into a routine with Hal as my lover, Vi and Larry as my closest friends. Hal was gone. Vi might be back, but that was not comforting. "I'll be fine." The word "desolate" popped up in my mind to replace "fine."

My thoughts must have showed on my face. Larry gave me a big hug, "Give yourself some space to grieve, but call me any time you need to talk or just someone to sit with. I could tell Bram was worried about you—I think he likes you, as we used to say in junior high." He winked.

"He's a wonderful person."

Larry volunteered to see some of my clients, and I didn't realize till he said it how much of a relief that was. I was in no condition to listen attentively to someone else's problems. After they left, I thought about how my friendship with Larry had lasted over several years—and in each of our cases several boyfriends.

I had met Larry at a retreat for Jungian therapists. Just the sort of thing I would normally avoid. My resistance was so low for the year after Mark died that I made it a point to stay upwind of any kind of salesmen or conference organizer. The few times I encountered one they instantly honed in on me like wolves attacking the weakest in the herd.

Larry had presented himself with his deceptively quiet face and ironic tone, brimming with more positive energy than I had seen in years. "My name is Larry Segovia, and yes, I come here often. Practically every bloody weekend as a matter of fact, and it has made a wasteland of what was once a modest social life. You might as well get used to me. You can tell me about yourself now."

I was so shaky and Larry radiated such warmth and kindness under his arch tones that I blurted out that my husband had just died. Larry said, "Oh, poor baby!" And without an instant's hesitation put his arms around me and comforted me with a hug. I hadn't realized till that moment how much I needed to be hugged. We became friends over the weekend. Our friendship deepened over the years.

And now I was lying to him about Vi's death.

The usual way to deal with death is to gather your loved ones around you, share memories of the person who had died, and keep busy making funeral and memorial service arrangements. I felt a flash of anger at Vi for embracing all things vampire and putting me in this situation. That was followed by a wave of guilt. If I hadn't led Sir John to her doorstep, Vi would still be alive.

I had some idea how to deal with death and no idea at all how to deal with a vampire best friend. Who was to say that the vampire life was better than no life at all? Until a week ago I wouldn't have said it was even possible.

A moist velvet nose nudged my hand on the chair's arm. Ariel, the little black tuxedo cat, had hopped up onto the table next to a long-cold tea mug, landing so softly that I hadn't known he was there. He stepped over to balance on the chair arm and looked at me with his intense green-eyed stare. He had a white chin, neck and chest that really did look like formal evening wear, and long white whiskers. I reached out and petted him, and he moved forward to my lap, curled up and began to purr. Soothing.

Sly emerged from his hiding place as well and moved onto the other arm of the chair. He started purring when I petted him. I relaxed a little more. A few minutes later Hamlet emerged from hiding under the chair I had been sitting in and stretched out on the floor, like a miniature black bear rug resting his head on my foot.

These particular friends weren't much on conversation, but they provided an unexpected amount of comfort as they settled in to wait with me through the next few days.

CHAPTER 51

FOR THREE DAYS I PUT DOWN ENOUGH FOOD for five cats, but I didn't see the two female ferals Vi had dubbed "the furry princesses." They must have waited to eat until I left the room. Ariel, Sly and Hamlet had no such scruples. They claimed me as their honorary can opener and litter box emptier, and clustered around me at every opportunity. Petting the cats soothed me better than any therapy I could imagine. When they purred I felt better, and they wouldn't brand me as delusional or give away Vi's secret.

I didn't realize that I was starved for human contact until I found myself replying to an email from a man who answered my online personal ad. The thought of Bram's kisses and his hands on me drove away any interest in online flirtation. I replied to Mister-Latte that there had been a death in the family and a lot of personal complications, so I was not available.

He didn't seem discouraged, and replied that I should feel free to email anytime. I recalled that his reply to the question about marital status had been odd. I looked again. He had written, "It's complicated." Oh. Probably married, but who cared? It only made me feel better about deleting his emails. As I did so I realized I hadn't thought of Hal in days.

CHAPTER 52

KRISTIN MARLOWE'S TYPED NOTES
AUGUST 23RD

A BLACK MERCEDES SEDAN CAR ARRIVED at the appointed hour with two men in the front seat. The driver was white—deathly pale, in fact, while the man in the front passenger seat was ebony black with a detached air. He came up Vi's front steps to ring the bell. "We'll take you to Mr. Morford's office," he said, and turned slightly to beckon me down to the car.

"Just a minute." I took a photo of both men and the car's license plate and emailed it to myself and Bram—captioned *will call later, or use this info*. "Just so you know that there's an official record of this ride."

Neither man replied or even acknowledged that I had spoken. The black man held the back door open. After I was seated he returned to the front passenger seat. They said no more until we reached our destination. I looked at the backs of their heads and hoped I wasn't going into a dangerous situation.

At Forest Hill Station the black man opened the door for me to get out, closed the door and nodded to the driver, who drove away. My escort led the way through the early evening Muni passengers down the funky steps to the train platform. He went to an obscure door I hadn't noticed and tapped in a code on a keypad. The door opened. He led me along a concrete-floored tunnel leading down. We seemed to be well below the level of the trains when the corridor leveled off. He opened another door that didn't seem to be locked, and surprisingly we walked into a marble-floored hallway that looked like a conventional old-fashioned office building, a hallway of wooden doors with frosted glass panels. One door read *Morford & Bates.*

The outer office contained only five straight chairs lined up against the wall opposite two more doors. A tall, thin man with black hair and eyes came out of one of the doors. He was dressed in an old-fashioned black suit.

"I'm Edgar Morford, and you must be Kristin Marlowe." He gave me a very cold hand to shake and nodded to my escort, who sat down on one of the chairs against the wall. Morford ushered me into the inner office and gestured to a chair across from a desk that looked as if it were made from solid ebony.

He leaned back in his chair and looked me over for a few seconds. "First of all, you'll be happy to hear that Violet Semmelweis did rise as we had hoped, at dusk this evening."

"She's alive?"

"She is undead."

"Can I see her? Where is she?"

"You'll see her very soon. She assured us that you could be trusted to help her. What we are about to discuss must remain confidential—for Violet's protection, and your own."

"She's my closest friend—of course I want to help. But I'd like to talk to her." Preferably away from Edgar, who did not inspire trust.

"One thing at a time, please."

"I saw her die, and those strange men came and took her."

"That was the beginning of the process Sir John set in motion. She's ready to make decisions about how to handle her . . . new existence."

"She's—one of them."

"One of us. Yes."

"But she always bitched about how fictional vampires are all young and built like strippers."

The lawyer spread his hands and a smile suddenly rose out of nowhere. I didn't see any fangs, but it was not a very broad smile. I got the feeling he didn't show amusement often. "Violet did ask if there was a dress code."

"I've always wondered that too. What's with the formal evening wear?"

"We find it useful to spread a bit of—how shall we say? Disinformation. Think of it as media hype. After all, you'd be on the alert if some gentleman in sideburns and an opera cape and an exotic lady all in black moved in next door, right?"

"Well, this is San Francisco. That wouldn't be too unusual."

"Yes, but you get my point. We focus attention on a cliché that doesn't exist. It would be more disturbing to think that anyone out after dark could be a vampire. The ordinary citizen behind you on the bus could be undead."

"So where do you keep the old ladies?" I kept arguing to keep from shaking, I was so nervous.

"At this hour they're out riding the buses, looking for a meal." He paused.

"I appreciate the effort at humor." I hoped he wouldn't try it anymore.

He raised an eyebrow. Maybe that hadn't been humor. "Some walk, take taxis or drive. At this hour most of them will have finished, or be pursuing their first meal upon rising."

He smiled again, and I began to see that he smiled when he was uncomfortable. "By our nature we are not subject to any kind of equal opportunity regulations. We make our own laws—and enforce them." He paused for emphasis, the smile gone. "It just happens that fewer senior females form relationships with vampires that then—transition into the undead state."

"Hmm. I wonder why."

"Kristin—may I call you Kristin?" He paused, didn't seem to breathe—did they breathe? I was pretty sure I remembered Sir John coughing and breathing. But this quiet office made me realize how much quieter vampires were than humans.

I nodded. "All right, then I'll call you Edgar." Somehow I doubted that I would.

"If you wish. Kristin, our organization protects an extremely vulnerable group. To put it bluntly, dead people have no rights. Even our charter as a foundation is framed in such a way as to evade scrutiny. Your friend Violet was lucky enough to die with property. Remember that old saying, 'You can't take it with you'? Our goal is to educate new vampires and find ways to protect our members' possessions, so they will have a small measure of security in their undead state."

"That makes sense. Rogue vampires would probably bring some

heat down on you."

"They could bring us attention that would cause all of us to be destroyed. By educating new vampires we protect our existence." His voice was stern. "Sir John is a case in point. Did he tell you the story of how he became a vampire?"

"You mean being hanged and burned as a martyr and rescued by a vampire?"

"Yes, he's told me about that too."

"He doesn't really seem like the religious martyr type."

"Is there a type? I always thought it was a matter of being stubborn in the wrong place at the wrong time." Morford cleared his throat.

"I know. I saw the woodcut."

Edgar smiled a little more broadly, still no visible fangs. "If that is true, it's one of the earliest documented examples of Vampire Disinformation—and a brilliant one, it's in the history books. But that may be as close as we'll get. After so many centuries, it's hard to know the real truth. Sir John is as much rogue as vampire, and I'm not sure which came first. But I do believe his story that he entered vampire life with less than the clothes on his back, and he has survived with grace and wit and inspired immortal plays and operas. Believe me, his recommendation is a high one." He cleared his throat, a little misty at the thought.

"I haven't seen Sir John since the night that Vi, that Vi—" My voice broke, determined not to show weakness in front of this man.

"Sir John always strays, but he shows up again." He pushed a box of tissues toward me, and I took one and quickly dabbed at my eyes. He cleared his throat. "Vi is awake now and impatient to see you, but we want to establish a secure nest where she won't be disturbed in the daylight hours. The logical choice would be the Clement Street property that she owned in life. We're completing the paperwork so she can transfer it to a special trust the SFUFO has set up."

"I don't see how it's possible, since she's dead and you say your organization doesn't exist in the real legal world."

"Technically all of that is true, and the date on the document might be suspect if it weren't for the fact that the signature on the will and trust documents are completely valid, as are those of the impeccable witnesses. First let's discuss the terms of Vi's will, or as we refer to it, her Undying Declaration."

He tapped the document spread out before me. "She hopes you can manage daytime feeding and caring for the cats. That includes spending at least an hour with the cats during the day, grooming, veterinary visits—interest income from the estate will cover the cats' care. It's all outlined in the document. During the evening, you can simply leave the basement door open and Vi will take care of them."

I was suddenly afraid. "I'll try it. But I can't guarantee I'll be able to handle it."

He nodded sagely but said nothing.

"If I change my mind, what will Vi do?"

'If you should refuse, you could still rent the cottage as you do now. The organization has reliable daylight employees who would take care of the cats. They were Violet's primary concern."

I smiled—that would be what Vi worried about. "I'll let you know how it goes."

"Vi has asked that no formal death notice be published. Something about the books she writes. She told me was that it was hard enough to get an agent when she was alive and she doesn't want to risk losing one simply because she's dead. You say only one or two people know she has transitioned. Are they are trustworthy?"

"One of them was there when Sir John brought her over, and the other one I just told she died suddenly. Those two don't know any of Vi's other friends. Oh, and the cat ladies. They just wanted to be sure someone was looking after her cats."

"She has only a few local connections, and she's going to email them that you'll be looking after her pets while she's traveling and doing research in Eastern Europe. She'll be able to continue to communicate via email."

I laughed for the first time in days. "That sounds like Vi."

"Let's see, what else? An accountant who works for the trust will consult with you about expenses, but your name is already on her checking account."

"It is?"

He seemed smug. "A great deal can be accomplished outside of bankers' hours if you know what you're doing. If you'll sign this card for the bank records, that will be completed. We have an accountant who will work with you if you need help on anything related to the property. Let us know if it doesn't work out and we'll go to plan B. Right now we need you to go to the house and wait for Vi's arrival."

I rose, and he reached across the desk. His hand was icy cold. "If you have any questions, don't hesitate to call."

He ushered me into the outer office and nodded to my escort, who stood. "They'll arrive before midnight."

CHAPTER 53

KRISTIN MARLOWE'S TYPED NOTES
AUGUST 23RD CONTINUED

ABOUT HALF AN HOUR AFTER MY SILENT ESCORT dropped me off at Vi's house two men wearing coveralls with a Midnight Movers Service logo stood on her doorstep. Neither was tall or muscular and both had pale shaven heads and visible piercings in several places. They didn't look strong enough to be hauling heavy loads, but I would never have guessed they were vampires. "Delivery for Kristin Marlowe. We need you to sign."

He waited while I signed. I handed the clipboard back.

"Now we need you to give verbal consent for us to bring the crate in and install it as per Mr. Morford's instructions."

"Don't you mean instructions from Violet Semmelweis?"

He studied the clipboard for a moment. "Yes."

"Okay." I stood aside and he waited.

"Um, you have to invite us or we can't cross the threshold."

"Oh, sorry. Come on in."

Both of them looked around wildly. "Don't ever do that!" the first man said. "Make it very clear who you're inviting, or you could be in a world of trouble."

"Sorry. I'm new to this. Should I use your names?"

The first man shrugged. "It wouldn't hurt. I'm Jeff, he's Toby."

"Okay, Jeff and Toby, I hereby formally invite you two Midnight Movers employees to come in for the purposes of bringing Violet home."

Jeff nodded. "Okay, Toby. We're good to go."

They went back down to the van, opened the back of it and tipped a rectangular box onto a large dolly. They got it up the steps and into the hall in short order.

"It says here that she requested installation in the basement." Jeff nodded approvingly. That's a good location. No chance of light in the daytime."

I directed them to the basement door, opened it and stood aside. Jeff and Toby each took an end and started down. I had only been in the basement once or twice to use Vi's washer and dryer, but the bare, windowless space gave me instant claustrophobia, so I preferred to use the Laundromat two blocks away.

Now I followed the men down the narrow stairs to the concrete-floored space with bare wood beams above. The basement ran the length of the house, with timbers sunk into the concrete and braced to retrofit it against earthquakes. Near the stairway, next to the light switch, a washer, dryer and a hot water heater sat next to utility shelves with tools, boxes of nails, cleaning supplies, light bulbs, old pots and pans and general unidentifiable clutter.

Shelves across from the stairwell held Vi's remainder books, still in the shipping boxes, neatly labeled by title and number of copies in black felt tip pen. I directed them to put her coffin there. It just seemed to me Vi would want to be near her books.

The two men pulled out crowbars and hammers and opened up the top of the crate. Then very gently they lifted the coffin out, rested it on the dolly for a moment while they flipped the crate over and tested it for stability. Then they set the coffin on top of it. It fit perfectly.

"You've done this before."

"Yeah," Jeff said. "We do most of them here in the Bay Area. There aren't that many, but sometimes, like tonight, we'll have two in a night. Toby custom cuts each crate into a base according to the client's height, so it's easy to get in and out of the casket."

I watched them a little queasily, fascinated, but dreading what came next.

"We won't know if it's exactly right till she tries it out here, though."

He opened the coffin's lid with a flourish. Vi sat up.

I managed not to faint—just barely.

CHAPTER 54

KRISTIN MARLOWE'S TYPED NOTES
AUGUST 23RD CONTINUED

I SAT DOWN HEAVILY ON THE LOWER STEPS of the staircase. I must have looked shocked enough that Jeff and Toby hovered over me. "Are you okay? It can be a shock sometimes."

I managed to look at Vi. She had climbed out of the coffin, and stood with her back against it and her arms crossed in front of her. I had looked forward to running to hug her, but unexpected fear and suspicion flooded me. The last time I saw her she had been in bed in her pajamas, dying—dead.

Now she wore slacks and a sweater that were too big for her and didn't look like anything I'd ever seen her wear. Her hair was the same rumpled salt and pepper gray as usual, and her face was pale, but not waxy and sickly like the last time I'd seen her.

"I'm sorry, Kris. I didn't mean to—" She didn't sound any different than usual. Not that faint whisper I had heard from her when she begged me to be sure she wasn't cremated.

"No, Vi, I'm glad to see you." Looking at her made me feel dizzy. "You'd think it wouldn't surprise me after all we've been through. But—I guess I've been going on autopilot lately, feeding your cats—" Before she could ask, I said, "Yes, I'm feeding the ferals too. Everyone's fine."

Jeff and Toby stowed the last of their tools. "Do you like this spot, ma'am?" He gestured to the coffin. "I don't mean to rush you. Take your time and see if it's where you want to lie during the daylight hours. We can move it and set it up anywhere."

Vi looked around, as if seeing her own basement for the first time.

"This is good."

"Are you sure?" Jeff held out his clipboard to her. "I need to get your signature, ma'am, that your installation suits your needs and your friend—" He looked over at me briefly and cleared his throat. "It seemed like a bit of a shock—is your friend going to be able to handle it?"

Vi's eyes pleaded with me, but she straightened up and took the clipboard. "Kris, if this is too much for you, Edgar said he can send a daytime staff member over tomorrow to help out."

"I'll be okay. I just need to get used to it."

The delivery guys looked relieved. "Like I said, we've got another client to install before dawn," Jeff muttered while Vi signed her part of the form. Toby used a cloth to remove a phantom speck of dust from the coffin and stood up to go.

Jeff shook Vi's hand, and Toby followed suit. "We're just glad to see Sir John claiming one of his own," Jeff said. "He hasn't made a vampire in—well, I've never heard of him ever doing it. It's a small, twilight world, Violet, and we protect our own." He sketched a rough salute. "We're honored to set up the coffin for someone Sir John brought over."

"Thank you." Vi smiled, showing her new fangs. She saw me staring and stopped smiling.

I must have been shocked to the point of babbling. "But what about the Others?"

"The Others?" Jeff and Toby turned eyes on me that suddenly were cold and flat.

Oops.

"What do you know about the Others?" Jeff's tone was hostile, almost threatening.

"I—I—" Behind them Vi put her finger across her lips to caution silence. "I don't know. I just heard the term."

"You should be very glad you never met those things, lady. Or you'd be undead, but not snug in a coffin in some nice, dry basement." Jeff laughed nervously.

Toby did not laugh. "We don't talk about those things. We don't think about those things." He turned to Vi. "We don't look at those things if they show up in front of us. Don't go thinking you're immortal now. Lots of things can destroy you. Go to your orientation classes starting tonight to find out how to protect yourself. In the meantime keep your eyes to yourself and just ignore anything that crosses your path until you get to class tonight. Mrs. Battle will teach you how to survive."

Once you got him started, Toby was hard to shut up.

Jeff tapped him on the shoulder. "Come on, we've got to get back to work. Say hi to Sir John when you see him." Reluctantly he turned to include me as well. "Call Mr. Morford's office if you need help." To Vi, he said, "The number is posted on the inside of your coffin."

Vi stayed on the basement stairs, but I escorted the men out and watched them through the not quite closed door.

"What is that woman doing talking about The Others!" Toby said, putting the dolly into the back of the van and slamming the door. He suddenly looked wildly around, as if someone might be observing him.

"I wonder where they heard about that." Jeff got into the driver's side of the van.

Toby got in the passenger side. He didn't seem to notice me watching—perhaps the door looked closed. "You gonna tell Mr. Morford?" The van door slammed before I could hear Jeff's reply.

I closed the front door, locked it and double-checked all the windows. Going back to the basement, I noticed that all the cats were crouching around the door. For some reason I didn't want to go back down there. "Vi. Your cats are all up here, looking down into the cellar."

That got her. I knew it would. She came up to look, and I instantly regretted having said anything. The cats heard her footsteps on the stairs and ran to hide. I had forgotten how afraid they were of Sir John.

She came upstairs and looked around. No cats.

Our eyes met. "Um, they just ran away."

"Well, I must smell different now, and it's all about scent for them. Did you feed them?"

"Yes, this morning and earlier tonight."

"Are they coming around to get petted?"

"Yes." I was sad about that all of a sudden, as if I were alienating her cats' affection.

"Well, I'd better get to my orientation meeting."

"Where is it?"

"It's out at Land's End."

"Do you want me to drive you?"

"The strange thing is, Kris, I feel great now. I know I look the same as when I died."

"Actually, you look better."

She smiled, but without fangs. "I haven't felt this energetic since I was a teenager. I could probably run to Land's End, but I'd better not. Somehow a gray-haired old lady sprinting down the street might get the wrong kind of attention." She stretched to demonstrate—yep, flexible and graceful. "I'd better go find out about getting something to eat."

A sudden wave of fear washed over me. "You haven't, um, eaten?"

"Don't worry, they gave me a couple of pints from a blood bank when I first woke up." Vi smiled again. Seeing the new fangs didn't reassure me. "Vampire fast food."

We both laughed, the first time in what seemed like forever.

"My orientation meeting starts in half an hour. I'll drive myself. Are my keys still on the hook near the door?"

I nodded and only shuddered a little when she brushed past me to go out. "Don't worry, I won't bite." I managed a weak smile in return. "Don't wait up for me."

CHAPTER 55

MINA MURRAY'S JOURNAL
RED DIGITAL VOICE RECORDER AUGUST 25TH

HAL FOLLOWED THE OLD MAN out of Kris' yard and I watched him beg Sir John to make him a vampire. When he got no answer, Hal swore he would go to the Others again. I left and went back to my own apartment. I never expected to see or hear from Hal again, and I was too angry to care. But I missed him.

Six days later Hal called and begged me to talk to him. We went for coffee at Louis' and then we walked along Ocean Beach. The minute I got close to him, I wanted him as much as I ever had. We were only a few blocks from his house and I was grimly determined not to wind up in bed with him. Usually I was afraid and he was confident, but now he seemed to be almost afraid to talk.

"I want another chance, Mina. I know I screwed up, but I don't want to lose you forever." I didn't know how to ask what he was frightened of, but it was clear in the way he hugged me that Hal suddenly needed me desperately in a way he had not before.

Damn. How could I resist him?

We ended up in bed, and before we got out of it—several hours later—the engagement was back on. I cried when he persuaded me to put it on, and he gave me a couple of other pieces of jewelry with an almost frantic desire to please. That might have been a turn-off, but it made me feel secure for once in my life. The man I wanted more than anything wanted me desperately. Almost too good to be true, but I took it.

I began to relax and feel safe with him again, but I drew the line at spending the night at his house even with the thing in the shed gone.

I know the vampire's name is Sir John, and the one time I met him he didn't scare me. But something about the house still gave me the creeps.

Hal said he would do anything to keep me. This was the moment to suggest selling the house, but I waited.

Over the next several days we settled into a honeymoon period. Sometimes we made love all afternoon in his big double bed. It seemed to inspire him to new heights of sensuality. He was trying to make it up to me, and I decided to let him. From the moment we got back together I was drunk on his love—the wild sex didn't hurt either.

Hal told me he was going to D.C. to talk to the agencies doing the funding and firm up the details for his latest contract. After that he would probably be going overseas for several months.

So we drank a farewell bottle of wine with lunch and after a long afternoon in bed. We drowsed as if we were floating.

"Mina, we could get married right away. You could come with me."

I stopped stroking his hair and examined his face. He seemed totally relaxed, but underneath it he was trying to push me.

"You're saying I should quit work and leave everything and everyone I know."

"You're not close to your family here. We could relocate to the DC area. It's closer to my work anyway. You don't like this house. I'll put it on the market." It's not practical to hang onto it, and with the ocean view, someone will buy it simply for the location.

"Hmm—that's a thought." Could it be that easy? I didn't even have to suggest it.

"You don't like your job anyway. You could find a better one in D.C. if you want—or don't work at all, come with me when I go overseas."

"The idea of being totally dependent scares me."

"Totally dependent on me, you mean."

I was so drained from sex, I didn't see how he got enough energy to pout.

"On anyone." The room seemed darker, and I looked up to realize that it was late. "It got dark outside when I wasn't looking." I was too tranquilized by wine and sex to feel as anxious as usual.

"It does that." Hal didn't say anything for awhile. I realized he was snoring. I had to smile. Maybe I had tired him out for once.

There was a noise outside the window. A faint scratching like a tree branch. Hal insisted on pulling the curtains shut even though I hadn't minded the sunlight while we made love.

It had been a warm September night. Hal's second story window looked out at the ocean. I got up and opened the curtains. I stood there naked for a moment, feeling unafraid in the moonlight. No one could see in because there was nothing between the house and the ocean—passing ships would be too far away and the window was dark, lit only by the light of the full moon. I thought about how unashamed Lucy always had been to be naked, any time, any place. I hadn't seen her since the night when Sir John yelled at everyone—nearly two weeks ago.

My eyes focused on the window to see a face pressed against the glass, outside—two stories up.

It was Lucy.

She was naked. Her blonde hair gleamed silver in the moonlight, and swirled around her as if in some spectral breeze. Her eyes glowed red and her skin seemed to glisten a luminescent pearl gray color.

Floating in the air at eye level two stories above the ground.

She was not alone. At first I saw vague shapes surrounding her and pulsing in a mass, as if buoying her up. What were they? They were shaped like humans but with slick gray skin that glistened like sea creatures. Then like a field of lights going on all at once, they opened huge round, red eyes. Their eyes bored into me. The mass of bodies clustered around the window leaped into focus as a flock of pale gray creatures, gleaming slippery in the moonlight.

Their red eyes pulled me closer to the window. I put out a hand and touched the glass and instantly they clustered around it. The more I looked into those eyes, the more they seemed like flowers with a myriad of neon red petals opening like straws, drawing me in.

The scream died in my throat and I gasped and tried to back away.

The creatures' eyes held me helpless, staring out the window. Several of the creatures pushed Lucy aside. She bobbed away as if floating in water. They pushed their smooth gray faces against the window—opened their mouths.

Teeth.

They had more teeth than I thought a mouth could contain. Several of them fastened their red mouths to the window glass and began to suck. I felt my life starting to drain out of me in a thousand threads.

I gasped as I felt terror and a tremendous surge of life leaving my body in a rush.

At the same time there was a glorious floating sensation of pure pleasure.

That afternoon, the afterglow from all the lovemaking with Hal, faded. This volcanic hot red joy made sexual ecstasy seem like a faint, cheap imitation. I wanted to scream, but I couldn't manage more than a faint whimper as a giddy languidness came over me.

Was I dying? Did I care if I was? A desperate, faint wailing came from somewhere in the depths of my being.

NO!

I thought I screamed, but it came out as a faint moan. Hal woke up, scrambled out of the bed and yanked me away by the shoulders.

A wave of pain and darkness crashed over me as the connection broke. Hal stepped between me and the window. His breathing was hoarse. I could feel his terror. He was shaking. He hugged me and reached behind him to pull the curtains. I weakly trying to push past him, to dive back into that ecstatic molten pond.

"Don't look at them." But I couldn't help but turn away from his grim face and struggle back to the window.

He wrapped both arms around me, walked me back to the bed, sat me on the edge and crawled in, pulling me up against him. I didn't have the strength to resist, didn't have the energy for hysteria.

"Lucy was out there, floating with those—things. Gray—red eyes—red teeth."

"I know. Mina, I'm sorry. I am so sorry. I was sure you couldn't see them and you'd be safe."

"You mean they've been here all along? You've seen them?"

"They come here at night. Lucy tries to get in." He shuddered. "We were looking for power when we first found them. But what they did to Lucy—" He shook his head. "The thing is. I don't know how to get rid of them."

"Can you ask that old vampire?"

"I can't find Sir John."

"I want to go home."

"You can't go outside now, Mina. Once you see them, they can follow you. They drank a lot of your life force—they did that to Lucy."

I started to cry. No words came. I felt violated to the core, and some deep, raw, evil part of me wanted them to take more or give more.

Hal was angry. He laid me down carefully on the pillow. I was literally too drained to move. He got up and began to pace. I watched him, half horrified, half wondering if I could get past him and reconnect with those creatures.

"Damn it, I'm leaving tomorrow. I want you to come with me, Mina."

"Can't."

"How about if you go to your father's place? That way I'll know someone is looking after you."

"No. I never go there except for holidays. I don't trust my father, and his new wife doesn't like me."

"At least call in sick to work tomorrow."

"Okay."

"I'll take you home in the morning before I go. They don't come out in the daytime. I'll sell the house. I don't think they can follow us if we move in the daytime."

I started to cry, but I was too weak to continue for long. Hal held me and stroked my hair. I slept and mercifully did not dream.

The next morning Hal was packed and ready to go and I was still very weak. But he drove me to my apartment in my car and took a cab to the airport from there.

I went inside, heading for the bedroom. I sat down on the sofa to rest first and never made it all the way to bed. When I awoke it was dark again. I glanced at the window and saw red bicycle reflector eyes clustered around the edge of the curtain.

They had followed me. I hid my head under the sofa pillow in terror. The darkness descended on my mind again, but I turned my face away from the window, clung to the sofa and slipped into a world of nightmares.

CHAPTER 56

THE DAYS AFTER VI ROSE AS A VAMPIRE blurred into hours of bright sunlight and disorientation for me. It was good that I had taken time off from seeing clients, because I was functioning just well enough to call the people in Vi's phone book whom she wanted told that she was dead. The ones whom she had decided to email and see in the evenings was a much smaller list. She told me that those two groups didn't overlap at all, so there was no danger of a friend hearing she was dead.

I was oddly grateful I had written Edgar Morford's suggested words down. I recited, "She died at her home, very suddenly of heart failure." The people who heard the words heard the numb shock from me. That was genuine.

I did that all morning, and around noon the doorbell began to ring. Friends and neighbors who had known Vi came over. Most of them brought food or drink. Some hugged me, even though I'd only met a few of them. Most sat for awhile, talking about Vi.

Three of the legendary Feral Cat Ladies came in a group, and appeared to be sixty-something, seventy-something and eighty-something respectively. The eldest spent most of the time talking to Vi's three tomcats, who ventured out to sniff them cautiously.

The youngest, Pamela, interrogated me while Ariel sat on the back of her chair and nuzzled her hair, which made her smile. The other two women played with Sly. Even Hamlet gave up his hiding place to check them out from a safe distance, stretching out his neck and his whole body to sniff Pamela's outstretched hand. "Who is taking care of Vi's cats?" she asked when Hamlet had settled down to observe them.

"I am. When she was alive Vi asked me to take them in if anything happened to her. I'm glad to do it."

All three women nodded their approval, perhaps with a tinge of relief. If I had hesitated or seemed unequal to the task, I guessed that they had cat carriers in the car ready to rescue them on the spot.

"How about the ferals?" Pamela asked. "Vi told me she fed a couple in the mornings in the back yard."

"Oh, I've been feeding them too. I can keep doing that."

"Are you sure, dear? It's a major commitment. Please, let us know if you need help."

"All right, I will." I was distantly amused that they were treating me like a possibly flighty youngster, and looking at how this situation would affect the cats. They left some sweet rolls and a couple of extra jugs of kitty litter. "You never want to run out," Pamela said.

For the next two days I was on a split shift. In the daytime more people visited Vi than I had ever seen in the house when she was alive. I was anxious about how Vi intended to tell some people she had died and not tell anyone in the writing community.

She rolled her eyes when I asked. "Writers and publishers live in different worlds," she said. "The writers are thinking about their own work, and the publishing world only hears from me when I finish a book. It might be different if I lived on the East Coast, but I could have been dead for years and no one would have been the wiser as long as I send email and meet my deadlines. It's three hours earlier in New York, so I can even call them on the phone before it's dawn here."

"Amazing."

Vi told me she would move her office down to the basement so she could work closer to dawn. She said she had so much material now, but she hadn't touched her computer since she came back from the dead.

As long as I had known her she had been obsessed with writing, and now she seemed to totally forget it. I didn't ask. Perhaps it was because she was living what she had only imagined on paper before.

The vampire orientation sessions took up her nights the first week. She left every evening at dusk and by the time I came over in the morning to feed her cats she was down in the basement, safely tucked away in her coffin.

I also noticed that the cats were hiding when I came in every morning. When I fed them in the evening, I waited till dusk to say hello to Vi when she arose, but the cats vanished into their hiding places the moment they heard her step on the basement stairs.

"Vi, have you seen your cats?"

Vi looked at me strangely. "No. Are they all right? They seem to be hiding. Do you see them when you feed them?"

"Yeah, they come out for meals. "

Neither of us said anything. I still wasn't used to how quiet Vi could be now that she was undead. I never had a clue what she might be thinking.

"The cats are still a little standoffish with me," I said.

"But they let you pet them?"

"The boys do."

"They won't come near me now." Her face looked very solemn. But she said no more and went out to feed and go to class. I never asked where she was getting the blood, or from whom. I went home and went to bed early.

Something woke me, not a sound but a feeling of pure terror stronger than the worst nightmare of my life. I sat up, heart pounding, short of breath for no known reason. I looked around. My bedroom was the same. The bedroom door to the hall was open as I had left it.

I was alone in the room. Nothing I could see explained what had wakened me. But the feeling was one of real danger. The large digital clock numerals read 2:00 a.m. I got up and went down the hall to the front of the cottage where the kitchen window and my office window faced Vi's house.

There was a faint sound in the garden between my house and Vi's and a flickering red light outside the window. Could it be from a police car out on Clement Street in front of Vi's house?

I pulled the curtain aside and looked out the window, the way I had a thousand times before.

A seething mass of gray bodies swarmed over Vi's house. I couldn't believe what I was seeing. Then a flickering of red that seemed to be gleaming eyes turned toward me in that writhing carpet of bodies.

I ducked back behind the blinds. That was what had wakened me. The terror gripped my heart again, as if to confirm it.

But there was no sound. No rustle of animals moving in a huge group. I had to look again, but I hid behind the curtain, hoping they would not see me.

Not bats, certainly not rats. They were bigger, much bigger. Built like humans, two arms, two legs, various sizes of body—some smaller than a child, others large as a big adult. These creatures swarmed in mid-air, floating without wings and diving down to join the mass blanketing the house.

They covered the two-story house in a living, crawling mass that billowed and moved in waves. Some crawling over each other. Some floating up, as if buoyant, to circle about and return, like pigeons rising from a flock and settling back down again.

The glints of red were huge, round eyes in otherwise featureless faces.

One of them left the pack and zoomed toward me—red eyes, burning like coals. It seemed to see me behind the curtain. I dived down straight down to the floor without a moment's hesitation. A moment later I heard a rustling at the window and a gentle bumping against the glass as if someone were tapping on the window with a balloon—bizarrely light, considering that they seemed to be the size of humans.

I could see the reddish glow on the floor reflected from the luminous eyes peering into my window. I backed up along the floor until I was at the opposite wall, where they should not have been able to see me. Occasionally one of them bobbed past the gap between the curtains and I caught a flash of moving, shark-gray flesh and neon red eyes. They didn't seem able to break the glass—they encountered it like fish at the edge of a tank, puzzled, interested. There was a faint slithering sound along the exterior wall of the cottage.

My mouth was so dry, I could barely swallow. I made myself take deep breaths and stayed on the floor as I scrambled into the next room. What were they? How could I keep them out? Were these creatures of the night, like vampires, who would be gone with the morning light? I wanted to talk to Vi, worried that they might be hurting her—not that I knew how to stop them if they were.

I called and got Vi's voicemail. I huddled on the floor. Faint bumping noises outside and I saw the red light of the creatures' eyes reflected on the wall opposite as they clustered at the window. I looked over to the door and saw the same red flickering around the edges of the door.

The digital clock on the wall read 2:30. I called Larry.

"I sincerely apologize for calling so late." Even I could hear the fear vibrating in my voice.

"Hi, Kris, don't worry about the time. What's going on?"

"That's just it, Larry. I'm not sure what's happening, but I need to talk to you about something I'm seeing. It's either a hallucination—or, I don't know what." I explained about the floating creatures outside Vi's place and my window.

"How very William Blake."

"Don't go Joseph Campbell on me, Larry."

"No, hon, I was trying to make you laugh. What you describe sounds terrifying. Shall I come over?"

"Okay, but Larry—"

"Yes, dear."

"If you see anything that looks dangerous, turn around and run like hell. Call me from home. Don't put yourself at risk."

"Hang in there, Kris. I'll be right over."

CHAPTER 57
KRISTIN MARLOWE'S TYPED NOTES
AUGUST 27TH PREDAWN HOURS

TEN MINUTES LATER I BUZZED LARRY through the gate and he walked past the hordes of floating monsters as if they did not exist. I pulled him inside without a word and shut the door on the creatures hovering just outside.

Hugging Larry made me feel much better. But the specter bobbing curiously at the window over his shoulder made me feel much worse.

Larry clearly didn't see it, and his presence didn't stop my seeing it.

"Let's start by turning on a few lights," he said. "You're sitting in the dark."

I let him turn on a lamp. The light masked the creatures outdoors, but it made me feel more vulnerable, a victim targeted in a spotlight.

"You've just been through an awful tragedy, Kris."

We went into my small kitchen—the window over the sink and counter faced Vi's garden and the back of her house, but I purposefully sat in the little breakfast nook facing away from the window. Larry sat facing me, ignoring the creatures outside the window.

"Do you think I'm having a breakdown?"

"Tell me what you see now."

"I'm making a point of not looking, but whenever I do, they're there. I realize that by telling you this I'm putting myself in a vulnerable position."

He squeezed my hand. "You can trust me not to abuse your confidence. All I can say for starters is that you're definitely seeing a reality that I'm not seeing. Have you been eating regularly? I know you're grieving, and if you forget to eat, that can put you in an altered state."

"Some of my neighbors brought food. I've been eating."

"You aren't on any medications that might explain what you're seeing?"

"No."

"Would you like to be on some medications? I brought my prescription pad and some sample packs of anti-psychotics. But I would also be happy to drive you to the emergency room of your choice and talk to the docs there. If we do that, I'll stick around and back you up, however you want."

I hugged him again. "You're a true friend, Larry, and I really appreciate that offer. But as a friend, I would ask you to not do that for the moment. I'm freaked out, but I'm hoping whatever it is will just go away and not come back."

"You've never had this kind of hallucination before?"

"Never."

"I'm not an expert on this particular area, but it does seem late in life to begin visual hallucinations, unless there's some kind of toxic mold in the house that's starting to affect you. Maybe you've got a brain tumor." He saw my face and patted my hand. "Just trying to cheer you up. Maybe someone slipped some hallucinatory drugs into a chicken noodle casserole in a misguided attempt at comfort food. Did anyone bring you suspicious brownies?"

I had to laugh, which made me feel a little better. I hated to withhold the information about Vi's death, but he hadn't seen it, and he didn't see the monsters swarming on the house now, so I hesitated. He already thought I was hallucinating—bringing up vampires would convince him I was totally delusional. "Did Bram Van Helsing talk at all about Vi's death?"

"No. He went back to Arizona to clear up some details and get his car. From everything he said, Vi's sudden illness and death must have been very traumatic. He did say he was very touched to have been able to help you, and he was coming back here this weekend." He smiled a little mischievously. "He asked me not to be offended at how hurt he was that you thought he was gay."

"I apologized for that, okay? I've been living in San Francisco too long."

"I had a feeling he liked you, and this just confirms it."

"Thanks, that cheers me up. I'm looking forward to seeing him again."

"And seeing more of him next time." Larry winked.

I had to laugh. Somehow Larry had accomplished the impossible and made the terror fade just a little.

He patted my shoulder. "Okay, Kris. Now that we've got your love life back on track, let's do an assessment. You told me what you see. Do you hear anything? Voices? Whispers, unusual sounds?"

"No." Now that he mentioned it, I considered how odd that the mass outside was so amazingly silent. Suddenly I took comfort in the possibility that this was a passing hallucination.

"How about other senses—do you feel as if anything is touching you? Like a crawling sensation on your skin?"

"You're creeping me out even more, Larry." I shuddered. "No tactile sensations, but thanks for suggesting it."

"It's very common for people who have recently lost a loved one to experience hearing their voice or briefly seeing them."

I shuddered. "Yes. I've heard of that." I was pretty sure Vi's vampire life was not a delusion, but would I know if it was?

Larry put his hand on my forehead. "No sign of a fever—infections can cause hallucinations. We could take your temperature, but your forehead is actually cool and not clammy. No outward signs of shock. No hot and cold feelings?"

I shook my head.

"You're shaking a little, though."

"Scared," was all I could say.

Larry got up and came over to hug me again and sat down next to me on the padded bench of the breakfast nook keeping an arm around my shoulders. "You've had such a rough time the last few days. Are you sure you don't want to come back to sleep in my guest room, just to get away from this place for awhile?"

I sighed. "No, thanks, I'd better stay. I've got to feed Vi's cats in the morning."

"You're shivering. How about if I tuck you in with an extra blanket and warm up some milk for you with toast. In my handy dandy drugs sample bag I have a mild sedative if you'd like it—no?"

I shook my head and managed a shaky laugh. "I might warm up

some milk. I'm better now, thanks, Larry. You should go home—you've got my clients to see as well as your own tomorrow. But thanks for coming over at this hour and listening to me without judgment. I think I just needed to hear a professional verdict of sanity."

"Relative sanity, Kris. Everything is relative."

"Thank you, Doctor Einstein."

He left soon after. I watched him go through the gate, and a few inches away on the other side of the window the red-eyed creature stared at me. I made eye contact and for a dizzying moment I was pulled into the human-looking iris in the middle of the neon-red eyeball.

The thing opened a mouth that was crowded with razor sharp teeth and smashed it up against the window pane with a solid thunk. Then it began to suck. Each one of those needle-like teeth opened up, drawing energy out of me. I could feel it, almost see the life force draining out of me in a tangible gush. I staggered a step forward.

The phone rang and I jumped. That broke whatever link had been established. I heard a loud pop. It might have been the creature peeling away from the window glass. I resisted the urge to check, and backed away. It didn't seem to be breaking the glass or coming in, but I felt drained. The damn thing had been sucking my life force through the window.

I turned and scrambled for the phone.

Vi's voice was loud and harsh on the line. "Stay away from the windows. Keep your back to them. Any attention draws them. Their eyes kill. Don't look."

She hung up.

I held the phone stunned for a moment, then remembered that Sir John's voice had somehow reached me to say something similar when I was pulling Vi away from the window. The night she got sick. Two nights before she died.

The trembling had been replaced by a bone-deep weariness. I went to get some duct tape out of a drawer and taped the edges of the curtains down so not even a trace of window could be seen. I couldn't help but think of a schizophrenic woman I'd met working at a free clinic, who lined her coat and hat with aluminum foil to ward off dangerous thought wave transmissions. Somehow that didn't seem so crazy to me at this point. What if I had told Larry that a phone call from a dead woman had given me suggestions about warding off red-eyed, energy-sucking creatures.

I looked at my watch. It was nearly 4:00 a.m. I sat in the chair, well away from the window, and tried to think clearly. Finally I pulled out my purse and dug out Edgar Morford's card. The vampire lawyer's number was the same as the one I had copied from Sir John.

If midnight was noon in the vampire world, as Sir John had told us, then 3:45 a.m. would fall toward the end of his business day.

CHAPTER 58

KRISTIN MARLOWE'S TYPED NOTES AUGUST 27TH 4:00 A.M.

MORFORD ANSWERED ON THE FIRST RING. "Kristin." Either a psychic vampire, or one with caller I.D.

"Edgar, something weird is happening."

"Describe it."

"I can see the back of Vi's house from my front window. It's covered in a swarm of huge gray—things with red eyes. I think they saw me and now some of them have come over to my window." I couldn't disguise the raw edge of hysteria in my voice.

" You just had a narrow escape. You must have known not to look in their eyes or you wouldn't be talking to me. " His voice grew cautious."I think I know what you're dealing with, but just to be sure, describe these things."

"Red eyes, different sizes, but they look somewhat human. Except they float. They're bumping up against my window like moths. I think—" My throat was so dry I could barely speak. "I think one of them was draining my life force when I made eye contact."

"Never do that, and don't give them the slightest invitation to come in."

"They could get in?"

"Only if you are insane enough to invite them."

"That won't happen."

"Then you should be safe if you ignore them."

"But they're crawling all over Vi's house."

"That is puzzling." His voice tone was chilly. "We don't know a lot about them. Studying them is dangerous. It's not unheard of for living humans to see them if they have been vampire-bit. Sir John drank your blood—any vampire can tell this when they meet you. But the horde you describe only swarm when living people invite them. You didn't invoke them somehow, did you, even by accident?"

"My God, no!"

"They can bring humans over into a kind of undeath. We call them the Others but they do not speak to vampires except to kill us. No one knows where they came from or how to destroy them. I cannot imagine why they would attack Violet's house. It was Sir John who brought Violet over, was it not?"

"Yes. He did. I saw it."

"Eyewitness testimony is persuasive." His tone was dry, as if he suspected me of not telling the whole truth. "Violet rose up like a vampire—that I myself saw."

"Can they hurt Vi? They're all over her house."

"She's going to her orientation meetings, isn't she?"

"Of course she is. She wouldn't miss them."

"Don't worry, then. From the first night she has received instructions about how to deal with them."

"But you said your organization takes care of vampires in need."

"Not the Others—or their spawn. Avoid them. They will kill you. Or worse." He hung up on me.

Bastard. So there was some kind of class war going on among vampires. British vampires with titles and their guests got preferential treatment. Vampires with property got custom coffin bases and an education. Bring us your tired, your poor, your correctly bitten humans, okay. But if you get bitten by seething masses of inhuman, fiends with red eyes glowing like coals, you're on your own.

I was shaking again, but a large part of it was anger. I hate to prejudge any creature. But they had almost killed Vi and now they were back to finish the job. I gazed at the curtain. On the other side of it the vague shapes were hovering, bumping against the window gently. Red light flickered around the edges of the door as they explored the cracks.

Vi said looking at them made them stronger, but it was hard to turn my back. I made my way back to the bedroom and closed the door to the hall. Suddenly I went from hyper alert to exhausted. I had a lot of questions for Vi—if we both survived the night.

CHAPTER 59

KRISTIN MARLOWE'S TYPED NOTES
AUGUST 27TH CONTINUED

I AWOKE TO FULL DAYLIGHT WITH A START, looking around for some kind of attacker. The morning was quiet, wrapped in fog. I put on a terrycloth robe and crept to the front window, unpeeled the duct tape and looked out into the garden. The only eyes that met mine in the cold gray light of dawn were the two feral cats waiting for their morning handout.

I got dressed and grabbed the shoulder bag where Vi kept food and water for them. Meanwhile, in the house, Vi's cats had come out of hiding. All five of them, including the shy mother and kitten sat in the window. When I went into Vi's kitchen they all clustered around my feet loudly demanding breakfast. I found a note from Vi taped to the cupboard where I couldn't miss it.

Dear Kris, I think the Others might kill the cats. I can't protect them much longer. Please get all of them out of here now. Don't feed them till you get them in the carrier. Call Pamela and explain you have to move the house ferals. She'll lend you a trap. They're taking my words, Kris. I don't know how long before they take my self. Kiss my babies for me. Tell them I loved them as long as I could. I know you will take care of them.

There was a faint red blot on the page, as if from a blood-tinged tear.

MOVING THE CATS took hours.

I started with Ariel. Vi had once told me he was so smart he would hide the minute he knew what was up. I ferried him across the garden to my bedroom and closed him in there.

Hamlet tried to resist going into the biggest carrier, but he was so terrified that he just froze and I hefted him in and locked the door before he could back out. He was heavy enough that I had to use both hands and brace the carrier against my thighs crossing the garden.

Sly accepted the relocation with only a few despairing mews on the trip across the garden.

Then I brought over all but one of their litter boxes, food and water bowls. I called Pamela about borrowing the trap, but she was out for the day, and it began to get closer to dark. The female cats would have to spend one more night at Vi's. I left a tiny amount of food and some water for them and went to comfort the other cats.

The office where I saw my clients seemed too close to the Others outside. I hauled the carriers back to my bedroom at the back of the house. It had heavy curtains over the window, and that put two doors between us and the silent horde. I opened the carrier doors and there was a pause. Each cat exited his carrier the same way, belly to the ground, eyes wide, looking for a place to hide. The bed was close and they sneaked under it and hunkered down. I put out food and water, installed a litter box on some newspapers.

The first of the Others came swooping across the sky as I left a brief note for Vi. I was not going out again that night. Neither was Vi, evidently. She was going to stay and protect the girl cats.

I lay on the bed, but there was no sound from the cats underneath. It was going to be a long night for all of us. I found myself touching the scar on my neck. Where was Sir John when we really needed him?

The phone rang. It was Vi.

CHAPTER 60

I GOT INTO WASHINGTON, D.C. LATE in the day on the 25th. It was dark by the time I checked into my hotel. I tried not to think about leaving Mina alone with those hordes of monsters. Until the night before I had assumed she was safe because she couldn't see them. I could only hope she would follow my instructions and be okay.

As unpacked my suitcase, I heard a knock at the door. I looked out the peephole, half expecting a hotel employee or messenger, and saw two official-looking men, one African American, one Asian. They wore dark suits. The black man held up a photo ID. "Mr. Roy, I'm Agent Fowler," he said through the closed door. "This is Agent Park. We need to speak to you."

"What's this about?" My first thought was a security check for my next assignment but the ID didn't seem quite right. I kept the chain on the door. "What agency are you with?"

"We're with the FVIA, sir. The Federal Vampire Investigation Agency."

"Is this some kind of joke?" I was totally lost. Such a practical joke made no sense. I had never breathed the word "vampire" to anyone Washington. The only people I'd ever told about Jack were my friends in San Francisco and since we'd encountered the Others, any hint of playfulness was gone.

"May we come in?"

I had wanted to meet other vampires. Maybe they could help. I unchained the door and stepped back. They waited. They appeared to need an invitation.

"You two gentlemen can come in."

Agent Fowler stepped in and Agent Park followed him and closed the door. The hotel room had a table and chairs and an armchair. I sat in the armchair and gestured to my two visitors to sit. They ignored the invitation and continued to stand.

"We have reason to believe that you are responsible for an infestation of alien vampires into the San Francisco area. We need to ask you some questions about that."

I wondered if they could tell that my guts clenched up like a fist. I waited for a couple of long breaths. Took a few breaths. I didn't see any evidence that they were breathing. "You say you're a federal agency, but I've never heard of a vampire branch of the government."

Agent Fowler smiled. "We're not listed in any official directory. But many secret services could make that same statement. We report to a different authority, but we are just as real as they are. Secrecy insures that we are free to get information in any way we choose. Answer the question, Mr. Roy."

"I think I need to call my lawyer."

"Edgar Morford?" This time when he smiled I saw the fangs. "He is one of us. He knows we're here. He knows what you did." His eyes were cold as black stones.

"Mr. Morford is worrying about saving his own skin at this point," Agent Park said.

An icy shiver went down my spine.

"We'd like you to come in with us now. We have some questions."

"Much as I'd like to help you boys out, it's late and I have appointments first thing in the morning."

"Not anymore. We've cleared your schedule," Agent Fowler said. "Cooperating with us just might result in your survival."

I WENT WITH THEM. Didn't have a choice, really. They seemed to know about the Others in general terms—they just wanted all the details. The first night I answered hundreds of questions. One thing they didn't ask was why I did it. Maybe it didn't matter anymore.

CHAPTER 61

MINA MURRAY'S JOURNAL
RED DIGITAL VOICE RECORDER AUGUST 27TH

I PACKED MY OVERNIGHT BAG AND SOME CLOTHES in a shoulder bag. As I faced the door I wrapped a scarf around my head, as if that could shield my eyes.

"Don't look at them," I kept repeating as I headed out the door, car key in hand. They bounced along, swarming around but never quite touching me. I looked at the ground. When I got to the car, I slipped in and slammed the door, half expecting them to try to get in as well, but they did not.

I started the engine and suddenly my windshield was full of gray bodies, massing around the outside of the car, staring in. I made it a point to look anywhere but in their eyes, peering out between the arms and legs and faces that writhed around the car.

None of the other cars on Geary noticed the swarm that covered my car. Clement Street was crowded, but people going to and from the restaurants gave no sign that they saw a horde of red-eyed monsters closing ranks around me when I parked the car, got out and started walking down the sidewalk.

The gray things followed as I walked. I looked at the pavement, ignoring them, peering between their bodies as I slowly made my way to ring the buzzer at Kristin's gate.

CHAPTER 62

KRISTIN MARLOWE'S TYPED NOTES
AUGUST 27TH

I BROUGHT THE PHONE INTO THE FRONT PART of the house and looked out the window, careful to look between the creatures that swarmed over Vi's house and the cottage. Vi stood at the window. Did her eyes have a faint red tinge, or was that my imagination?

"Be careful, Kris."

"Don't worry. I called Morford and he told me you should have learned how to protect yourself."

"I'm learning. But Morford doesn't know they killed me."

I hesitated. "I told him about those things, but not about how you met them before you died."

There was a long pause. "Maybe it was . . . a bad idea to tell him."

"Someone has got to help us. Sir John has done a disappearing act. Morford said he'd be in touch."

"I got your note about the trap. I'm staying in tonight to protect the girl cats. Please trap them and bring them to your place tomorrow. I'm sorry to ask, but it's too dangerous here."

"I'll do it. Don't worry."

"I don't know how long I can hold out." She hung up. It was full dark now, and the red in her eyes was bright as neon. Why hadn't I seen it before?

There was a spark of red behind her. She did not turn. But over her shoulder I could see the impassive face and round red eyes of one of the Others.

They were in the house with Vi now.

I jumped at the sound of the front gate buzzer.

As it buzzed, my phone rang again. I answered the phone first, thinking it might be Vi.

It was Mina. "Kristin, I'm at your gate. I'm in trouble. Please buzz me in."

After I pressed the button to open the gate, I watched her carefully pull it closed behind her. It would have swung closed, but I was glad to hear it click shut.

Mina walked down the path with her head bent down, as if dodging a heavy rainstorm.

"Hi." I opened the door and pulled her in without ceremony, terrified that inviting her in would bring in the Others.

She didn't hesitate. The minute I closed the door we looked at each other. I almost didn't have to ask. "Do you—?"

"You see them too, don't you?" She looked around, her eyes settling on the duct tape.

I sighed with relief. "Yes, I do."

"Hal's house is covered with them. They followed me to my apartment and then here."

"Let's go in the office. We can talk there."

Mina laughed a shaky laugh. "You're right. It would make me feel safer not to see them, even though I know they're out there."

We instinctively took our places as if for a therapy session, myself in my chair, Mina on the sofa, but this time both of us were sitting forward, leaning close. Her fear had come home to inhabit me. "What can we do, Kris?"

I was still clutching my cell phone. "I'm going to try calling for help."

"Who could help?"

"Maybe the local vampire organization."

"Wow, Kris. When I first told you, I wasn't sure you even believed me about the vampires. Now you've got their phone number."

"It seems like forever ago." We both laughed. "I just hope they'll help us."

Morford answered the phone on the first ring. "Edgar, it's Kristin. I spoke to Vi earlier. She was bit by the Others before Sir John brought her over. She's afraid they might get into her house."

"Is she planning to invite them in?"

"No! Of course not. But I think you should help us."

"What you've told me indicates that our contract may have been breached, and we may be forced to terminate our arrangement."

"Thank you so much—I'm glad to hear that your first priority is your contract. If you just let them kill us, won't they come for you next?"

"You are most persuasive." Morford's voice was cold as dry ice. "We have one expert on this. It's too late to reach him tonight. I will speak to him tomorrow night. I'm sure he'll want to talk to you both."

"How about some ideas about how to survive this night?"

"I've told you as much as I know. All vampires can see these creatures, but we cultivate mental skills to remove our attention from them. Some vampire-bitten humans see them and feed them, and then it is very hard to eradicate them. I have never seen a horde so large as you describe. This is most—disturbing. We will be in touch tomorrow night. Distract yourself till dawn, don't go near them, and try not to talk or think about them too much. It makes them stronger."

"I guess we'll see you tomorrow night then—assuming we're still alive. Do you know how to contact Sir John?"

"You would know that better than I, since he fed from you."

"How would you suggest—hello?" I put the phone down and looked at Mina. "The bloodsucking bastard hung up on me."

Mina laughed. "I've never heard you swear."

"I'm having a bad night."

She laughed again. "Me too." Then her face grew solemn.

"You might want to wait here. I want to check on my friend." I approached the window cautiously, unpeeled the tape and peeked around the corner of the curtain. The mass of Others who covered Vi's house were seething, concentrating on windows and doors. Could they really get in? The windows had a rosy glow that seemed as if lit by a red light bulb. I didn't like the look of that.

A couple of Others popped up on the other side of my window glass, and smacked gently at the window.

I slammed the curtain shut, resealed the duct tape and turned my back on them. Back in the office, I closed the door behind me firmly.

"They can't seem to get in," I reported.

"Yet," she added. "They're like that at Hal's, and then they followed me home." She leaned back languidly. "I wonder if they followed Hal's jet to DC." She seemed almost entertained by the prospect.

The phone rang. I sighed and answered.

"Kris, it's Bram Van Helsing."

"It's a friend who might help us," I said. "Hang on, Bram." Mina nodded, but she seemed to be half asleep already. "Feel free to nap on the couch, Mina. I'll take it this call in the other room."

I sat down in the kitchen with my back to the window.

"Larry told me what you're fighting—or as he put it, hallucinating," Bram said. "I'm coming over."

"I didn't know you were in town."

"I just got in. I didn't want to show up on Larry's doorstep unannounced, so I got a hotel room over on Van Ness. Then I found that message from Larry on my voicemail. You should have called me, Kris."

"You're right, I should have—not that there's much you could do from Arizona, or even here. You may not be able to see these things, Bram. Some people can, some people can't. Larry couldn't."

"Well, I did some research and I have a weapon. I don't know if it will work."

"Mina is here with me. She can see these things too, which makes me feel a lot saner, even though we're both scared. I think we should sleep."

"Tomorrow, then?"

"Yes. Come before sunset. Maybe they won't even show up and we can all go out to dinner."

Bram's voice was gentle. "Either way, we'll be ready."

Neither of us believed it was over.

Mina had fallen asleep on the client couch. I brought her a pillow and spread a blanket over her and went to my bedroom. Even with the heavy curtains over the windows, flickers of red danced under the door and behind the curtains. I must have slept, because I dreamed, and the dreams were almost as bad as the reality.

CHAPTER 63

KRISTIN MARLOWE'S TYPED NOTES
AUGUST 28TH

IN THE GRAY DAWN I PUT OUT SOME DRY FOOD for Vi's cats, who were still hiding. I passed by the door of my office and heard faint snoring as Mina slept. I got myself a cup of coffee and fed the ferals in the garden where they sat waiting patiently in the usual spot.

Then I had to face Vi's house. It seemed deserted. No signs of damage. I had no idea what it would look like if the Others had killed Vi permanently.

It was the first time I had been down in the cellar since the coffin was installed. My heart beat faster with each step down the stairs. The cellar was the same, the coffin on its stand. Vi had not brought the computer down here. Her note to me had been handwritten. She had not written a word on her book in progress since she became a vampire, so far as I could tell.

I raised the coffin lid a little and looked in to see Vi in the same dead condition that Sir John had demonstrated on his first night in Vi's house. Only Vi looked more gray than waxy pale.

The harsh front door buzzer startled me. I dropped the coffin lid with a crash. I apologized to Vi—not sure whether she could hear it or not. I went upstairs, sighing in relief to close the basement door. The buzzer sounded again.

On the front steps stood Pamela, the unofficial head of the unofficial feral feeding group, holding a long narrow steel mesh contraption by a suitcase-style handle on top. "I brought the humane trap," she said. In the other hand she held some supermarket shopping bags. I let her in.

"Thanks for loaning me this. Vi told me not to feed the ferals before trapping them."

"Vi told you?" She looked at me oddly.

Oops.

"I helped her trap them the first time, and then again to go to the vet to be spayed."

"Oh, of course. It's good that you've got some experience."

Pamela had clearly been in the place before, because she talked as she walked straight back to the kitchen. I followed her. She put her bags on the table. "I know everyone's bringing you food, but these are from the farmers' market—apples, grapes, lettuce, onions and potatoes." She glanced around. "Didn't Vi feed the cats here?"

"We've got repairmen coming in, so I took all the tame cats next door," I said, improvising. "I don't want these girls sneaking out and going feral again."

Pamela nodded approvingly. "Let me show you how to set this up."

Once I had demonstrated to her satisfaction that I could open and prop the trap door, set the triggering device and reset it when it sprang, she sat back on her heels—she was very limber for a woman in her sixties.

"Did you know that Violet wrote vampire fiction?"

Pamela smiled. "I heard that, but I haven't read any of her books."

"Would you like a copy? I'm sure she'd want you to have one."

Pamela nodded, and followed me into the front room. It looked forlorn, although the furniture was still in place. She went directly to the mantelpiece to look at the portraits—and ashes. I explained that those were cats that had died.

"Maybe they're together now."

I looked at her sharply. Oh, she meant in the afterlife.

"She really liked black cats. I used to tease her that those looked like pictures of the same cat. So she would give me the rundown on how Othello loved to drink honeydew melon juice, Ophelia was a purebred Persian who liked her tummy rubbed, and Portia was a tiny, half-Siamese who ruled the household with an iron paw."

Pamela examined the pictures solemnly. "Vi was an amazing woman."

I felt guilty deceiving Pamela, who seemed like such a nice person.

But I couldn't imagine telling her what really happened. "Vi always wondered why all the vampires in books look like teenaged underwear models."

"Maybe old women can recognize a deal with the devil when they see it. Or maybe the vampires are too afraid of us."

We both laughed. "I like that idea. Thanks for listening to me," I said as she got up to go.

She gave me a hug. "Call if you have any problems with the cats. When you're finished with the trap I'll come get it."

She left the bags of produce on the kitchen counter with instructions not to store the onions and potatoes next to each other, because the fumes from the onions would make the potatoes rot. Or maybe that was vice versa. My kitchen chemistry comes back to me in fits and starts.

After she left, I put out a teaspoon of food on a small paper plate inside the trap and went to take the groceries Pamela had brought over to the cottage. Mina was taking a shower.

I left her a note to help herself to anything she wanted, and went back to Vi's.

The cat food in the cage had been consumed. I put down another teaspoon, and this time when I left the room I watched from behind the door. It took a few minutes, but Lady Macbeth, a chubby silver and gray striped cat, sneaked out from a hiding place behind the stove. Her daughter, Juliet, followed, crouching down cautiously. Lean and long, with a lovely dark marbled coat, she pressed up as close as possible to her mother for safety, and lashed her long, fluffy tail anxiously.

After they went into the cage together and ate every molecule of food, they wandered out, retreating from the room when I went in to put more food in. On the third teaspoon of food, I sprang the trap. Lady Macbeth stood up instantly and started to try to back out. Not possible. The cage door was solidly shut. Juliet began throwing herself at the sides of the cage. I dropped a blanket over it as Pamela had instructed, and sent a silent prayer of thanks to whatever angels watch over feral cats.

I hefted the cage in both hands out of the house and across the way to the cottage. The metal mesh shook in my hands, but neither cat made a sound. Vi told me that ferals don't cry because they did not expect rescue. They would escape by any means possible, but they would not risk drawing attention by making noise. To them, I was the predator.

I put the cage down in the bathroom and set up the litter box, food and water. Then I opened the cage and left, closing the door. I heard some thumps and thuds and when I next went into the bathroom, both cats had discovered the linen closet and hunkered down there, hissing when I peeked in the door. For the moment the bathroom would be their new home.

My office door was open, the blanket had been neatly folded on the sofa, and a note from Mina said she had gone to work, but would like to come back afterward.

I called her at work. "I had to get out and do something," she said. "I'll be back before dusk."

CHAPTER 64

SIR JOHN FALSTAFF'S WORDS
ON BLACK DIGITAL RECORDER, UNDATED

DEATH SEEKS ME THAT ONETIME did flee from me.

Again adrift. Walking, the midnight streets, the Others surge in stronger numbers.

Too close, too close by half. New dangers from my lovely prey. Last night when I rose, I came across my new hostess dragging my old great-coat out of my box to be cleaned. Disaster!

She said t'was dusty. Indeed it is, as befits a grave.

No, never wash that coat. The coat holds more than secrets.

It was not always so. I found the coat in some European battlefield, its owner dead. Now my cherished grave dust lines its secret pockets. That soil engrained in every fiber holds me to this world. My old coat holds the dirt that's irreplaceable for such as me that live by moonlight. Not much of it. I've outlived many graves and often need to travel light. Many's the time that coat and a length of good old velvet were all that stood between me and the killing sun of the day. Wash that coat and wash me away.

But what's this? A familiar scent. Mistress Kit's perfume unraveling like a scarlet thread to the steps of a house. Hmm, old enough to have a basement or windowless closet. Up the steps and ring the bell. A man of simmering energy answers. Not young, but perhaps not so wise in some dangers.

He smiles when I say Kit Marlowe told me to meet her here. I spin a tale of looking for new lodging, mayhap a basement or windowless closet—the word has a special power for him.

"Staying in the closet is not the only choice, sir, even for a senior.

Would you like to come in and wait?"

He invites me in. I am careful to leave no visible marks. His basement is secure, his mind disbelieves my very existence. This will do for awhile.

CHAPTER 65

KRISTIN MARLOWE'S TYPED NOTES
AUGUST 28ᵀᴴ CONTINUED

BRAM VAN HELSING SHOWED UP BEFORE SUNSET, carrying a huge duffel bag. He put it down inside the door to the front room. We hugged like old friends. "How is it going?"

"It's scary. What did Larry tell you about the night I called him? "

"About what you'd expect."

"He really wanted to take me to the local ER for a psych evaluation."

"I might agree with him, if I hadn't seen Sir John rise from the dead. So I've got an open mind, even if it was forcibly ripped open. Maybe I'll be able to see these guys—and then persuade them to go away."

"I hope so, but be very careful about looking at them." I looked into his eyes. "That's what killed Vi, and the vampires say the more attention you pay to them, the stronger they get." I told him about feeling that they were draining me through the window.

"So the vampires can all see these things?"

"And most humans can't. The vampires learn to block them out. Or at least that's what Vi's vampire lawyer says."

"Her vampire lawyer?"

We sat in the garden on the stone bench for awhile and I filled him in on the first week of Vi's vampire life.

"I brought a weapon that may work on your infestation, but I need a flat surface to assemble it."

"Let's go inside."

"I remember these characters." Bram said as Ariel and Sly ventured out to greet him, sniffing the duffel bag and wrinkling their noses at it. Bram reached down to scratch Sly's chin. "How'd they get over here?

"Vi is afraid the Others will destroy the cats."

"So now you have all these cats in this small cottage." He laughed, and scratched both cats' ears as they rubbed against his hand so he could do them in sequence.

"They really like you. Would you like the grand tour? The grounds are not extensive. This is the kitchen."

"Nice touch with the duct tape around the curtains, by the way."

"It made a lot of sense at the time."

"The room just beyond the entryway must be your office."

"How did you guess?"

"The couch has that therapeutic look to it."

"There's the bathroom further down the hall. We have to keep the door closed because that's where I have got Vi's feral female cats on lockdown for the moment, so they don't sneak out "

"I need a flat surface to assemble this weapon."

"So for a flat surface, you can use the desk in my office—it's bigger than the table in the kitchen."

Bram unzipped a duffel bag all the way around until it lay flat on the desk. Then he began to bring out and assemble parts. There was a hose and a fuel tank. The finished product looked lethal enough.

"I looked around for things that would kill vampires, and I put together some specs and got the local pyromaniac—Three Fingers Revere, over in the physics department at the U, to help me put it together. He gave me a crash course in using it."

"Three Fingers?"

"Used to be Four Fingers, but he had a bad rocket season a few years back."

Full dusk arrived and Mina buzzed at the door.

"Remember the woman I told you about the first day I met you? The one with the vampire fixation? Turns out she was right. She can see these things too."

She hurried down the path as the first wave of Others poured out of what looked like a rift in the rain clouded sky.

"Do you see them?" I asked Bram as they surrounded Vi's house.

"No. I don't see anything." He sounded disappointed.

"Okay. Please don't try. It's not a skill anyone wants to develop."

"I think we can still use my flame shooter. When Larry said he couldn't see your intruders, I thought about how we could get at them if I couldn't see them either."

I hustled Mina through the door and introduced her to Bram. She stared at him as he strapped on a heavy vest.

"Fire proof," he said.

She looked at the flame shooter. "Can you see them too?"

"No, I can't," he said, pulling down the vest. "But in the vampire lore, which is all I have to go by, fire is one of the few things that totally destroys a vampire. Kris is going to direct my aim, all right?" He turned to me.

"Okay." At that point I would try anything.

He handed me a duplicate vest. "Asbestos," he said. "And here's a fire extinguisher. Have you ever used one?"

"I have. I was the safety warden for fire drills when I worked at a clinic."

"Great. Good to have experience if something should catch fire."

"Or when."

He gave me a grim look. "Do you want to try this or not? You'll have to direct my arm to where they are."

I sighed. "Okay, let's try it."

"Where are they?"

"Right outside the door. They sort of float and bump into it, but they can't seem to come in without an invitation. We shouldn't talk about them much because it makes them stronger. Let's just do it. Mina. We're going to step a few feet outside the door."

Mina shuddered sympathetically.

Bram opened the door and we stepped out into the drizzly night. Vi's back porch light was on and it illuminated the yard and cast huge shadows. The Others milled about, lit by their own faint luminescence. They seemed untouched by the porch light or the shadows.

I stepped up close behind Bram and used my arm to aim his flame shooter at the Others nearest us. It was an intimate position. I had to press against his back to move his arm to point at the creature right in front of us. If I hadn't been terrified and trying to avoid the red eyes, I'd have been very aroused.

He liked it, too. "We'll try this again—later without the asbestos vest, okay?"

"Okay," was all I trusted myself to say.

Straight ahead several of the gray shapes bobbed in front of us.

"Directly in front of you, point blank range, about two feet away, between you and that tree."

"Gotcha!"

"Go ahead." I snatched my hand back. My voice sounded steadier than I felt.

Bram fired and a jet of flame roared out of the nozzle with an impressive *whump!*

The crowd of Others in its path instantly bobbed up several feet unharmed.

A small tree at the other end of the garden burst into flame.

"Stop!" I yelled. He put down the nozzle. I rushed over to douse the tree with the fire extinguisher. There was a lot of smoke in the damp air.

I caught a glimpse of Vi in the window. She looked sad.

Bram pulled off the Velcro straps of the flame shooter harness and came over to inspect the tree. "Did we do any damage?" he asked softly.

"Only to the tree." Looking up from the charred, foam covered tree, I saw Vi and Edgar Morford emerge from the house to stand watching from the back stairs. A short, heavyset man in an old-fashioned suit followed them. Another vampire.

CHAPTER 66

THE VAMPIRE WITH VI AND MORFORD surveyed the scene as focused as a small hawk, despite his portly build. His slicked back brown hair and huge mustache made him look like a refugee from an antique 1880s tintype.

The Others now swooped down, unhurt, swarming around the house and garden.

The three vampires walked down the steps and waded through the Others as if they did not exist, although I could see Vi trembling. The hordes parted to let them go through as if pushed out of the way, and closed ranks behind them.

The man with Morford went directly up to Bram and nodded at the flame shooter he was still holding. "This can do a lot of damage. It could kill a living human or a vampire, but not the Others, as you see." He inclined his head toward the swarming mass, without even turning to glance at it.

Bram nodded, "I actually don't see them, but you're telling me that this had no effect on them."

Morford stepped forward. "This is Dr. Quiller. He's one of our medical experts."

"I'm Abraham Van Helsing."

Morford and Quiller froze in their tracks and stared at Bram.

"Van Helsing, of the vampire hunting family?" Morford asked.

"Maybe."

Morford and Quiller exchanged glances.

Vi walked around them to hold out a hand to Bram. "Hi."

He took her hand in both of his. "Hi, Violet. I'm glad you're feeling better."

It began to rain, and we stood for a moment. The rain cleared the smoke from the air, thoroughly wetting the torched tree. The rain didn't seem to touch the Others—they moved through the night as if it did not exist. The rest of us, including the vampires, were starting to get wet.

"Let's go back inside," Morford said. "We need to talk without distractions." That was as close as he came to mentioning the Others. I was pretty sure he didn't mean the rain. "Just a minute—I'm worried about Mina being alone." I went back inside the cottage, carefully closing the door against the eager horde. "There are two vampire community leaders here. They want to talk about strategy. You can come if you want, or stay here."

Mina took a deep breath. "I want to go with you. I need to know what to do."

Morford and Quiller paused when I told them Mina would come with us. The expressions even in the dim, rainy night made their opposition to the idea clear.

"She sees them."

Quiller's nostrils flared and he made a motion of his head like a dog scenting the air around Mina. "She is unbitten and should not be seeing what she sees."

"The fact is that she does see," I said. "So she deserves help—if you have any to offer."

"If only we had," Morford said. But Quiller bowed politely to Mina.

We all trooped over to Vi's house. Bram and I stripped off the asbestos vests and left the damp fire shooter contraption in the kitchen. Soon we were sitting on the same couch where we had ended up kissing madly while Sir John drank Vi's blood in the corner. It was less than two weeks earlier, but it seemed a lifetime ago.

Mina squeezed in next to Bram and me on the sofa. Morford took the wing chair near the fireplace and Dr. Quiller took the straight chair next to him. Vi simply stood, looking half confused until Bram got up and pulled her computer chair over from the desk to join the circle. He gestured to her, and she sat in it.

"Vi, your case is unusual but not totally unique," Morford began. His eyes lighted on Mina. "Are you sure you want to hear this?"

"I'm just as scared of those things outside as you are. How can we stop them? "

"You have never been bit by a vampire," Quiller said to Mina. It wasn't a question.

"No, I haven't," Mina shuddered.

"When did you start to see the—things outside?" Dr. Quiller asked.

"About three days ago. I saw Lucy with them, floating outside the window of Hal's house. Ever since that they—" She gulped. "Followed me."

"Interesting," Dr. Quiller said softly. "This Lucy—you fed from her, Edgar?"

"Sir John introduced us and gave permission," Morford said, a little too quickly.

"Hal could see them, too," Mina said. "And he told me Sir John never took his blood—he was really angry at him for that."

"A normal vampire bite will begin the process of bonding between human and undead," Quiller explained. "The living are human and the undead once were human, so there is no incompatibility. But these Others never have been human. When they feed, they kill. If interrupted, they will return to resume, and that begins a process of assimilation into their life form."

"Cats are afraid of me now." Vi stared at the carpet. "Hide from me."

Morford looked down as if embarrassed. "Cats usually avoid vampires."

I felt a surge of anger. "You knew this when you set up her legal documents. You knew her cats would avoid her when she became a vampire."

"Ask Vi if she'd rather be dead." His eyes flashed with annoyance.

We all looked at Vi. She didn't seem to have heard the question.

"You called us. You wanted our help. She was already dead and primed with vampire blood when you called. She would have risen in three days and drained any human or animal she could find in the first throes of hunger. We protected you from that and set up the best arrangement we could."

"It was the property, wasn't it? Your foundation gets the property."

Morford shrugged a little stiffly. "Her property remains her own for the moment under our law, and she needed some help keeping it under the laws of the living."

"But you knew Vi's cats would run away from her. The plan wouldn't work."

"It has worked. Vi is able to know her cats are well taken care of. Animals instinctively avoid predators, and some vampires see cats as appetizers. Where are the cats, by the way?"

"I am taking care of them—don't worry about it." After that appetizer remark, I wasn't about to give him more information.

"You can continue to live in that cottage if you fulfill that condition of the trust. Vi, you can see your cats whenever you want. We never promised that your cats would continue to seek your company once you became a predator."

"Hey, we have a life-threatening crisis here—shut up about contracts!" I waved my hand impatiently. "Vi is in trouble. She seems to be losing her words, her capacity to think and write. Is that a vampire thing?"

Even with us talking about her directly, Vi seemed to be ignoring the conversation.

Dr. Quiller shook his head. "Vampires have no limitation on our capacity to think and write—although our authors must remain in the shade." He gave a rusty chuckle at his own pun.

No one else even smiled.

I was angry enough to take a step toward him, with no clear idea what I meant by it. "The only thing she lived for was the cats and her writing—now she's losing both."

"That is the least of what she will lose." Quiller pointed towards the back of the house. "You have seen them?"

I shuddered. "Yes."

"You looked into their eyes." He turned to Mina, "As you did also. I can feel it in both of you like a splinter of poison in your hearts."

"Eww," Mina said.

Both of us were shaken, but Mina seemed overwhelmed, I reached out to squeeze her hand. "Tell us something useful." I said. "You said you don't know much—what do you know?"

"You two are among the few humans to have survived an encounter." Quiller turned to me and looked me up and down with unnerving clinical precision. "Once a human has been vampire-bit, they are vulnerable to those creatures, who draw them in and drain their life force quickly unless the vampire master protects them at all times. Very few have the will and strength to break the connection once they have begun to drain a human. You are the first who has survived with mental facilities intact to tell us." He turned his attention to examining Vi.

I clenched my fists. I wanted to yell at him to let her alone. Bram put a restraining hand on my arm. I looked at him sitting next to me, our thighs almost touching. I took a deep breath. "How can you stay so calm?" I whispered.

"No worse than a particularly intense faculty meeting," he said out of the corner of his mouth.

"Dr. Quiller knows as much as anyone living or undead about the Others." Morford leaned forward to explain. "He was a man of science, and even to this day he uses a secure lab we have established for him to study the Others. It's quite an honor to have him go out into the field to examine a victim. He doesn't like to be taken away from his studies."

"If you're studying the Others, this would appear to be part of your studies," I said to Quiller. I could feel Bram's body tense beside me, and risked a glance. He had a neutral expression pasted on his face. I envied his composure.

Dr. Quiller drew himself up, frowning, as if making himself more formidable. "I should have been called in immediately." He turned his glare on Morford.

"It was near dawn yesterday, Nehemiah. We called you at dusk today."

"You two quit it! Look at Vi, she's fading away! Isn't there some kind of treatment for Vi, or way to keep the Others—"

"Hush!" Morford said loudly. "The more attention we pay to them, the stronger they get."

I was losing patience, "I don't know anything about this sort of entity—is that an acceptable way to talk about them?"

"If you must."

"I do know from the scientific training I have had, that you can't study something without examining it."

Dr. Quiller's face slipped into a serene expression that for some reason was more frightening than his frown.

"As to a cure—we have none yet. As to combating them—the reason we teach new vampires to ignore them is that is the best method. These—entities, as you say—can kill a vampire much more quickly than they kill a human. We can only accumulate enough life force to keep us going for a day or so, and unlike the living, we cannot restore it with food and rest. We spend the daylight hours dormant in our coffins, but then we awake, needing to recharge very soon. I have studied these—creatures—for over a hundred years. Usually they appear in small, isolated attack groups. I have never seen such a flock. Something is new here. Someone called them."

"Hal." Mina blurted out. Then she put her hand to her mouth and looked around.

"Sir John's human friend," Morford told Quiller.

Quiller leaned toward Mina with a force of will that everyone in the room could feel. "You saw this?"

She shook her head, "No, but Hal told Sir John he was going to go find them."

Morford turned to me. "You should have been honest from the beginning about Vi's contamination."

"Even now you seem to care less about Vi and more about yourselves." I couldn't keep the indignation out of my voice. "When I called to tell you about them, you told me it was our problem and hung up on me."

"Unwise, Morford." Quiller spared him a sharp look. "It is your problem, and ours as well." He took out a small notebook and leaned toward Vi. "Miss Semmelweis, how do you feel?"

"I need to feed," she said thickly.

She had been hunched over, staring at the rug, but when she raised her face her complexion was almost gray, and she was trembling. I wanted to go to her, but she terrified me. I didn't want her to drink my blood.

Quiller went to her and knelt by her chair. "Forgive me. I was so distracted by the larger threat, I neglected your care." He opened up his jacket and pulled out a small plastic bag filled with a red liquid—a unit of blood. "Drink this. Here, I'll hold it for you."

We all watched, mesmerized, as he held it up to her and steadied her hands and the bag as she cradled it and bent her head over it. "There now. Slowly, don't spill it."

For several moments there was only the sound of Vi sucking the contents of the bag. Finally, when she had drained it completely, he removed the empty bag from Vi's hands and handed it to Morford, who thanked him politely, raised it to his lips and used one fang to neatly slice the bag from top to bottom. Then he licked out the last few drops with relish and not a hint of self-consciousness. He folded it into a clean handkerchief and put it in his pocket. "Can't leave these lying around," he smiled at Mina, Bram and me.

We all turned back as Vi raised her head more strongly and looked around. Kneeling so close to her, Quiller gasped, and we all saw. Her eyes had a reddish, luminous glow. He swallowed audibly and asked her to turn her head this way and that while he examined her face and neck. He touched the scar that now stood out angry and red.

"Sir John." He said to no one in particular.

"Yes." Vi's voice was stronger. "I asked him to drink my blood, so he would be strong enough to tell me his stories."

"Ah yes, he's a great one for stories, isn't he?" Quiller's voice was as tender as a mother bathing a child. "What then? After he drank your blood."

"Then, at night, I saw them, outside—they—I can't remember, but it was glorious and painful, and then I was freezing to death. Dying, I think."

Quiller tapped her mouth. "Open, let me see your teeth and fangs."

Vi opened her mouth and we all gasped to see that her teeth were now pink. There seemed to be more of them, with her new fangs growing in above, pure white against the pink.

"Thank you, dear. Now, continue. You were dying, then what?"

"Hospital, transfusions. Came home. Sir John—drank my blood, I drank his. I died. Then I woke up—" she turned to Morford, who nodded. "They fed me. Talked about my new life. Came home, Kristin helped." A red tear stole down her cheek. "Cats don't like me anymore."

"And then?"

Her voice grew stronger. "Went Mrs. Battle's classes. Learned to feed, and to ignore—you know—them. But they were so many. They

214

hurt Kristin. I can hear them now."

"What?" Quiller and Morford both said at once.

"Faint. Not words. Like songs, or bugs buzzing far away. I block it out when I'm strong."

"Keep blocking it. Distract yourself as much as possible. We will talk about it later." Quiller went back to his chair, dropping his bedside manner and resuming his irritable expression.

In the profound silence that followed, the only sound was the breathing of the three humans in the room.

"We don't know what we're dealing with," Quiller said at last. "These things seem to exist on a different plane. Whether it is another dimension, or a kind of shielding that is beyond our current science to detect, I wish I knew." He cast another resentful look at Morford. "We could do some useful tests, although the Foundation hasn't seen fit to equip a lab properly."

"It's not the lab, it's the containment, Nehemiah."

"We have to grow our own experts." Quiller's voice was plaintive. "When Vi feels better, she may be able to help."

"Is Dr. Quiller the only researcher?" I had to ask.

Both vampires stared at me, then looked at each other. "Science is new to the vampire community," Quiller said. "Some in our community believe that studying these creatures makes them stronger."

"We still live by ironclad rules and taboos," Morford said. "Sir John broke several rules when he brought Vi over after she—uh—had that—um—encounter. But the highest authority in this area, the Night Court, would hold Quiller and myself and all of you responsible. Of course, the national and worldwide vampire community would blame our local group for inviting an infestation. All who have been touched by it any way would be hunted down and destroyed. They would sow salt in our graves and burn our remains to close any possible doorway into the realms of the creatures of whom we speak. Such is our law."

"Oh," I said, feeling a little faint just to hear it.

"Dr. Quiller feels this would not solve the infestation problem. Worst of all, it would cut off all possibility of finding a solution— which most likely will come from Dr. Quiller's lab."

Personally, I thought worst of all would be the part about destroying us.

"Sir John's protégé invited this upon us," Morford said. "Sir John must take the blame."

"When you say blame," I had to ask, "What does that mean, exactly? You mean that you would shun him?"

"We want to avoid bringing this to the attention of the Night Court. We may have to kill Sir John—permanently," Morford said.

He and Quiller got up and left without another word.

PART IV

THE DARK LADIES

CHAPTER 67

KRISTIN MARLOWE'S TYPED NOTES
AUGUST 28TH CONTINUED

I WATCHED THE TWO VAMPIRES WALK AWAY down Clement Street in the rain. They didn't have umbrellas. I hoped they got really wet.

"Friendly group," Bram said. "No wonder they don't make much scientific progress. Killing everyone who encounters a new phenomenon means you never get any enough info to find out how to deal with it."

"I shouldn't have told on Hal," Mina said. "I don't want them to kill him."

"They would have found out," I said. "They may have already known."

A screeching sound from the back of the house and a flood of hearty cursing made everyone jump. I went down the hall and looked, just in time to see Sir John shoving up the back window at the end of the hall—the one Vi told me was permanently stuck. He clambered in, kicking and thrashing with his fists at Others who tried to slip through with him. Once inside, he slammed the window down and turned to face us.

"Mistress Kit, I came with all deliberate speed." He wore the clothes I had bought him. The microfiber trench coat was wet. He took it off as we walked down the hall.

"Morford and Quiller just left," I told him.

"Indeed. I waited till they had safely gone."

"Vi is, she's—" I realized I was close to sobbing, and he stopped and enfolded me in an unexpected hug, wet from the rain. But, unlike

218

Vi's coldness, Sir John was unaccountably warm. I didn't want to think about whose blood and life force he had recently fed on.

"Come then. Let's see what's to be done."

We went back into the front room and there was a knock at the front door. Mina, Bram and I all looked up in alarm, fearing that Morford and Quiller were back, but Sir John seemed calm. "You'd best get the door, Mistress Violet," he said.

Vi went out into the hall to open the door.

"Oh, hello!" Her voice had a happy tone I had not heard lately.

A low, precise voice answered. "Invite me in, but limit the invitation to me."

"Mrs. Battle, I invite you to enter my home."

"That is correct, my dear."

Vi ushered in a short, very round, African-American woman. She wore a tan trench coat, which she took off to reveal a plain navy blue dress with an old-fashioned watch on a chain around her neck. Her navy blue fedora hat should have looked absurd, but somehow it looked extremely stylish on her.

She removed the fedora, revealing crisp salt and pepper hair twisted up in braids, knotted at the nape of her neck. She knocked drops of rain off the hat and, after a moment's consideration, put it on the mantelpiece itself. "That way I won't forget it," she said. "Well, then, introduce me—except to that rogue. I know him all too well."

Sir John bowed. "My dark lady. We meet again."

"This is my vampire instructor, Mrs. Battle." Vi introduced everyone else.

Mrs. Battle removed her wet trench coat and leaned down to look into the empty fireplace. As she did, we could all see the red eyes of several Others lurking behind the fire screen. Mrs. Battle instantly straightened up and draped her trench coat over the fireplace, covering it completely. "That should have been blocked before, but no doubt the gentlemen who just left were too busy quarreling and pointing fingers."

"You must know them," I said.

"All too well. Some things are remarkably consistent over the centuries." Mrs. Battle settled into the wing chair where Morford had sat. Sir John sat in the straight chair Quiller had occupied, and the rest of us returned to our previous seats on sofa and computer chair. "So did the gentlemen who just left have any ideas to cope with our problems?"

"Aside from blaming Sir John, you mean?" I said. 'No."

"Blame is a dangerous word." Mrs. Battle and Sir John exchanged glances. "Vampire laws are severe." Mrs. Battle shook her head. "Morford and Quiller are young in vampire terms. They lived as humans in the 1800s. I came from New Orleans nearly a hundred years earlier, yet, considering their prejudice, it is a miracle that they let me teach young vampires."

Mrs. Battle inclined her head slightly to the newbies—Vi, Mina, Bram and me. "When entering into the undead state some gain a new power, some preserve a native talent. Sir John brings us the gift of laughter. Rare in human life, rarer still among our kind. We honor him for that—or we should, if we had a lick of common decency. My gift—and my hunger—is history, finding out what happened to us. It's written in fragments, old letters and diaries. I also find it stored in old vampires' memories. I have to ferret it out, sift out the misinformation and save the truth to teach new vampires. Even if old in human years, we all start our undeath knowing very little."

Vi sighed. "Fascinating," she said. "You can see why I love to go to classes."

I nodded, relieved that once her initial hunger was satisfied, Vi's mind seemed to be waking up again.

"Thank you, Violet," Mrs. Battle said. She turned to me. "Your friend is an excellent student, and you are going to need everything I can teach you, because we all face a grave challenge. I expect Sir John will help us just as he did in 1939 at the Time of Relocation."

"What's that?" Bram asked eagerly. I could see him itching to interview Mrs. Battle and write down all this vampire history.

"It became illegal to bury people inside the San Francisco city limits in 1901. No new bodies were buried here, and existing graves were moved—mostly out here to the western fringes of the city. For nearly forty years most vampires lived in cemeteries that never changed. They were like neighborhoods. Rich society people in one, separate burial grounds for Catholics, Jews, Chinese and black. They were all over this part of town. Holy Cross, Lone Mountain, and Notre Dame and so on. The city kept expanding, and they moved the city limits further west.

"Every time that happened, they dug up the old graveyards and moved the bodies. Finally all the way out near the ocean to Golden Gate Cemetery—where the golf course is now.

"In 1939, nearly a century after the Gold Rush that brought everyone to San Francisco, the city claimed that final bit of grave land, carted off the tombstones and moved the bodies south. Down the peninsula to Colma. Or at least they moved some of the bodies. The rich ones who had family to pay for new plots were moved. Some poor people's bodies were dumped in mass graves, other were just left, their tombstones ripped out and used for paving materials, their graves covered over. Tens of thousands of Hungry Ghosts still rest under that golf course only few blocks from here. Vampires resting there met with a worse fate—their caskets cracked open in daylight. Every time the graves were moved many vampires were destroyed."

"How did Sir John help?"

"Sir John was the oldest vampire any of us had met. He had lived through hundreds of years of wars and uprootings in England. He helped us learn to be nimble and find shelter under the very noses of the living. Sir John saved our small piece of vampire civilization here. We'd be fools to sacrifice him."

"There's a kind word for the old man," Sir John said.

Mina leaned forward. She had been casting glances at Vi. "Mrs. Battle, this change that's happening to Violet—" She seemed at a loss for words, looking at Vi's neon red eyes and gray skin, beginning to go transparent.

"It isn't a bad menopause, I can tell you that much." Vi snorted with something approaching a laugh.

"So death is worse than menopause?" I said. "That's good to know."

"I've been dead and I've been menopausal, and I'll take hot flashes any day," Mrs. Battle said.

Now Vi was laughing. Did I imagine that a little of the red went out of her eyes and into her cheeks?

Mina shook her head at us as if half amused and half shocked at the jokes.

"You're getting your words back?" I met Vi's eyes.

"Some. Pulled by group mind, fighting." She stood and came to me, reached out unexpectedly and gripped my hand. Her grip was like iron. I gasped to find myself pulled close to those neon red eyes. "The girl cats—safe?"

"All five of your cats are safe with me."

"Good." She smiled, showing an array of unretracted fangs that sent Mina and me involuntarily scrambling back. "Go."

"Watch the cats. Ask the cats. They know. How." She dropped my hand and backed away. "Better go, bad night. Hungry again."

Mrs. Battle retrieved her hat. "Come along, then. I'm sure Dr. Quiller gave you a unit of blood, but that packaged fast food is dead food. Get your coat, Vi." She removed her coat from the mantel for a moment, then swept a Mexican blanket off the back of the sofa and draped it over the fireplace, arranging it carefully so that nothing showed. "Keep it blocked—they'll test the opening," she said. Then she turned to her fellow vampires. "Sir John, shall we hunt first and think later?"

"Yes, my lady." He ushered them out the front door.

"Take care, Vi," I called out. No reply. They were already gone.

We left through the back door. Mina and I started running and Bram followed along. Hordes of Others massing around the house swooped down on us. Their grasping hands brushed us, but they couldn't seem to grab hold. Having seen the teeth Vi was growing, I was trembling with fear. A few of them followed us to the cottage, but they bobbed around the entrance like fish at the edge of a fishbowl. I slammed the door shut and locked it.

CHAPTER 68

KRISTIN MARLOWE'S TYPED NOTES
AUGUST 28TH CONTINUED

"WE WERE RUNNING AWAY FROM——?" Bram asked.

"The things you can't see."

Bram offered to take us out to dinner, but neither Mina nor I wanted to go out through the swarm of others.

"I have to work tomorrow," Mina said.

"Okay, then. I'll get something to eat and go back to my hotel room to lick my wounds at another crushing defeat in front of the woman I most want to impress."

"He really likes you," Mina said.

"She's very perceptive," Bram said with a smile.

"I know." I smiled back a little shyly.

"All right. Either stay and we'll order a pizza or go, because I'm starving," Mina said. Bram said he was going, and we all hugged goodnight as if he was off to war. It did feel like that.

Mina followed me while I fed and inventoried the cats. All present and accounted for.

"It's really important to make sure the bathroom door stays shut till we sort it out with the things outside," I explained to Mina. "These cats might try to sneak out the door and get stranded with the things outside."

Mina nodded. Her eyes were as wide as the cats', and I wasn't sure how much of this she was tracking.

"Let's see what we have to eat," I said.

"Good idea. That cat food was starting to look pretty good."

But when we looked I found we had had finished the last of the dishes the neighbors brought, and I'd been too distracted to shop. A survey of my cupboards yielded the groceries Pamela had brought and a few cans of chicken broth.

"How about French Onion soup? I can make that from what I have on hand."

"Wow, really?"

I smiled. "Everything I can cook I learned from cookbooks after the age of 30. When I was your age I could scramble eggs, boil water and bake potatoes, and that was about it."

"I can do that much, and cook rice as well."

"That sounds good. After tonight you can add onion soup to your repertoire."

"Okay."

It was soothing to chop onions. The window over the sink and counter in the small kitchen looked out over the garden to Vi's house, but I kept my eyes studiously on my chopping block. The window had been stuck open about two inches for as long as I could remember. Vi had installed a set of wrought iron security bars outside it, so having it slightly open had never worried me till now.

The rain had loosened the duct tape around the opening, and I could hear the faint bumping noises and see the occasional flicker of red eyes around the window where the tape gapped.

Human beings can get used to an amazing amount of weirdness. As I chopped onions I reflected that I had adjusted to the idea that homicidal monsters tapped at the window sill less than three feet away. I didn't feel secure, but it seemed that as long as I kept my eyes away from the window and didn't invite them in, I would be safe.

Mina was poking around in the kitchen and found the little pottery garlic keeper. "Could we use some garlic too?"

"Why not? It's supposed to keep vampires away. We should probably be wearing necklaces of this stuff."

"Here, I'll chop the garlic." Mina picked up a knife and began to peel cloves of garlic. She sat at the table with her back to the window.

I had chopped one onion and it had made me cry, so I was just about to wash my hands before picking up the next when a strange sound made me look up. I peeled the duct-taped edge of the curtain away and cautiously peeked. One of the red-eyed creatures zoomed backward away from the window, long, thin hands covering its eyes, mouth open in a soundless scream.

I felt as much as heard a small explosion nearby and stared, transfixed, as the creature seemed to claw open a hole in the air, leap in and vanish from view. My attention went back to the onions when my eyes started to water.

Eyes. Onions.

"Kristin, what are you doing!" Mina had turned to see me looking up at the sound. "Don't look out there!"

I turned back to her, letting the curtain fall shut. "You know why onions make you cry?"

"The fumes?"

"Right. The gas that's released when you peel and slice the onion mixes with some enzymes and rises up to mix with the water in your eyes and form sulfuric acid."

"Really?"

"Yes. That's why peeling onions under water protects your eyes. Let's try an experiment. Can you bring that fan over here?" I pointed to the small fan on the counter for the very occasional hot days—and to dissipate smoke if I burned something while cooking. Mina brought it over. I raised the curtain a few cautious inches. A thin gray hand instantly moved over the screen and a red-eyed face gazed in, questing for an opening to drain our lives. Shivering at the thing's proximity without even window glass between us, I plugged the fan in and lifted the cutting board so the fan blew across the onions out into the garden.

The creature bobbing around the window frame backed away, clutching its eyes and then rubbing long thin hands over its face. Screaming soundlessly, it rocketed upward. The sky ripped open and it vanished.

Mina moved up to stand beside me. "Wow!"

"Let me get my food processor." We started dumping chopped onions into it. I let her finish. "Now I'm going to get my spray bottle."

"Yeah!" Mina processed onions and drained the juice into a measuring cup while I emptied the water out of the plastic bottle I used as a plant mister. A few minutes and some tears later, we had enough onion juice to fill the sprayer. Then we headed for the front door.

My heart beat wildly as I stepped outside the door. Mina half cringed behind me as we ventured forward. Three of the Others drifted closer, their red eyes curious—their shark-like mouths half open. My hands trembled. I aimed a wide spray toward their faces, looking between them rather than at them.

I felt a jolt when the onion mist connected with the creatures.

All three clutched their eyes and writhed in what looked like agony as they shot high into the air. A muted crash rumbled and the ground shook as a pinkish rift opened up over Vi's backyard. They rushed up into it, crowding each other as they went.

A ripple of hesitation ran through the swarm outside the cottage. As we advanced down the path, more creatures swarmed over to meet us and writhed away in agony when I squirted at them, sailing up into the opening above.

Mina came out of the cottage behind me, the paring knife still in her hand. "Let me do some!"

"Aim for the eyes, but be careful not to look into them."

I handed her the mister, and she sprayed at the faces of every creature within reach. Her face tense. With the plastic sprayer in one hand and the paring knife in the other, she looked ready to stab them if they didn't retreat. The stream of creatures away from Vi's house accelerated.

"It's almost as if they're suddenly afraid of us." Mina's face was swollen with tears from the onion fumes, but triumphant.

I half expected the creatures to come crashing back down, but their numbers were dwindling. Mina squirted till she had her fill of it and handed the bottle to me. I kept squirting, and the stampede into the pinkish cloud continued until a thunderclap marked its closing.

At last we stood on the edge of Vi's garden, and not one of the Others was in sight.

Mina came to stand beside me. "Could this be a weapon?"

"I don't know, but I think it's a start." I shook the bottle. "I've still got a little juice left."

A tapping sound in the quiet garden made me jump. I looked up and saw Vi standing in the window—back from the hunt rather quickly, it seemed. Her glowing eyes staring where the Others had gone. She looked down at me and raised her hand in a thumbs up gesture. I started toward the door, but she held a palm out to stop me.

"Come on, Kristin, we're going to need more onions. We don't know when they'll be back."

"We also don't know if the onions will keep working.

"Yeah."

"I wonder." I went over to the window. It was open just a crack, and I looked up at Vi standing there. She didn't move, but she watched me with the same wide-eyed caution that her cats did. "I'm going to squirt some of this under the sill," I told her, not sure whether she could hear me or not. "If you touch it, will it repel you, the way it repels—uh, them?"

She didn't answer, but watched me squirt some onion juice into the crack at the bottom of the window. It was too high for me to see whether it dripped in, but she looked down and touched it with a fingertip. She shut her eyes and winced, breathing in with some pain. Then she opened her eyes and nodded.

"Can I come in?"

She must have heard me, because she shook her head and pointed to the window. Effortlessly, she raised the sill up another two inches and slipped her hands out, palms down. She nodded. I sprayed her hands all over with onion juice, there was just a little left. Her hands trembled, but she turned the palms up and nodded, and I sprayed her palms.

Vi pulled her hands back inside and slowly raised them to her face. She rubbed the onion juice all over, as if she were rinsing her face in water. Then she made another oddly animal gesture, put her hands over her nose and mouth, and inhaled deeply. She began to cough, a deep, echoing sound like crashing footfalls in a huge empty room. She turned away from the window, waved me away and crouched down, still coughing. I waited several seconds after the coughing subsided. Finally her wan face appeared above the window sill.

"Later," she said. "Rest now." I couldn't tell if her pallor looked a little less gray and her eyes less red, but it seemed so.

"Wait, wait, Vi. Get your plant mister from inside. I'll give you the last of it, and I want to try one more thing."

"I want to try garlic juice," I told Mina while Vi went to get the plant mister and opened the window enough to hand it through to me. I poured the rest of the onion juice into it. "You may want to use that on anything that comes indoors," I told her.

"You knew they were inside."

"I saw them. But not when Morford and Quiller were in there."

"I hid them."

"You can do that?"

Vi just looked at me. Mina came back with a quarter cup of garlic she had pressed earlier. I dumped it into Vi's hand, which she stuck through the window. She rubbed it all over her face and arms and licked the last of it off her hands. It seemed to hurt her to do that, but she let out a quick puff of breath.

"Better. Feel better."

"We'll get more onions, and more garlic too."

"We could go to the grocery store," Mina said.

"I don't like to leave her." I said.

"I'm scared to go alone, but maybe we could ask Bram." She had a faint teasing note in her voice. "I'll bet he'd do it for you."

"You're right." I ignored the teasing. "He'll want to know about what we just did, and maybe he can bring us some more squirt bottles, too."

CHAPTER 69

KRISTIN MARLOWE'S TYPED NOTES
AUGUST 28TH CONTINUED

I JUST HAD TIME TO FINISH THE ONION SOUP when Bram arrived with three ten-pound sacks of onions, a huge bag of raw garlic, a Late Bake loaf of sourdough bread, salad ingredients in a bag, and some ice cream. He also carried a plastic contraption that looked like a bright yellow-and-purple rifle.

"What is that?"

"Water cannon. It's amazing what the concierge of a hotel can come up with on short notice at nine p.m."

Mina and I laughed. "Did he give you a strange look?" I asked.

Bram shook his head. "He was unflappable. I did ask if it was the weirdest request he'd gotten at night on short notice, and he said he wasn't at liberty to divulge guests' business, but this wasn't even close."

"Might as well bring it into the kitchen. We'll fill it up with onion juice if they show up again. For the moment we actually cleared the space of the things you can't see with just a mister full of onion juice."

"Good. Let's eat."

I heated up the soup while Bram and Mina brought dishes, salad and bread and set placemats on my office desk like a table. The tiny table in the kitchenette was too small for three. Eating dinner with Bram and Mina banked up the fires of humanity enough to push aside thoughts of the marauding creatures and whether they might return.

When we were all sated and the few dishes washed, Mina stretched and yawned. "It's after 11:00 and I have to work tomorrow. Can I sleep in your office on your couch? You guys can go talk in the bedroom if you want. It won't keep me awake. I feel safe with you here."

Bram looked at me, and I smiled, "Come on, I'll give you the tour. First we have to check on the reluctant guests." Leading the way back to the bathroom, I opened the closet door to give him a peek at the feral furry princesses. The sight of us brought forth a guttural growl from the mother cat.

"Okay, okay, enough!" Bram laughed. "The women around here are something fierce." He put his arms around me and pressed me up against the sink. "Fortunately, strong and fierce is just fine with me."

He leaned down to kiss me and I ran my hands down his back and just inside his belt. We kissed more deeply, pressing up against the sink.

"Listen," I said when we came up for air.

"What." His voice was husky.

"They're not growling any more. I think they're purring. The feral girls approve."

"Well, they're not getting any."

"Sorry, girls." I took Bram's hand and led him to the bedroom. Ariel, Sly and Hamlet were sprawled across the bed, but when they saw us they leaped up and ran to hide.

"Very sensible of them to get out of the way." Bram sat on the bed and leaned back against the headboard. I got into the bed beside him and he pulled me close. It felt like coming home.

"I know you couldn't see those things around the house, but having them gone feels like a immense burden was lifted."

"The way you all were acting gave me a chill. If I hadn't been through all that with Sir John, I might have wondered if it wasn't a kind of mass hysteria."

"I wish it had been. I'd prefer hallucinations to having those things be real."

He stroked my hair.

I sighed. "I love that you do that. It's something you can't really ask for, but it's so very nice." We kissed a little more, feeling the luxury of a whole night ahead.

"Thank you for coming back to help," I said between kisses.

"Which time?"

"Every time."

"I wanted to see you, and I wanted to do this. And this. Also this." We went beyond words.

Afterward, dozing in the quiet of intimacy under the covers, I wondered at how much more profound it was with Bram. For the first time I realized that Hal had been performing, while Bram was exploring. For a moment I thought he was asleep, until he asked, "Do you have any kids?"

"No. You said you had a son?"

"I have a son. My wife and I divorced when he was fifteen, and I've spent the past ten years getting reacquainted with him."

I told him a little about taking care of my husband during his long illness.

Lying full length touching each other made the questions a kind of continuation of the lovemaking. "Do you regret not having kids?"

"Some curiosity, but no regret. Do you regret having kids?"

"Only during the years from 15 to 25."

We both laughed. "My clients are like my kids in a way. Of course, they do get better and go out into the world and never call."

"And this is different from children—how?"

"So, are you a grandfather?" It seemed to be the thing to ask.

"Not yet."

With Bram in the bed, I slept peacefully for the first night in a long time. When I awoke, Sly and Ariel were stretched out on either side of us, while Hamlet snored softly draped over most of the loveseat next to the bed.

CHAPTER 70

KRISTIN MARLOWE'S TYPED NOTES AUGUST 29TH

BY THE TIME WE GOT OUT OF THE BEDROOM the next morning, Mina had gone off to work. Bram took a cup of coffee and watched in amusement as I walked around feeding cats—outdoor ferals, the three males in the bedroom. The two females in the bathroom stayed pasted up against the back of the closet when I peeked in.

When Bram and I took a shower, I tried leaving the door open a little so the steam would get out, but the three male cats immediately came in to investigate. More growling and hissing followed, so I got out of the shower, waved a towel to chase the males out of the room, and closed the door again.

Bram laughed. "Not one of those sensual morning-after shared showers."

"More like a turf war in a steam room."

"You have very complicated domestic arrangements, Kristin Marlowe."

"This is new to me, too."

"I know. But you're resourceful, and sexy, and never boring."

"And you are wise and open-minded and very inventive."

"You're not just saying that because I destroyed that tree yesterday."

"Not every experiment is going to work, and you did protect us from getting burned with the asbestos vests. The water cannons will be great to put the onion juice in if those things do come back. Though frankly, I'm hoping they never will."

"Amen to that."

We went out to breakfast. All the tension had drained away, to be replaced with that hollow, hallowed post-great-sex, infinite-possibilities feeling.

"I think I should stay with you until this is over."

"It will be crowded, but until we're out of the woods, I would feel safer with you here."

Bram went to the hotel to get his things.

While he was gone doing that, I got my first email from a vampire.

Of course. They could send email all night. This one had been sent around 2:00 a.m.

To: Kristin Marlow
From: Dr. Nehemiah Quiller
Subject: Last night's rout

Dear Ms. Marlowe,

It has come to my attention due to a brief report from Violet Semmelweis that you and your fellow human, Miss Mina, have defeated the entire contingent of forces besieging Violet's house by employing a spray apparatus filled with onion juice. I need to hear more of this, and request that you present yourself at my laboratory this evening.

Violet can bring you here. I must test her blood to see what effect the onion treatment you gave her has had. Her faculties are much revived or she would not have contacted me describing your encounter. I have never received an email from her before. Indeed, I was not aware that she had my address, so this shows a considerable improvement in her mental functioning over last night. Meanwhile, I have the honor to remain,

Your obedient servant,
Nehemiah Quiller, M.D.

I had to smile—even in his emails, he was an 1800s kinda guy. But was happy to hear that Vi was turning on her computer to write, even if it was just email. So far as I knew, this was the first she had turned it on since becoming a vampire. I longed to talk to her, but of course she would not arise till dusk.

Bram came back with a rolling suitcase and duffel bag of clothes. He worked for a little while on a laptop at my kitchen breakfast nook. Then he went out to talk to colleagues to let them know he would be in town again.

"What are you going to tell Larry?" I asked.

"As little as possible."

It felt odd, but somehow natural, to send Bram off with a kiss. I sat down with my notes. I was missing some of my clients, and concerned about a few of them. I called Larry, who had sent me an email recap of sessions with my clients during the week I took off.

"You told Luther to get a paid escort?"

"Now Kris, I didn't specifically recommend that he pay for sex. But I told him that since he intended to stay married, the least he could do was offer lots of goodies, like dining at the finest restaurants, fun day trips to the wine country. In the gay community a man in a similar situation might use code words like 'generous member of the millionaire club' or 'financially secure and enjoys finer things in life.'"

"And you say he took notes?"

"We talked tactics. I think he should be upfront from the beginning and focus on his strong points. I said he could say, 'friends say I'm distinguished looking,' because he is. Not bad, really—sort of a silver fox type. I hope I didn't scare off your client."

"Hey, you may have solved his problem. Lately his therapy has degenerated into him complaining about how his personal ads aren't working."

"Some times the man-to-man thing is useful. It balances out with some of your other clients, like Tammy, who couldn't wait a week to see you and then came in and wouldn't even talk to me."

"She's a little scared of men."

"Ya think?"

"I told her she could call me if anything serious came up, and she hasn't, so this should just give us another thing to consider next session. Thanks, Larry."

"Glad to help." He paused. "So, Kris, how are you doing on the hallucination front?"

"No hallucinations at all now. Thanks, Larry, for being there for me the other night."

When I checked my email again, I was startled to find that my anonymous suitor Mr_Latte had changed his ad. It now read: "Financially secure, married man, wishes to share the finer things in life."

He had emailed me to say he changed his ad, after getting some advice—and I was pretty sure where he got it. He suggested that if I was interested, once I was recovered sufficiently from my grief we might get together for dinner at one of San Francisco's finer restaurants, or even consider a fun day trip to the wine country.

Hmmm. I wrote him, saying that my personal life had taken a sudden turn and I was no longer looking for companionship. I wished him luck.

CHAPTER 71

MINA MURRAY'S JOURNAL
RED DIGITAL VOICE RECORDER AUGUST 29TH

WEIRD THINGS NEVER HAPPENED AFTER DAWN, so I was beginning to view work as a refuge. I had several voicemail messages from Hal since he left for Washington and I went to stay with Kris. Each time he said he couldn't get a callback where he was and he'd keep trying until he reached me. Finally he called and I answered.

"Mina, how are you? I keep missing you. I was worried."

"Are you in DC, Hal?"

"Yes, I'm filling in for some people here. I decided not to take any of the overseas projects. But I'll be staying here for awhile, cleaning up some loose ends."

"They followed me home, Hal."

There was a short silence. "Are you okay?"

"Yes. Did those things follow you to DC?"

"No." His voice suddenly changed. "No, they didn't. I'm sorry, Mina. You can't know how sorry. Look, I've got to go. I just wanted to see if you were okay. Stay safe. I love you."

"Hal—" But it was too late. The line went dead.

On impulse I dialed Ned. At first I got his voicemail, but he must have been screening calls, because he picked up the phone. "Mina, how are you? I was worried about you."

"I just talked to Hal."

Ned paused. "Oh, what did he say?"

"He's staying in DC for awhile."

"Oh."

"The night before he left, I saw Lucy floating outside the

window—with those gray things. Do you know what I'm talking
about?"

"Yes."

"Have you seen them?"

"Yes." His voice sounded infinitely weary.

"And do you have your own contingent? Did they follow you home,
too?"

"Mina, I know Hal wanted to protect you from those."

"Which is why he left town. You didn't answer my question, Ned.
Do you have the same things around your house as Hal has?"

"Yes."

"I think I know how to get rid of them."

"Does Hal know about it?"

"I didn't have time to tell him. He apologized and hung up and he's
not accepting calls. But I can tell you, if you want to know."

"You really have a cure for them?"

I told him.

"It can't be that simple." He didn't believe me.

"Fine, then. Live with them."

"How do you know all this?"

"We discovered it by accident, but so far it makes them go away.
One lady that nearly got killed by them seems to be getting better. It
might help Lucy if she's not too far gone."

Ned's voice was filled with pain. "She's too far gone, Mina. I've been
over to Hal's place to see her with them, and she looks more and more
like them every time. Last night I couldn't even pick her out. I don't
know if I want to send them away, because I keep hoping one of them
will be Lucy. I might even, you know—" he paused. "Let them drain
my life out, just to be with her."

"I'm so sorry, Ned."

"She never liked me as much as she liked Hal. I think she's still part
of the mob that swarms over his house every night. I try not to go, but
I always end up there."

"Be careful, Ned."

He didn't answer for a moment, but I could hear him taking a deep
breath at the other end of the line. "Mina, there's one thing you should
know about Hal."

"What?"

"He'll use you if he can, and he lies about everything."

I didn't say anything for a minute. It hurt too much. "Do you think he lied about those things following him to DC?"

"I don't know, but if he thought they'd help him, he'd buy them a first class ticket."

CHAPTER 72

KRISTIN MARLOWE'S TYPED NOTES
AUGUST 29TH

THE MOMENT THE SUN SLIPPED UNDER the horizon, my phone rang. It was Dr. Quiller.

"Miss Marlowe, I may not be able to meet with you tonight. After I wrote to you last night, I acted on impulse and went to see Violet for myself. She said you gave her both onion and garlic. I wondered if it might be the antibiotic properties of those.

"The myth of garlic repelling vampires is untrue. So I had no reason to study these things. The vampire venom that gives us eternal life kills all infection, so when the human researchers developed penicillin in the 1940s, I paid very little attention." He paused, and his voice took on a defensive tone. "I qualified as a doctor in the 1850s, and I became a vampire during the Civil War. My specialty now is vampire burns from exposure to sunlight, water retention from leaky coffins, that kind of thing. But if the Others can be repulsed by onion and garlic, stronger antibiotics might be useful."

I mentioned the enzyme that combines with water to make sulfuric acid, thinking that as a medical man he should know that,

"Interesting." His tone was dismissive as if he had made up his mind already. "Some experiments are in order," he said

I didn't like the sound of that—experiments on whom or what? "Do these kinds of infestations happen often?"

"They are rare. But, as you have observed, highly disruptive."

"Um, you know sulfuric acid can be pretty dangerous, maybe even to vampires."

"Please allow me to be the judge of what is dangerous to vampires."

He hung up. So much for the Victorian courtesies. He didn't seem too concerned about dangers to humans. I was just as glad to not be seeing him at his lab.

As soon as I hung up there was a knock at the door and Vi stood there. I was so glad to see her that I impulsively reached out and hugged her. Bad idea. She was cold as ice. She stayed outside the door, at arm's length.

"I need you to give me a formal invitation before I can come in, Kris—make it specific to me, just to be safe." She looked around for a second and both of us smiled to see no signs of the Others.

Her face was redder than it had been, and her eyes were clearer.

"Violet Semmelweis, you are welcome to enter." Even with no visible swarm, I wasn't about to take any chances. "You want to go into the office and sit down?"

"There's no time. I need your help."

"To do what?"

"Come with me to Quiller's laboratory."

"Oh, he just called and asked me not to come."

"That's why we need to go now, while he's not there. Please come now. We can talk about it on the way."

Except that once we got in the car, she didn't want to talk about it. Her face was grim. I drove.

We parked near Forest Hill Station, and she led me to the same maze of corridors that had brought me to Morford's office. Vi took a different turn in the underground maze. No marble floors and office doors here, just walls and floors painted battleship gray. I was lost by the time we arrived at a steel door.

Vi punched in a security code to a keypad, and the door clicked open. We went down a concrete stairway that led to another security door then down-sloping tunnel. Behind that was a modest set of rooms with literally no decoration. Bare pipes overhead and concrete floor. It smelled of animals. I began to get a sick feeling in the pit of my stomach.

"Don't look—" Vi began.

"—in their eyes. I know. Oh, my God."

Most of the cages were glass boxes occupied by gray blobs of substance with round, red eyes. They were all sizes. A set of tables held cases small enough to hold mice, and a few more for slightly bigger animals. A really big one in the corner held a gray blob that was nearly as large as a human. They had few identifying features, and I didn't dare examine them too closely for fear of getting hooked. They did not look happy. "What are they?"

"Others in embryo," Vi said grimly. "They once were mammals of some kind—too small for humans. Dr. Quiller has been trying to treat them, but he admitted he'd had no success. I was the only one who ever got better—maybe because of Sir John's blood and the onion juice."

She paused in front of a set of regular wire cages. Only one was occupied. A normal-looking, thin gray cat with orange eyes stared out at us. "He's a vampire cat," Vi said. "I just wanted you to see." She looked around. "Usually there are attendants."

I looked at my watch. "Can we leave now?"

"In a sec. We've got to work fast." She cast another look around the room. "What the hell," she said, and snapped the lock off the cage as if it were a toothpick. She reached in and pulled the cat out.

"Here, hold him for a minute." Vi put the cat in my arms and reached into her coat pocket to pull out her sprayer of onion juice. Then she saw the cat sniffing the pulse points on my wrist and up along my arm with interest. She stopped, reached out and moved the cat's head away. "No, no. No biting. We'll find some mice later."

The cat looked at her steadily and did not return to sniffing my arm.

The lab had five cages filled with Others in various stages of metamorphosis. Vi sprayed onion juice into the air vents of each of the cages and the small Others, who all resembled caterpillars with huge staring eyes, shrieked, and each one vanished with the popping sound that had grown familiar.

She took the cat back from me and slipped him under her jacket, tucking her blouse around him and into her jeans to support him. It made her look somewhat pregnant. An audible purr rose up in the quiet room.

We left immediately, walking upwards this time. The tunnel was deserted, but when we got to the first landing Dr. Quiller suddenly stepped in front of us. I hadn't seen him approach—he seemed to have simply appeared in our path. Short and upright, he wore the same immaculate tweed suit and huge mustache. He radiated power that was almost visible, like the air trembling on a hot day.

"What have you done?"

"What I had to." Vi was an inch or so shorter than Quiller, but her iron resolve met his power aura with a palpable feeling of engagement.

"The animal under your jacket is our property. He has to be returned to the lab. We still need to perform experiments to make sure that we have a weapon we can use."

"No more cats, Dr. Quiller."

Quiller's eyes glinted dangerously. "Who are you to tell us what to do and what not to do?"

Vi fixed her eyes on his, and they began to radiate redness like red hot heated metal.

I had to turn away a little from it, but Quiller felt the full impact. I looked out of the corner of my eye and saw him stagger, and then fall to his knees. Veins stood out in his neck and forehead as he tried to break the eye contact.

"No!" he screamed. He shuddered all over.

I took a step away from Vi, pierced with terror by the glowing in her eyes.

His eyes still locked on Vi's, Quiller fell down to lie on the grimy concrete walkway. Vi finally released him from her gaze.

The only sound was Quiller's labored breathing, and that unearthly purring from the gray cat under Vi's sweater. It took Vi several breaths to come back to herself. I kept my eyes down on Quiller's pitiful frame.

"Dr. Quiller." Vi's voice was soft, but more sibilant than usual, as if it were coming from beyond her. There was a sort of echoing buzz in her words. "Dr. Quiller, do you hear me?"

"Yes," he whispered, barely audible.

"Leave the cats alone. We will find a neutral place where you can test my blood. You will never use a cat or a dog, or a mammal, again. Do you understand me?"

"Yes."

"Good. Because neither of us wants to have the conversation again. If you disobey me, I will send you where you can observe the Others firsthand."

"No, please."

"Do you doubt that I can do it?"

"No."

"Good. Now do you agree to leave the cats and other animals alone?"

"Yes."

"I will know instantly if you disobey me. Do you understand?"

"Yes."

"If you find another vampire cat, you will let me know, and I will claim it. If you find a cat that has been attacked by the Others, let me know, and I will treat it. Do you agree?"

"Yes."

"Then we understand each other."

"Yes."

"Will you be able to get home, or can we help you to get to safety before dawn?"

"Help." His voice was faint.

She helped him up as if he were a sack of feathers. They were close enough in height that she could support him with her arm around his waist and his arm around her shoulder. I held open the doors for them as we took our tortuous way back up to the surface and to the car, where she gently settled him in the back seat. I drove and Quiller whispered directions to an old Victorian on Laguna and Pacific. We helped him up the steps, held his hand while he worked the key in the door. The place was jammed with ornate Victorian furniture, with lacy doilies on every chair and legions of gilded doodads on every flat surface.

We settled him in his ornate bronze coffin on a pedestal in a back bedroom.

"He probably decorated that place back in the 1870s," Vi commented back in the car.

I drove her home, half expecting to see some kind of vampire police force following us, but none did. The cat popped his head out of her jacket, looked around a little, and then snuggled back in.

"Was the cat on his way to getting like those caterpillars?"

"I don't know. Maybe I was too."

"How are you going to save him?"

"I already let him drink my blood when I went to the lab to scout it out. I also rubbed him down with onion juice. He hissed when I did it—living cats hate onions, too—I think they're toxic to them. But this guy licked it off his fur, and now he's better. I'm going to keep giving

243

it to him and taking it myself, just in case. I think this little guy was a vampire before Quiller got him. Some vampire brought him over and then either got killed or maybe they just dumped him. Even after death some people are irresponsible. If I can stop Quiller, things will be at least a little better for the animals."

"I'm totally with you on that." But I wondered what we might have got ourselves in for.

When we reached the house, we both saw.

The Others were back.

CHAPTER 73

THE OTHERS SWARMED AROUND THE HOUSE in greater numbers than before. Several broke off from the main swarm and crowded around the car.

"Keep your head down." Vi said.

"I know, maybe we should run."

"Walk fast, but be careful. If you fall and cut yourself, they can kill you faster." Walking from the car to the house seemed to take forever. Vi kept the cat close under her jacket, and finally we got inside. A few followed us in. I gasped to be in the same room with them.

Vi shook her head. "Don't say a word," she whispered. "That just makes it worse." She picked up her onion juice primed plant mister and zapped the creatures floating nearest her. They did their silent shriek and vanished, tearing a hole in the air right in the living room. She cast around for more victims and found that the place was now clear.

"Wait here." She went down to the basement with her new cat. "There you go," I heard her say to him. "You can sleep with me in this nice coffin."

I could hear the purring all the way up the stairs.

From the back yard I heard a hose-squirting sound and the whump of Others being hit and ascending into the odd pink cloud rift in the sky. Vi came to stand beside me.

"Wow."

Bram and Mina were standing just outside the doorway of the cottage with water cannons. They were both sighting and hitting the Others with great effectiveness. They might have cleared the garden easily if there hadn't been such a horde out there.

"Vi, do you think that what you did to Quiller—?"

"Brought them back? Maybe. Even if it did I had to rescue that cat."

"I know." On the kitchen table I saw one of the garish plastic water cannons, smelling strongly of onion juice. "Look, Mina and Bram must have left this for you. May I?" I picked it up.

"Be my guest."

I whirled on the Other floating around Vi, spraying the juice full in its face.

A more muted *whump* sound, and the Other screamed and rushed away to wherever they went. I adjusted the stream from the stream and squirted it several times to dispatch an Other that had been hovering around the ceiling.

Vi unexpectedly hugged me. She was so cold that I started to shiver. She saw and stepped back. "Thank you, Kris. Please thank Bram for me. I'm going out to hunt now. I'll take this big squirt gun bottle with me."

"I'll leave you another bottle of fresh onion juice so you can refill."

CHAPTER 74

KRISTIN MARLOWE'S TYPED NOTES
AUGUST 29TH CONTINUED

GOING OUT VI'S BACK DOOR I WALKED through swarms of Others, kept my head down until I got to Bram and Mina. Their faces were flushed and damp—with tears, I realized. They were creating clouds of onion spray.

Bram wiped his face with his arm and handed me the water cannon. "Here, take this. I've got another loaded inside. Be right back."

"Get wet dish towels," I said, "for our eyes." I stood next to Mina and began firing at Others. They disappeared up into the cloud with regularity, but there were still many swarming Vi's house, although they had cleared away from my cottage.

"Did you notice?" Mina said. "Bram can see them now."

"He can?" I turned to look at her and paused while she expertly sprayed one of the creatures who followed my head motion to bob beside her, trying to catch my eye. The Other screamed soundlessly and jetted up into the cloud escape route.

"Yeah. I think I figured out why."

"Why?"

Mina winked. "Think—what happened last night that was different?"

Before I had time to react, Bram was back with a freshly primed water cannon. The three of us started working together. Mina was right. It was clear from how deftly he was aiming that Bram could see them, all right—and he never seemed to be tempted to look them in the eye.

It took another half hour for the three of us to clear the yard. Then Bram and I went along with Mina back to her apartment. She persuaded us to swing by Hal's house on the way out. It was just an old house in the dark—no sign of the swarm of Others there.

It felt like a good night's work. We left Mina at her apartment with a juice-loaded water cannon, ten pounds of onions and a small food processor. A week earlier none of us would have thought of this as armor.

"Suddenly you can see them," I said to Bram on the drive back to the cottage.

"Mina asked what was different." He gave me a significant look.

"You mean sex is the answer?"

"Depends on the question, but that's a pretty good answer," he said.

I was driving, so I couldn't hit him on the arm. "Seriously. It seems that sex with someone who can see the Others can communicate that ability."

"You say those things can feed through window glass without making physical contact. We don't have enough information to know what it takes to see them. But it's sure easier to shoot them if you can see them."

"If we're very lucky, maybe they'll just go away."

"We'll have to take it one night at a time."

So we did.

CHAPTER 75

KRISTIN MARLOWE'S TYPED NOTES
AUGUST 30TH

THE NEXT EVENING VI CAME OUT to meet me with the thin gray cat balanced on her shoulder. His eyes had less orange and more pale green as he regarded me with the same insolence he had shown the night before.

"There's one cat who's not afraid of you," I said.

"I don't think he's afraid of much. We went out hunting last night and he stalked a pit bull terrier." Vi reached up and scratched under the cat's chin. It stretched its skinny neck out and began a loud, rusty purr.

"That's not funny."

A pained look came over Vi's face. "We don't kill our victims. Mrs. Battle taught me that only a certain amount of blood and a large helping of life force are necessary to survive. We can harvest a victim off of any Muni bus, and we can make it a pleasant experience for all concerned. He's adopted me now."

"Have you thought about names? What about Fang the Wonder Cat?"

Vi petted the cat from head to tail, and it stood on her shoulder and purred louder. "His name is Brutus now."

"*E tu, Brutus.*"

"I'll teach him to be much nicer to his prey. I'm starting a new organization with some of the other vampires in my orientation class. We're going to call it—Vampires for the Ethical Treatment of Prey."

I hadn't seen Vi so happy since—well, since she died.

"I think I've figured out why they don't recruit more older women for the ranks of the vampires," she said.

"Why?"

"They don't want their authority challenged."

"And older women are more likely to do it." I finished up the thought. "I guess it's too late now. The vampire establishment is in big trouble."

Vi smiled, revealing that her teeth were no longer that scary pink, although the vampire fangs still showed. She was smiling more now, but when she took a step toward me, I instinctively stepped away.

"Are you afraid of me too, Kris?"

"Vi, I saw what you did to Quiller. "

Her voice was meek. "I promise you, Kris, I would never do anything to hurt you. But Quiller was trying to hurt this kitty and other animals. I had to stop him from that."

"You would have killed him. Sucked his life force out and killed him."

"I meant that about sending him to the Others. He knows that now."

"You could do that? When you do that thing with the eyes?"

"I've done it before with prey—don't freak out, we practice feeding without causing harm on birds and mice, but mine kept disappearing. I didn't know what it was until Mrs. Battle explained that normal vampires don't do that. It's like the vampire feeding without drinking blood, except that the Others do it without physical touch. Now that I know what it is, I can control it—some."

"Control it some? Oh my God, Violet!" Without meaning to, I put my hands over my face. I rubbed my eyes and looked back up cautiously.

"You don't have to be afraid. I can look you in the eye without draining you. I don't use their way of feeding. A few more came back in the house when I got back from hunting. I think it draws them in when I use that power." She gazed sadly at me.

"I thought you were cured with the onion juice?"

"I don't think it's a cure, Kris." Vi stepped closer to me and I started to shiver, fighting an instinctive thrill of fear, and the cold. Nowadays, standing near her chilled me—except just after she had fed. I wanted to step away, but I managed to stand my ground.

"I've been taking the onion juice and garlic juice whenever I feel the

Others rising in me," Vi said.

"Oh, God."

"I think that's one reason they've stopped swarming the house. Their eyes are much more vulnerable than the rest of them, and the onion fumes hurt them. Rubbing it all over me is creating some kind of thin barrier. I'm learning how to fight them off, but without that barrier, I might be lost in their world."

"What do you know about their world?" This was the first I had heard of that.

"I got as far as the entrance. It was like standing on a small ledge above a great dark plain, or on the rim of an active volcano, looking down into the caldera. There's an almost irresistible pull down into the darkness—all I could see down there were a lot of red fissures. I don't know what they are. They looked like hot lava with a small crust of cooler black on the top, but there was no feeling of intolerable heat. It's heavier as if there were more gravity. It might be a gateway into another planet for all I know. It was darker, which is why they only come here at night. Their world looked like hell to me. You brought me back with the garlic and onion juice—I only pray it keeps working."

CHAPTER 76

KRISTIN MARLOWE'S TYPED NOTES
AUGUST 31ST

THE ONION JUICE STOPPED WORKING the next night. The Others began to filter back. Looking cautiously at them, we could see a kind of film around their eyes. It looked like a transparent visor or shield completely covering their eyes. Either they had grown a membrane or created a covering that could be worn with no signs of straps or other attaching devices.

Bram and I tried the water cannons first with onion and then garlic juice. The spray just bounced off their new shielding.

"A true scientist would test whether they could still drain the life out of you with those eye protectors on." Bram said thoughtfully.

"No!" My response was instant and heartfelt.

"Don't worry, I won't experiment." Bram put his arm around me and hugged me reassuringly.

"Let's just assume, in the interests of survival, that if they could do it through a windowpane, whatever shielding they've got would allow them to attack us, either with their eyes or their teeth or both."

Mina buzzed my doorbell not long after. They had returned to her apartment, too.

CHAPTER 77

HAL ROY'S SPOKEN NOTES
SILVER FLASH DRIVE/VOICE RECORDER
AUGUST 31ST

THE FVI CHECKED ME OUT OF MY HOTEL and set me up in a small dorm-style room at their headquarters. The door was locked from the outside. They brought me a phone to make a few monitored outgoing calls, but not to receive any. I called Mina. Afterwards I regretted that. Had I just betrayed her to them?

At first I hoped that giving them information would do my career some good. But the questions sounded more like a criminal interrogation, although no one directly accused me of anything.

"The question you need to answer to our satisfaction, Mr. Roy, is how you could even see the creatures." The vampire who sat across the table to interrogate me was a degree or two less cold than the two silent vampires who stood against the wall unspeaking—the difference between standing in a windstorm and standing in a windstorm on a glacier.

"I don't know why."

"Usually the Others can only be seen by a vampire, or one who has been bitten and injected with vampire venom." All three vamps tensed a little when he said "the Others."

I didn't have much going for me, so I tried to observe them, but it was like observing marble statues. I didn't say anything. After all, he hadn't really asked a question.

"But you say you were never bitten."

"I understand that you can tell that I never was."

The interrogator hesitated. I could feel the other two tensing up.

Then he smiled and leaned forward, so that I could see his fangs close up. "The purpose of our investigation is not to give out information, but for you to provide it."

"A vampire told me that he could tell I hadn't been bitten."

"And that vampire's name would be?"

"Morford."

"Ah, yes, your lawyer." They weren't taking notes. Of course, our conversation would be recorded. "You are not a vampire and have never been bitten. How could you see the Others?"

"Maybe a third category would be someone who has sex with someone who has been bitten by a vampire."

"Most intriguing, Mr. Roy. We'll need names and contact information."

Finally I told them how Lucy, who had been bit by Morford, drew the attention of the Others when she cut her knee. By sleeping with Lucy, I seemed to have opened up some kind of way for the Others to get to me as well.

No flicker of emotion showed on the vampire agents' faces but I could feel a visceral shudder pass through them.

"You know that these creatures steal life from vampires. Having a woman with bites from both is dangerous. We need to hunt them down at the source. Would you happen to know what death gate they came through?"

"I don't even know what a death gate is, and you say there's more than one?" Now I shuddered at the thought.

"There are several. They seem to be vectors into whatever it is they came from. Where did you see them first?"

I told them what happened on the Golden Gate Bridge.

CHAPTER 78

KRISTIN MARLOWE'S TYPED NOTES
AUGUST 31ST TO SEPTEMBER 1ST

MINA STOOD ON THE STREET OUTSIDE the gate, but the Others swarmed over the house and cottage, hovering over the garden in between like an army of floating gray, with sparks of red eyes glowing. It was chilly and wisps of fog floated around the mass of creatures. I called Mina's cell phone and told her to go on up the steps and knock on Vi's front door. Bram and I would meet her there.

Bram and I set out across the garden through mobs of Others bobbing around us. They floated aside without touching when we walked through. It was unnerving.

"Goddamn paparazzi," I muttered.

"Or gigantic mosquitoes."

We both laughed. I hadn't known I still could joke. But the crowd pressed closer, as if encouraged. "Sorry. Shutting up." I said.

Bram put his arm around my shoulder and I slipped mine around his waist. We walked bent over, as if through a windstorm.

Mina and Vi were waiting for us in the front room. Sir John came in a few minutes afterward and sat in the wing chair, Vi in the straight chair next to him. Mina had brought the computer chair over with no prompting. Bram and I sat close together on the sofa. The body contact seemed to give us both more courage.

"We have a little grace time before the Night Court meets and decrees our death," Sir John said solemnly.

"Our death? Why are you so sure they'll decide that?"

"They fear contamination. This horde started at Hal's, followed over here and to Mistress Mina's abode. For now they only swarm us.

But if the local vampire rulers allow them to spread, the national vampire organizations will move to stop the contagion by destroying every vampire in the city and every human who can see these creatures."

The front door opened and a moment later Mrs. Battle appeared, this time wearing a blue trench coat and a tan fedora.

She looked at me as if I had spoken. "Once we have permission to enter, Kristin, vampires have no need to knock. I cannot stay long." She gave a cursory check that the blanket still blocked the fireplace and nodded her approval, but she kept the hat and coat on.

"I must persuade those with influence in the Night Court to postpone your hearing till tomorrow night. They wish to dispose of you quickly before they get blamed for this infestation. All I can do is delay—unless you have a new weapon." She looked at us hopefully.

"We haven't come up with anything to get through the critters' new eye defense," I said. "Dr. Quiller had an idea to use antibiotics, based on the antibiotic properties of garlic. I think he's just discovering antibiotics about sixty years after everyone else."

"Dr. Quiller has not been seen lately. He seems to be feeling poorly." Mrs. Battle looked at Vi as if she expected a confession, but Vi and I both kept silent.

"There is one thing we might use against them." Sir John had a sheepish look on his face. "Didn't think of it till now. I've seen a hundred battles over turf in the past six hundred years. But fighting through that mob outside reminds me of the Hungry Ghosts. They might do our work for us."

"What are Hungry Ghosts?" I asked.

"Displaced spirits," Sir John said. He deferred to Mrs. Battle.

She nodded. "That might work, Sir John." She sighed and removed her trench coat and sat on the sofa, but kept her hat on. "Most of our Hungry Ghosts died here a hundred years ago or more—some from the 1850s Gold Rush days. They had no relatives living near to give them burial rites. Mostly Asian, but some black, some Indian, some white—all poor. If they had died among their kinfolk, their families would have offered rituals, or tended their graves at the least. They got buried out beyond the city limits—twice. They didn't get moved the last time they the cemetery was dug up. There they lie, forgotten, their graves unmarked. No family to pray or burn candles and incense. No one to feed them on feast days, or ring bells. They rise up and drift in the fog, hungry and seeking."

"You say Hungry Ghosts—what do they eat?" Bram leaned forward, fascinated.

"Subtle-bodied creatures that they are, professor, they live on scents," she said. "They are not physical, but they consume anything in their realm."

"Creatures that'll steal a human's last breath—like the long pork you know." Sir John managed a weary chuckle. "I hear they like common roasted pork as well. They wander into restaurants and drool. Poor sorry things."

"Can you see them?" Mina asked.

Sir John looked at Mrs. Battle. She shrugged. "Knowing where to look, I can. Most vampires can. Though they hide well. They come upon humans from the side or behind. They lurk on property lines, fences and walls, guarding their last scraps of residence, even after the graves are long gone."

"Do they destroy vampires?" Bram was curious.

"They'll snuff an unwary vampire like a candle," Sir John said.

Mrs. Battle didn't say anything for a moment. "They are among the dangers I teach young vampires to avoid. They haven't fangs and venom to take life as a vampire does, but they can steal the breath from a man or a vampire and kill him if they catch him unawares."

"Do you think they might eat the Others?" I had to ask.

"They might if we can summon them from their graves," Sir John shrugged. "We must needs bring the Others to their table."

"That horde of creatures follows us, so that might be possible," Mina said.

"Smart young lady. At dusk tomorrow, then. Bring incense and a bell—a Chinese altar bell, if you can find it—and steaming hot barbe-cued pork." Sir John's voice was solemn.

"You're joking." I waited for the laugh that would say he was not serious.

"I never joke on the matter of roasted pork."

Mrs. Battle, Vi and Sir John went out. "Feel free to stay," Vi said. "I'll be back well before dawn."

"I think we'll sleep better in the cottage."

"Okay." She put on her coat, stuffing the gray cat under it. His head popped out the front just above the top button. Then she turned and went out. Somehow the sound of the door closing made me realize that the Others were not held at bay by windows and doors, but by something like the vampire law of permission.

Mina, Bram and I went back through the mobs of Others in the garden.

Mina settled in on the couch in my office again

"We'll just be a few yards away. Call if you hear or see anything weird," I said hesitatingly. There wasn't much any of us could do if the Others found a way in here.

"I'll be okay." Mina held up her cell phone. "If I can't yell, I've got you on speed dial." She pressed the button and my cell phone rang.

IT WAS A NIGHT OF FITFUL SLEEP until dawn, when the tension eased and I slept until I woke in bed with Ariel standing on the pillow staring solemnly at my face. He meowed and another cat echoed the call for breakfast.

I came into the kitchen to find Mina dressed for work, eating at the breakfast nook. Bram was cooking at the stove.

"He makes a good breakfast," Mina said, winking at me. "Hang onto this guy."

"After I have some coffee maybe I'll be able to think of a snappy comeback, but for now I'll just agree with you."

"Too late. I'll be on the bus to work by then. We're eating in shifts, because of the size of your kitchen," Mina said. "I'm going up on Grant Street to get a Chinese gong at lunch today. It's not far from where I work."

I smiled at her, and realized suddenly that as frightened as we all were, the terror she had felt that had brought her into therapy seemed to have vaporized. She looked like a woman with a mission.

"I've got to go," Mina put her plate in the sink. Bram waved her on, and I said I'd wash the dishes.

"We'll get the stuff we need for tonight—except for the pork," Bram said. "I think we should go to a restaurant with good barbecue for dinner and get a mess of takeout."

After feeding the cats I sat with my coffee and ate some of the toast and jam Bram had got out. Then I looked up to realize he had left the room several minutes ago, and not come back.

I got up and first looked outside. The garden seemed deserted in the daytime. No sign of him. Then I made my way back to the bedroom where he had laid down and now was snoring gently. I curled up next to him, and after a little while a few of the cats joined us.

We slept for awhile and woke to make love with the urgency of those who are not sure they will live to see another day.

Larry consented to go to lunch at short notice, and I was nearly moved to tears to see how happy he was that Bram and I had found each other.

"You both deserve to be happy," he said kindly. "Now we'll have to find a bigger flat for you two."

"No argument there," Bram said. "I'm up to my elbows in cats at her place."

Our eyes met and shared the fear that we might not make it through the night. Mina called to say she'd found a gong, complete with rope and drumstick. I realized I'd forgotten to ask her if she'd got incense, so we went down to a one-stop-shopping import store on Clement Street. We could have gotten the barbecued pork in the Chinese deli next door, but we decided to wait till closer to evening. We walked past the mansions of Sea Cliff, stood awhile looking at the Golden Gate Bridge from China Beach. Then we walked back to the cottage to shower and change.

Mina came home from work before sunset, carrying a package with a flat brass gong about 17 inches across, suspended from a small rope. There was a padded drum stick that went with it, and it made a penetrating *Bong!* sound when struck. We set up matches and incense ready to use. They seemed like fragile tools to combat the gray hordes.

We walked back down Clement Street looking for the ideal restaurant. Waiting for sunset, we ate a meal that was carefully vegetarian—none of us wanted to eat anything that might attract ghostly attention. The waiter gave us an odd look when we asked for a huge takeout order of barbecued pork.

Vi arose at dusk, and the Others appeared in the garden, swarming all over the house. Only a few were inside, but they were harder to ignore. When Sir John and Mrs. Battle arrived, the Others who were indoors followed us outside to join the crowd in the garden.

Sir John led the march. The Others followed, like a crowd rushing down on the field at a sporting event, mobbing the players. They floated all round us and never touched us, but we had to avoid eye contact from hundreds of eyes.

CHAPTER 79

KRISTIN MARLOWE'S TYPED NOTES
SEPTEMBER 1ST CONTINUED

AS WE STARTED DOWN THE SIDEWALK, three official-looking vampires walked up to the house. One wore a blue coat and trousers that had a vaguely uniform look to them without any identifying badge or marker. The other two wore conservative black suits. I would have said they were FBI if I hadn't known that they were part of the vampire world.

All three men held themselves very stiffly and were careful where they directed their eyes. I'd be willing to bet that they had never seen so many Others together in one place. They may have mastered the art of the blank expression, but the swarming hordes were scaring the hell out of them. Me too. But I'd been scared for weeks now, so I had more practice.

"Sir John, you know me," the man in blue said.

"Indeed, sir, you are the Bailiff of the Night Court."

"We have called you to a reckoning, Sir John, and you have not appeared."

"Excuse me, gentlemen, but I had other pressing matters." He gestured to the crowds of Others. The creatures swarmed around the three vampire officials, who appeared to be clenching every muscle to continue to stand there and not acknowledge them.

"Sir John, I summon you to the Night Court. You, Violet Semmelweis, and any human companions." The man in blue looked uncomfortable. "Mrs. Battle. I didn't expect you here." He turned back to confer with the other two vampires.

The older of the two men in black moved to stand in front of Mrs.

Battle. "Identify yourself, please, ma'am."

"I am Mrs. Amanda Battle—Instructor in Elementary Vampire Life," she said. "Violet Semmelweis is my pupil."

The man in blue brought a folded document out of his vest pocket. It looked like a legal document, except that the cover was black rather than blue. The three men examined it. "You are not listed on my warrant, Mrs. Battle. This warrant specifically states Sir John, known as Sir John Falstaff, Violet Semmelweis, and any humans in their company should be brought before the Night Court of San Francisco."

"You're the Bailiff—who are these two?" I asked.

"We are Federal Vampire Investigators here to accompany the local authorities. We may need to deal with you ourselves as risks to the greater community."

Sir John nodded as if conferring a favor. "Gentlemen, we will honor your warrant, but you must come with us first. We have the means to deal with a certain infestation, of which you must be well aware." He jerked his head toward the mass of Others swarming around us. "Surely we'll all be more comfortable after these rascals are banished."

"You can do that?" the younger FVI man blurted out. His companion gave him a nasty look.

"Come and see."

"You must see this in the interests of science and public safety, gentlemen," Mrs. Battle said with a calm air of command.

"Very well, our writ can wait till you do this, as long as you don't leave our sight."

Sir John said to light the incense.

Bram produced a lighter, and I held out a few joss sticks of sandalwood. The smoke began to rise, but it had no effect on the Others. None. They simply pressed closer around us, ignoring the incense.

Vi's house on Clement was about fifteen blocks from the former cemetery and now golf course. We started out to walk toward it with Sir John and Vi in the lead. Bram, Mina and I followed. I carried the incense, she carried the gong, and Bram carried two big white bags holding four steaming orders of barbecued pork. Mrs. Battle walked with the officials, talking softly to the bailiff and FVI agents.

The Others floated and eddied around us. There were so many that it was hard to see the sky or the houses on either side of the street.

I kept the incense burning. The smoke drifted slowly backward in narrow trails as we walked. It was a rare San Francisco night that was cold and clear, without a breath of wind or a patch of fog. The first stick finished as we neared the golf course. The main entrance was a few blocks away, but we stopped where the grounds began.

The south side of Clement Street was all houses—looking across the street at the thicket of trees and very high chain link fence that marked the beginning of the golf course. It was hard to imagine that all of this had once been a cemetery. But in the dark night, even the street lights couldn't dispel a chill of dread. I looked at the row of houses, their windows lit against the darkness, but shut away from us and unable to help, or even see, the danger that we faced.

"Do we have to go into the golf course?" Mina asked.

Mrs. Battle's voice was low but penetrating, "No. The fence, trees and roadway came later. We stand on their graves even now."

"What about the takeout?" Bram held up the bags.

"Leave it capped for now. We'll need it in good time." Sir John's voice sounded hollow. "Smoke'll draw 'em. Light more incense."

Bram pulled out his lighter and held out a handful of sticks of sandalwood incense. The smoke rose straight up. Still no wind.

The night was eerily clear and cold. Then suddenly gray mist began to rise. But not from the west, like the ocean-bred fog.

This fog poured through the bushes surrounding the golf course.

"Should we call them somehow?" Mina held up the gong. "Tell me when to hit it."

"Hungry ghosts, we wish you well," Bram said, as if he had been preparing something. "We bring you incense."

"And sounds," Sir John bellowed out. He nodded at Mina. "Now!"

Mina hit the drumstick to the gong she carried. The sound was clear, high pitched, resonating on the cold air.

"We invite you to feast on these tasty creatures from another dimension," Bram said.

"Bram!" I didn't yell, but spoke louder than I expected. "You don't want to offend them."

"No. They are well pleased," Sir John said. "Ring the bell again, and keep ringing it until I say to stop."

Mina hit the gong several more times

"Stop now." Sir John's voice was calm. "Look. They come."

I felt it. We all felt it. Mina froze with the stick halfway to the gong.

The air grew suddenly so much colder that the humans among us could all see our breath. Mist rose from the ground and poured toward us, rustling the bushes and trees.

The Others froze uncertainly. I had never seen them hesitate. The fog enveloped them and us. For the first time their red eyes dimmed, wrapped in a fog that excluded the humans and vampires.

"Can I put the gong away?" Mina asked Sir John.

"Yes, do so." Sir John said.

She shoved it in her shoulder bag.

"Quickly get back!" Sir John, cried out. "Across the street out of the fog."

A crowd of half-formed, vague shapes materialized out of the mist, outnumbering the Others tenfold.

It was oddly silent. I heard a voice whispering. Mina had dialed her cell phone and was talking to someone. Even as she talked she kept her eyes riveted on the gray cloud that was surrounding the Others, and I turned my eyes back there.

For the first time we were able to get away from the mass of Others. Something in the fog that grew thicker and thicker around them was holding them back from following us.

Mina snapped her phone shut and put it in her pocket.

In total silence we could see ghostly figures swarming around each of the Others.

In total silence they began ripping them apart. Strangely glowing silver blood began to flow from the Others wounds and puddle in the street. I wanted to turn away, but couldn't.

A second battalion of misty forms swept through the trees into the street as if drawn by the silver liquid that poured from the Others. Ghosts that were crowded out swarmed on the wet ground, crouching down to lap up the spectral blood.

We watched from the sidewalk on the other side of Clement Street.

Some of the Others tried to escape the fog to reach us, but dozens of cold white arms wrapped round them and pulled them back. The ghosts grew clearer as they devoured the Others, taking on vaguely human shapes made of fog.

Still the gray forms, rose from the golf course, poured through the fence and trees, riding on a nonexistent wind.

"Ten thousand, did you say?" I asked.

"Some say more." Mrs. Battle murmured.

"All they have left is hunger," Sir John said. "Seldom something comes into their sphere that they can eat. Most times they make do with fumes from cooking, and strangling the unwary jogger."

I could hear a very faint, woeful vibration. My ears heard nothing, but I felt a soundless wail pierce my bones. From a distance the fog might have been formless. But from just across the street we could see the Hungry Ghosts circling the Others, falling upon them, tearing them limb from limb, and fighting over every scrap. The night grew colder and colder and the fierce mists of an army of ghosts grew clearer and clearer to our sight. Stalking and ripping at the Others, who struggled in their clutches.

The Bailiff and the FVI agents stood as paralyzed in awe as the rest of us.

No noise reached us, although some of the Others screamed, scrabbled to fight back, their life-draining eyes and mouths flickering and snapping.

"Why can't they drain them—like they do to humans and vampires?" Mina asked softly.

"No life to drain," Mrs. Battle answered even more softly.

In the total silence we heard the creak of a bicycle and saw another horde of Others approaching, a huge mass around Ned, and more trailing behind as he pedaled Lucy's bike so fast that he nearly fell when he got near us and braked to a halt.

"Bring them into the fog and then move out!" Sir John yelled, with a tone of command I had never heard before.

Ned rode toward the fog, and the crowd of Others around him piled in as well. Some seemed to sense the danger immediately and tried to get away, but it was too late. They were quickly enveloped by thickening fog.

"Ned. Quick, come over here!" Mina called. We all called out to him, and he came slowly out of the fog, wheeling the bicycle. When he reached our little group on the sidewalk, he turned back to look and saw what the ghosts were doing. Now they had captured the whole group of Others Ned had brought.

"It's ones who were swarming Hal's house," Mina whispered.

Ned's hoarse breathing from his bike ride was the only sound for a minute. "What are they doing?"

No one answered him.

"They're killing them," Ned cried out. "No!"

"That's what they were trying to do to us," Vi said.

Ned looked around wildly. "Mina, you didn't say that they were eating them." He started back toward the horde. "Lucy!"

Sir John simply reached out and restrained him with one hand.

Ned struggled for a moment, then stopped and stood with the rest of us. Watching figures made of insubstantial fog rip the gray bodies apart, devour their sleek gray skins and fight over pieces. Silver blood puddled on the ground and another group of ghosts crouched around the pools, running long, gray fingers along the ground to sop it up and devour it. Even with the Others Ned had brought, there were ten ghosts for every Other.

A yawning abyss opened in the sky above, in answer to some distress call from the Others.

"Do you see it?" I asked Vi.

"Yes," Vi said faintly. "It's a gate to the Others' home."

Now as the few surviving Others left intact struggled to reach it, dozens of ghosts got there first and blocked the escape route.

Ned began to sob openly. "I didn't know, Mina. I thought you could send them away, not slaughter them. They killed her. They've killed them all. I would have rescued Lucy. But I couldn't tell which one she was anymore." Mina put her arms around him. He was so tall he buried his face in her hair and wept.

At last the rift in the sky to the Others' realm began to close, and within less than a minute the night sky was perfect, as if it had never opened. The Hungry Ghosts turned to us.

"Wave the incense, ring the bell," Mrs. Battle urged.

"Put the pork on the ground. Right here, on this citizen's lawn. Open the lid. Push the incense sticks into the earth so they still burn," Sir John commanded. "Now we must back away, slowly. They will take humans or even vampires if they can catch them from behind."

We all felt the cold like a bitter wind as the Hungry Ghosts approached.

"Keep backing, slowly. Don't turn away till we get further off."

The fog thickened as the ghosts massed around the open containers of steaming barbecued pork until the container disappeared from view into clouds of mist.

We were starting down the hill now, away from the golf course, when Sir John paused. "Right now I need your lighter, Professor. When I say so, everyone turn and run as fast as you can."

Bram struck his lighter as Sir John pulled a long string of red firecrackers from his pocket and held it out for Bram to light. The fuse sputtered and caught and Sir John threw the string toward the thickest of the fog.

"Now, run!"

The firecrackers went off with gunshot-loud explosions.

Bram grabbed my hand and we all turned and ran, except for Ned, who climbed on the bike and pedaled beside us. When we got as far as the next block, Geary Boulevard, Sir John called out to stop. We turned to look back up the slight hill.

The fog totally obscured the street, the golf course, and the fence. The rest of the night was still clear and still. The pork and incense were cut off from view. Then the mist slowly began to retreat back into the bushes and trees, into the manicured lawns that held their bodies and their still hungry spirits.

"Did the firecrackers scare them off?" I asked.

Sir John was still out of breath. "Distracted 'em, so they wouldn't think to follow. Not sure how far they would get, but I didn't want to chance it."

Ned and Mina spoke quietly together. His face had the pale sheen of someone in shock. "Later we can go to my place and talk," Mina said. Ned nodded. "Now we have to go with these men."

"Can I come?" Ned still held his bike with one hand, but kept the other wrapped around Mina's shoulders.

"Can Ned come too?" Mina asked the Bailiff.

The Bailiff laughed—a short bark. "No one ever asks to come to the Night Court, young man. You will share your friends' fate if the verdict goes against them."

"I don't care if I live or die."

"A useful attitude. You may accompany your friends."

Sir John, Vi, Mrs. Battle climbed into the Bailiff's van. The FVI agents had their own rental, and no one wanted to go with them. They followed us to where I had parked my car and fell in behind as I drove Mina, Ned and Bram, following the Bailiff's van to Night Court.

CHAPTER 80

KRISTIN MARLOWE'S TYPED NOTES
SEPTEMBER 1ST CONTINUED

THE VAN LED US UP TO THE PARKING LOT at Coit Tower on top of Telegraph Hill. Only a few cars remained in the lot at this hour, and I didn't see anyone walking around. "Closed at 6:00 P.M." was noted on the locked door to the first floor of the tower. The Bailiff led us around the curve of the tower to another, unobtrusive door labeled "No Entry." It seemed at first like a janitor's closet. But the Bailiff raised a trap door to reveal a staircase leading down. He led us, with FVI contingent bringing up the rear, down to an iron-barred wooden door set into solid rock.

The door was unlocked and opened into a small room, like a tiny semicircular amphitheater with perhaps 100 seats cut into the rock. The seats sloped down to face a paved floor that contained only a plain wooden table with an armless teacher's chair behind it. The Bailiff closed the heavy door behind us with a tremendous crash and locked it from the inside.

In the first row facing the table sat a few vampires—one of whom was Edgar Morford. The Bailiff led us all down to sit in the first row off to one side. The FVI guys moved off a few seats, but within easy reach.

The higher rows were nearly full of spectators, a random sampling of a San Francisco crowd with a rainbow assortment of skin colors and dress styles, more men than women. Their utter stillness and they way they examined us as potential prey let us know that they were all vampires.

A tall, thin young man came in from a door in the wall behind the desk. He sat at the table. His complexion was the color of white candle wax, in stark contrast to his carefully combed, chestnut colored hair and the mutton chop whiskers that stuck out oddly from his narrow face. His eyes were pale blue and he wore half glasses over them as he looked down at a book that had been left open on the desk. He was dressed in a threadbare woolen coat with a plain white shirt, and trousers with suspenders. Abraham Lincoln would have been comfortable in the suit. The man's expression was serious and reserved. Mrs. Battle whispered that he had been studying law in Virginia when he went off to the Gold Rush in 1849, and he had been turned into a vampire before he reached the age of 22.

Edgar Morford came up to Sir John and quietly asked if he could represent him. Sir John nodded.

A man came in through a door on the side leading Hal by the arm. Wearing his best gray suit and a blank, emotionless look on his face, Hal didn't look around to see who else was there. Without meaning to, Mina and I exchanged a glance. I wondered if she felt the same mixture of anguish for Hal, and a shameful satisfaction to see him in some kind of custody. Not that we were much better off.

The vampire with Hal, whether he was another FVI agent or some kind of prosecuting attorney, pushed him forward as if he were a sulky child. "Tell the judge what you told us."

Hal's voice was flat. "I went to the middle of the Golden Gate Bridge at midnight. I invited the Others to come through the gate. Lucy fell and cut her knee and then the Others came."

There was an audible gasp from the vampire audience.

"Were there other surviving witnesses?" The judge asked.

"There are two," the agent said. "Lucy Westenra and Ned Harker-Poins, but we have not found them."

Ned looked up, as if in a daze. "I'm Ned Harker-Poins," he said, as if just discovering the fact. "Lucy is dead."

Hal turned to meet Ned's gaze. "Hi, Ned."

"Hi, Hal."

He gave no sign of registering Mina and me standing together with Sir John and Vi.

Another official in a blue outfit similar to the Bailiff's came up and ushered Ned down to stand before the judge.

"You were there when Henry Roy called the Others through the

Death Gate?" the judge asked.

"Yes, sir."

"Who else was there?"

"Our friend Lucy was there. She fell and skinned her knee, and that's when the Others got her. She went over to them over the past few weeks. Only she died tonight. I saw it."

"Lucy?" Hal's voice was stricken.

"That will be all," the judge said to Ned. "Go back to your seat." The second bailiff followed Ned to where he had been sitting.

"You fed from Lucy, didn't you, Morford?" Mrs. Battle asked.

Bram whispered to me, "How can they tell?"

I whispered back, "I don't know, but they can."

That earned us a look from the judge that nearly stopped my heart. Bram squeezed my hand.

The judge turned his ire on Morford. "Unlike Sir John's actions with Miss Violet here, you made no move to try to save humans you made vulnerable."

Sir John took a small step away from Morford. The judge turned an equally severe look on him. "You, sir, must share the blame."

I noticed everyone in the room winced at the word "blame." A dangerous thing in this group.

"You brought this young fool along to the point where you should have brought him over or eliminated him," the judge continued. "Now your human protégé has managed to unleash the Others. Who will pay for that error in judgment?"

"What if Sir John was responsible for finding a way to eliminate the Others?" Mrs. Battle spoke up.

"I'm as fond of Sir John as anyone," the judge said, with what sounded like petulance. "He's most amusing. But it hardly seems likely that he destroyed the Others."

Sir John raised his head. "These deeds have witnesses."

"They have indeed, Your Honor. Ask these gentlemen." Mrs. Battle pointed at the Bailiff and two agents who had gone with us.

The Bailiff spoke up. "She's right. We just saw two hordes of Others devoured by Hungry Ghosts at the golf course on Clement Street. So far as we know, the infestation has been wiped out because of Sir John's action."

There was a faint buzz of comment in the room, which the judge silenced with another nasty look. No need for a gavel here. Young as he seemed, his pale eyes made crystal clear that he would silence any disrespect of the court—probably permanently. Nothing like the threat of total annihilation to silence a room.

"Sir John, Violet and her human friends here took real steps to solve the problem," Mrs. Battle said. "Edgar?"

Morford shuffled forward as if reluctant to speak. "Mrs. Battle is correct. My client, Violet Semmelweis, is recovering from an Other attack solely due to action on Sir John's part, and quick thinking and ingenious treatment by Abraham Van Helsing, Kristin Marlowe, and their associates whom you see here."

"Van Helsing!" The judge exclaimed. The name caused another stir in the room. "Vampire hunters helping vampires?"

"This gentleman is from the American branch of the family," Morford said hastily. "He will testify that he has never hunted vampires, and indeed, he has befriended Sir John." He turned to Sir John, who smiled, nodded, and put an arm around Bram and hugged him for the judge's benefit.

Bram stifled a faint "oof!" at the energy of the gesture, but smiled, though his smile was a little sickly.

The judge was mollified enough to be curious. "You humans came up with a treatment to cure attacks by the Others?"

"And some ways to fend off Others when they attack," I couldn't resist saying.

The judge turned to me again with only a little less ice in his eyes—I realized I was the first non-vampire to say anything without being asked first. "Sorry, sir," I apologized too late.

"The court has read Dr. Quiller's report on these strategies," the judge said. "This action is worthy of mercy in the court's eyes." He nodded to the Bailiff. "I will rule on this case now."

The Bailiff raised his voice. "All stand for the verdict."

Everyone in the room got to their feet.

"Leave this court and cause no more disruption. We may not be so lenient if there is a next time. Mr. Morford, inform the court of any other developments." He took off his half glasses, folded them up and stowed them in a small pocket in his jacket. He swept the room with another searching look, and I realized the glasses were a formal ceremonial remnant of his humanity. "Also let us know of any further infestations." He turned and left without another word.

The man accompanying Hal took him out through the door they came in by. As he left, Hal cast a mournful look at Mina, his eyes widening in surprise as he finally realized Mina and I stood together. I wasn't sure where they took him. He seemed to be getting a lot more personal time with vampires, but I got the feeling it wasn't giving him the power he had been seeking.

The Bailiff unlocked the door and led us up and out the tunnels to the surface.

As we walked into the parking lot with no more official escorts, Mrs. Battle said in a solemn, low voice that this was the best verdict we could have gotten. "Night Court verdicts are usually either instant death, or banishment to another country."

"I'm kind of glad I didn't know that going in."

"They do let you choose the country you're banished to—usually," Mrs. Battle said with a wry smile.

I offered to take everyone home in my car, but it was clear we wouldn't all fit. Bram suggested to calling a cab.

"No need to have our feast delivered, young man," Sir John said. I realized that the meal he was referring to the cab driver. He turned to Vi and Mrs. Battle "Who will hunt with me tonight?"

The three vampires decided to walk down the Filbert Steps to go out hunting in North Beach.

"Fertile ground indeed," Sir John said with gusto. "Wine-besotted lovers, disoriented tourists, blind-drunk sailors—marinated for our pleasure!"

As they left, Sir John pulled me aside to say, "'Twas not the time to tell you before, but only fair for you to know. Hungry Ghosts never stray far from their graves. No matter that they be unmarked graves."

"So the only way to get the ghosts to kill the Others was to bring them there."

"Indeed. If they had not followed us—" He let the words die out, and winked at me, bowed and held out a hand to Mrs. Battle and Vi. The three of them set off down the Filbert Steps to a vampire feast in North Beach.

CHAPTER 81

KRISTIN MARLOWE'S TYPED NOTES
NEW YEAR'S DAY

I RETURNED TO MY CLIENTS THE WEEK AFTER our Night Court hearing. I received a surprise picture from my online suitor, Mr_Latte. As I suspected, he was indeed my client Luther. Luther and I had a serious talk at his next appointment, and he decided to try Larry's suggestion and use the money to fund a better benefit package to attract prospective girlfriends. He casually mentioned exploring some New Age massage services. He left with a spring in his step that I had never seen before.

Mina found a new apartment that had no memories of Hal. She began to get on with her life. Ned came by often to see her. Bram and I took them out to dinner. We looked at some of his new cartoons and bought a CD from his band, which he had re-named Tragic Consequences. Mina told me he seemed to be slowly dealing with his grief over Lucy.

Mrs. Battle reported that the vampire hierarchy interested itself in Hal's career. Talks were under way to marry him off to a French vampire of royal blood. They also sponsored his diplomatic career in order to keep a close eye on him.

Vi continued to recover from her encounter with the Others, and started to use her computer again, although most of what she wrote was vampire activism literature. Brutus, the vampire cat, sat on her shoulder while she wrote.

Bram decided to move to San Francisco to finish his book on the vampire-obsessed subculture. We started looking for a larger place— one that would have room for five cats and be close enough to feed Vi's ferals every morning.

In late October I received a package via courier. Inside I found the silver-framed picture of my mother, along with three words written on plain white paper: "Sorry. Love, Hal."

Sir John disappeared from time to time, notably when Dr. Quiller came around to ask questions about his defeat of the Others. He also reappeared in Vi's living room from time to time for no known reason, but invariably in the best of spirits.

This book is dedicated
To El Nino, the gentle giant and alpha tomcat,
who taught me so much

ACKNOWLEDGEMENTS

I DEEPLY APPRECIATE THE USUAL SUSPECTS, friends and neighbors whose caring and support have kept me alive and writing. Thanks to my brother Mike Murray, friends Jacqueline Stone, Barbara Landis, Merry vonBrauch, Jaqueline Girdner, Gregory Booi, Laurie Toby Edison, Ann Reasoner, Ronald Russell, Arlene Cooper Russell and David Cooper.

Special thanks to Peggy Elam, Ph.D. and Pearlsong Press for sharing the dream to make life-sized fiction available to the world at large.

I am also most grateful for the online feedback on the first several chapters from critters at Dr. Andrew Burt's critique exchange site at http://www.critters.org/ and particularly from Carolyn, who undertook to critique the entire manuscript.

Thanks to Terri Bischoff, of Midnight Ink, for useful suggestions on some contents to the package on page one!

ABOUT THE AUTHOR

LYNNE MURRAY IS THE AUTHOR OF the award-winning Josephine Fuller mystery series. Lynne knew she wanted to write a novel about a woman of size who doesn't apologize when she read one fat joke too many in a mystery. She found the trick to creating a positive fat fictional character was to become a self-accepting woman of size in the process of writing about one. *Larger Than Death*, the first in the series, won the National Association to Advance Fat Acceptance (NAAFA) Distinguished Achievement Award.

Lynne's romantic comedy novel *Bride of the Living Dead* was published by Pearlsong Press in 2010. Her humorous short pieces have appeared in magazines and newspapers. Many of her articles, including her interview of Darlene Cates, star of *What's Eating Gilbert Grape,* are available on her website at www.lmurray.com.

Lynne has written two ebooks for Holly Lisle's *33 Worst Mistakes Writers Make* series: *The 33 Worst Mistakes Writers Make About San Francisco* and—based on years of working in law firms—*The 33 Worst Mistakes Writers Make About Courtroom Law.*

Lynne and fellow mystery author Jaqueline Girdner also collaborated on an ebook of encouragement: *Writer to Writer Reminders, Tickles, Tips and Tricks for Writers.*

A longtime San Francisco resident, Lynne received a B.A. in psychology from San Francisco State University. The city is the setting for most of her fiction since her first book, *Termination Interview,* was published in 1988.

Lynne shares an apartment with a small group of extremely mellow cats, who are all either rescued or formerly feral.

ABOUT PEARLSONG PRESS

PEARLSONG PRESS IS AN INDEPENDENT publishing company dedicated to providing books and resources that entertain while expanding perspectives on the self and the world. The company was founded by Peggy Elam, Ph.D., a psychologist and journalist, in 2003. Pearls are formed when a piece of sand or grit or other abrasive, annoying, or even dangerous substance enters an oyster and triggers its protective response. The substance is coated with shimmering opalescent nacre ("mother of pearl"), the coats eventually building up to produce a beautiful gem. The self-healing response of the oyster thus transforms suffering into a thing of beauty.

The pearl-creating process reflects our company's desire to move outside a pathological or "disease" based model of life, health and well-being into a more integrative and transcendent perspective. A move out of suffering into joy. And that, we think, is something to sing about.

PEARLSONG PRESS ENDORSES Health At Every Size, an approach to health and well-being that celebrates natural diversity in body size and encourages people to stop focusing on weight (or any external measurement) in favor of listening to and respecting natural appetites for food, drink, sleep, rest, movement, and recreation. While not every book we publish specifically promotes Health At Every Size (by, for instance, featuring fat heroines or educating readers on size acceptance), none of our books or other resources will contradict this holistic and body-positive perspective.

WE ENCOURAGE YOU TO ENJOY other Pearlsong Press books, which you can purchase at www.pearlsong.com or your favorite bookstore. Keep up with us through our blog at www.pearlsongpress.com.

FICTION:

The Season of Lost Children—a novel by Karen Blomain
The Fat Lady Sings—a young adult novel by Charlie Lovett
Syd Arthur—a novel by Ellen Frankel
Fallen Embers & *Blowing Embers* (Books One & Two of The Embers Series)—paranormal romance by Lauri J Owen
Bride of the Living Dead—romantic comedy by Lynne Murray
Measure By Measure—a romantic romp with the fabulously fat by Rebecca Fox & William Sherman
FatLand—a visionary novel by Frannie Zellman
The Program—a suspense novel by Charlie Lovett
The Singing of Swans—a novel about the Divine Feminine by Mary Saracino

ROMANCE NOVELS & SHORT STORIES FEATURING BIG BEAUTIFUL HEROINES:
by Pat Ballard, the Queen of Rubenesque Romances:
   Dangerous Love | *The Best Man* | *Abigail's Revenge*
   Dangerous Curves Ahead: Short Stories | *Wanted: One Groom*
   Nobody's Perfect | *His Brother's Child* | *A Worthy Heir*
by Rebecca Brock—*The Giving Season*
& by Judy Bagshaw—*At Long Last, Love: A Collection*

NONFICTION:

Fat Poets Speak: Voices of the Fat Poets' Society—edited by Frannie Zellman
Ten Steps to Loving Your Body (No Matter What Size You Are) by Pat Ballard
Beyond Measure: A Memoir About Short Stature & Inner Growth by Ellen Frankel
Taking Up Space: How Eating Well & Exercising Regularly Changed My Life by Pattie Thomas, Ph.D. with Carl Wilkerson, M.B.A. (foreword by Paul Campos, author of The Obesity Myth)
Off Kilter: A Woman's Journey to Peace with Scoliosis, Her Mother & Her Polish Heritage—a memoir by Linda C. Wisniewski
Unconventional Means: The Dream Down Under—a spiritual travelogue & memoir by Anne Richardson Williams
Splendid Seniors: Great Lives, Great Deeds—inspirational biographies by Jack Adler

HEALING THE WORLD ONE BOOK AT A TIME